He stood in the main fortress of a threatened, perhaps a doomed land. The age-old fortress of Estcarp was menaced from the north and from the south, and also from the sea to the west. Only because they were the heirs of age-old knowledge were the dark people of her fields, her towns and cities, able to hold back the press. Theirs might be a losing cause, but they would go down fighting to the last blow of sword from the last living Guardsman, the last blasting weapon man or woman could lay hand upon.

And the hunger which had drawn Simon under the rough arch in Petronius' yard into this land was alive and avid in him once more. They made no appeal to him, their pride was unbending. But he gave his allegiance to the woman who had questioned him, chose sides in that moment with a rush of a boy's openhearted enthusiasm. Without a word passing between them, Simon took service in Estcarp.

. . . And so begins a saga of magic and peril, of power and adventure on a distant world of enchantment—

ANDRE NORTON
WITCH WORLD

ACE BOOKS, NEW YORK

WITCH WORLD

An Ace Book / published by arrangement with
the author

PRINTING HISTORY
Eleventh printing / January 1986
Twelfth printing / February 1988

All rights reserved.
Copyright © 1963 by Ace Books, Inc.
This book may not be reproduced in whole or in part,
by mimeograph or any other means, without permission.
For information address: The Berkley Publishing Group,
200 Madison Avenue, New York, New York 10016.

ISBN: 0-441-89708-8

Ace Books are published by The Berkley Publishing Group,
200 Madison Avenue, New York, New York 10016.
The name "Ace" and the "A" logo
are trademarks belonging to Charter Communications, Inc.
PRINTED IN THE UNITED STATES OF AMERICA

20   19   18   17   16   15   14   13   12

PART I: VENTURE OUT OF SULCARKEEP

I

SIEGE PERILOUS

The rain was a slantwise curtain across the dingy street, washing soot from city walls, the taste of it metallic on the lips of the tall, thin man who walked with a loping stride close to the buildings, watching the mouths of doorways, the gaps of alleys with a narrow-eyed intentness.

Simon Tregarth had left the railroad station two—or was it three hours ago? He had no reason to mark the passing of time any longer. It had ceased to have any meaning, and he had no destination. As the hunted, the runner, the hider—no, he was not in hiding. He walked in the open, alert, ready, his shoulders as straight, his head as erect as ever.

In those first frantic days when he had retained a wisp of hope, when he had used every scrap of animal cunning, every trick and dodge he had learned, when he had twisted and back-trailed, and befogged his tracks, then he had been governed by hours and minutes, he had run. Now he walked, and he would continue to walk until the death lurking in one of those doorways, in ambush in some alley would confront him. And even then he would go down using his fangs. His right hand, thrust deep into the soggy pocket of his top coat, caressed those fangs—smooth, sleek, deadly, a weapon which fitted as neatly into his palm as if it were a part of his finely trained body.

Tawdry red-and-yellow neon lights made wavering patterns across the water-slick pavement; his acquaintance with this town was centered about a hotel or two located at its center section, a handful of restaurants, some stores, all a casual traveler learned in two visits half a dozen years apart. And he was driven by the urge to remain in the open, for he was convinced that the end to the chase would come that night or early tomorrow.

Simon realized that he was tiring. No sleep, the need for constant sentry—go. He slackened pace before a lighted doorway, read the legend on the rain-limp awning above it. A doorman swung open the inner portal and the man in the rain accepted the tacit invitation, stepping into warmth and the fragrance of food.

The bad weather must have discouraged patrons. Maybe that was why the headwaiter welcomed him so quickly. Or perhaps the cut of the still presentable suit protected from the damp by the coat he shed, his faint but unmistakable natural arrogance—the mark left upon a man who has commanded his kind and been readily obeyed—insured for him the well-placed table and the speedily attentive waiter.

Simon grinned wryly as his eye sped down the lines of the menu, and there was a ghost of true humor in that grin. The condemned man would eat a hearty meal anyway. His reflection, distorted by the curving side of the polished sugarbowl, smiled back at him. A long face, fine-drawn, with lines at the corners of the eyes, and deeper set brackets at the lips, a brown face, well-weathered, but in its way an ageless face. It had looked much the same at twenty-five, it would continue to look so at sixty.

Tregarth ate slowly, savoring each bite, letting the comforting warmth of the room, of the carefully chosen wine, relax his body if not mind and nerves. But that relaxation nurtured no false courage. This was *the* end, he knew it—had come to accept it.

"Pardon . . ."

The fork he had raised with its thick bite of steak impaled did not pause before his lips. But in spite of Simon's iron control a muscle twitched in his lower eyelid. He chewed, and then he answered, his voice even.

"Yes?"

The man standing politely at his table might be a broker, a corporation lawyer, a doctor. He had a professional air designed to inspire confidence in his fellows. But he was not what Simon had expected at all, he was too respectable, too polite and correct to be—death! Though the organization had many servants in widely separated fields.

"Colonel Simon Tregarth, I believe?"

Simon broke a muffin apart and buttered it. "Simon Tregarth, but not 'Colonel'," he corrected, and then added with a counterthrust on his own, "As you well know."

The other seemed a little surprised, and then he smiled, that smooth, soothing, professional smile.

"How maladroit of me, Tregarth. But let me say at once—I am not a member of the organization. I am, instead—if you wish it, of course—a friend of yours. Permit me to introduce myself. I am Dr. Jorge Petronius. Very much at your service, may I add."

Simon blinked. He had thought the scrap of future remaining to him well accounted for, but he had not reckoned on this meeting. For the first time in bitter days he felt, far inside him, the stir of something remotely akin to hope.

It did not occur to him to doubt the identification offered by this small man watching him narrowly now through the curiously thick lenses, supported by such heavy and broad black plastic frames that Petronius appeared to wear the half-mask of eighteenth century disguise. Dr. Jorge Petronius was very well known throughout that half-world where Tregarth had lived for several violent years. If you were "hot" and you were also lucky enough to be in funds you went to Petronius. Those who did were never found thereafter, either by the law, or the vengeance of their fellows.

"Sammy is in town," that precise, slightly accented voice continued.

Simon sipped appreciatively at his wine. "Sammy?" he matched the other's detachment. "I am flattered."

"Oh, you have something of a reputation, Tregarth. For you the organization unleashed their best hounds. But after the efficient way you dealt with Kotchev and Lampson, there remained only Sammy. However, he is slightly different metal from the others. And you have, if you will forgive my prying into your personal affairs, been on the run for some time. A situation which does not exactly strengthen the sword arm."

Simon laughed. He was enjoying this, the good food and drink, even the sly needling of Dr. Jorge Petronius. But he did not lower his guard.

"So, my sword arm needs strengthening? Well, doctor, what do you suggest as the remedy?"

"There is—my own."

Simon put down his wine glass. A red drop trickled down its side to be absorbed by the cloth.

"I have been told your services come high, Petronius."

The small man shrugged. "Naturally. But in return I can promise complete escape. Those who trust me receive the worth of their dollars. I have had no complaints."

"Unfortunately I am not one who can afford your services."

"Your recent activities having so eaten into your cash reserve? But, of course. However, you left San Pedro with twenty thousand. You could not have completely exhausted such a sum in this short interval. And if you meet Sammy what remains shall only be returned to Hanson."

Simon's lips tightened. For an instant he looked as dangerous as he was, as Sammy would see him if they had a fair, face-to-face meeting.

"Why hunt me up—and how?" he asked.

"Why?" Again Petronius shrugged. "That you shall understand later. I am, in my way, a scientist, an explorer, an experimenter. As for how I knew you were in town and in need of my service—Tregarth, you should be aware by now how rumor spreads. You are a marked man and a dangerous one. Your coming and going is noted. It is a pity for your sake that you are honest."

Simon's right hand balled into a fist. "After my activities of the past seven years you apply that label to me?"

It was Petronius who laughed now, a small chuckle, inviting the other to enjoy the humor of the situation. "But honesty sometimes has very little to do with the pronouncements of the law, Tregarth. If you had not been an essentially honest man—as well as one with ideals—you would never have stood up to Hanson. It is because you are what you are that I know you are ripe for me. Shall we go?"

Somehow Simon found himself paying his check, following Dr. Jorge Petronius. A car waited at the curb, but the doctor did not address its driver as the machine carried them into the night and the rain.

"Simon Tregarth," Petronius' voice was as impersonal now as if he recited data important only to himself. "Of Cornish descent. Enlisted in the U.S. Army on March tenth, 1939. Promoted on the field from sergeant to lieutenant, and climbed to rank of Lieutenant-Colonel. Served in the occupation forces until stripped of his commission and imprisoned for— For what, Colonel? Ah, yes, for flagrant black market dealing. Only, most unfortunately the brave colonel did not know he had been drawn into a criminal deal until too late. That was the point, was it not, Tregarth, which put you on the other side of the law? Since you had been given the name you thought you might as well play the game.

"Since Berlin you have been busy in quite a few dubious exploits, until you were unwise enough to cross Hanson. Another affair into which you were pushed unknowingly? You seem to be an unlucky man, Tregarth. Let us hope that your fortunes change tonight."

"Where are we going—to the docks?"

Again he heard that rich chuckle. "We head downtown, but not to the harbor. My clients travel, but not by sea, air, or land. How much do you know of the traditions of your fatherland, Colonel?"

"Matacham, Pennsylvania has no traditions I ever heard of—"

"I am not concerned with a crude mining town on this continent. I am speaking of Cornwall, which is older than time—our time."

"My grandparents were Cornish. But I don't know any more than that."

"Your family was of the pure blood, and Cornwall is old, so very old. It is associated with Wales in legends. Arthur was known there, and the Romans of Britain huddled within its borders when the axes of the Saxons swept them to limbo. Before the Romans there were others, many, many others, some of them bearing with them scraps of strange knowledge. You are going to make me very happy, Tregarth." There was a pause as if inviting comment; when Simon did not answer, the other continued.

"I am about to introduce you to one of your native traditions, Colonel. A most interesting experiment. Ah, here we are!"

The car had stopped before the mouth of a dark alley. Petronius opened the door.

"You now behold the single drawback of my establishment, Tregarth. This lane is too narrow to accommodate the car; we must walk."

For a moment Simon stared up the black mouth, wondering if the doctor had brought him to some appointed slaughterhouse. Did Sammy wait here? But Petronius had snapped on a torch and was waving its beam ahead in invitation.

"Only a yard or two, I assure you. Just follow me."

The alley was indeed a short one and they came out into an empty space between towering buildings. Squatting in a hollow ringed about by these giants was a small house.

"You see here an anachronism, Tregarth." The doctor set a key in the door lock. "This is a late seventeenth century farmhouse in the heart of a twentieth century city. Because its title is in doubt, it exists, a very substantial ghost of the past to haunt the present. Enter please."

Later, as he steamed in front of an open fire, a mixture his host had pressed upon him in his hand, Simon thought that Petronius' description of a ghost house was very apt. It needed only a steeple crowned hat for the doctor's head, a sword at his side, to complete the illusion that he had stepped from one era into another.

"Where do I go from here?" he asked.

Petronius prodded the fire with a poker. "You shall go at dawn, Colonel, free and clear, as I promise. As to where," he smiled, "that we shall see."

"Why wait until dawn?"

As if being forced into telling more than he wished, Petronius put down the poker and wiped his hands on a handkerchief before he faced his client squarely.

"Because only at dawn does your door open—the proper one for you. This is a story at which you may scoff, Tregarth, until you see the proof before your eyes. What do you know of menhirs?"

Simon felt absurdly pleased that he could supply an answer the other obviously did not expect.

"They were stones—set in circles by prehistoric men—Stonehenge."

"Set up in circles, sometimes. But they had other uses also." Petronius was all unsuppressed eagerness now, begging for serious attention from his listener. "There were certain stones of great power mentioned in the old legends. The Lia Fail of the Tuatha De Danann of Ireland. When the rightful king trod upon it, it shouted aloud in his honor. It was the coronation stone of that race, one of their three great treasures. And do not the kings of England to this day still cherish the Stone of Scone beneath their throne?

"But in Cornwall there was another stone of power—the Siege Perilous. It was one rumored to be able to judge a man, determine his worth, and then deliver him to his fate. Arthur was supposed to have discovered its power through the Seer Merlin and incorporated it among the seats of the Round Table. Six of his knights tried it—and disappeared. Then came two who knew its secret and stayed: Percival and Galahad."

"Look here." Simon was bitterly disappointed, the more so because he had almost dared to hope again. Petronius was cracked, there was no escape after all. "Arthur and the Round Table—that's a fairy tale for kids. You're talking as if—"

"As if it were true history?" Petronius caught him up. "Ah, but who is to say what is history and what is not? Every word of the past which comes to us is colored and influenced by the learning, the prejudices, even the physical condition of the historian who has recorded it for later generations. Tradition fathers history and what is tradition but word of mouth? How distorted may such accounts become in a single generation? You, yourself, had your entire life changed by perjured testimony. Yet that testimony had been inserted in records, has now become history, untrue as it is. How can anyone say that this story is legend but that one a fact, and know that he is correct? History is made, is recorded by human beings, and it is larded with all the errors our species is subject to. There are scraps of truth in legend and many lies in accepted history. I know—for the Siege Perilous does exist!

"There are also theories of history alien to the conventional ones we learn as children. Have you ever heard of the alternate worlds which may stem from momentous decisions? In one of those worlds, Colonel Tregarth, perhaps you did not turn aside your eyes on that night in Berlin. In another you did not meet with me an hour ago, but went on to keep your rendezvous with Sammy!"

The doctor rocked back and forth on his heels, as if set teetering by the force of his words and belief. And in spite of himself Simon caught a bit of that fiery enthusiasm.

"Which of these theories do you intend to apply to my problem?"

Petronius laughed, once again at ease. "Just have the patience to hear me out without believing that you are listening to a madman, and I shall explain." He glanced from the watch on his wrist to the wall clock behind him. "We have some hours yet. So, it is like this—"

As the little man began mouthing what sounded like wild nonsense, Simon obediently listened. The warmth, the drink, the chance to rest were payment enough. He might have to leave to face Sammy later, but that chance he pushed to the back of his mind as he concentrated on what Petronius was saying.

The mellow chime of the ancient clock struck the hour three times before the doctor was done. Tregarth sighed, perhaps he had only been battered into submission by that flood of words, but if it *were* true—And there was Petronius' reputation. Simon unbuttoned his shirt and drew out his money belt.

"I know that Sacarsi and Wolverstein haven't been heard of since they contacted you," he conceded.

"No, for they went through their doors; they found

the worlds they had always unconsciously sought. It is as I have told you. One takes his seat upon the Siege and before him opens that existence in which his spirit, his mind—his soul if you wish to call it that—is at home. And he goes forth to seek his fortune there.''

"Why haven't you tried it yourself?'' That was to Simon the weak point in the other's story. If Petronius possessed the key to such a door, why had he not used it himself?

"Why?'' The doctor stared down at the two plump hands resting on his knees. "Because there is no return—and only a desperate man chooses an irrevocable future. In this world we always cling to the belief that we can control our lives, make our own decisions. But through there, we have made a choice which cannot be cancelled. I use words, many words, but at this moment I cannot seem to choose them rightly to express what I feel. There have been many Guardians of the Siege—only a few of them have used it for themselves. Perhaps . . . some day . . . but as yet I have not the courage.''

"So you sell your services to the hunted? Well, that is one way of making a living. A list of your clients might make interesting reading.''

"Correct! I have had some very famous men apply for assistance. Especially at the close of the war. You might not believe the identity of some who sought me out then, after fortune's wheel spun against them.''

Simon nodded. "There *were* some notable gaps in the war criminal captures,'' he remarked. "And some odd worlds your stone must have opened if your tale is true.'' He arose and stretched. Then went to the table and counted out the money he took from his belt. Old bills, most of them, dirty, with a greasy film as if the business they had been used for had translated some of its slime to their creased surfaces. There remained in his hand a single coin. Simon spun it in the air and let it ring down on the polished wood. The engraved eagle lay up. He looked at it for a moment and then picked it up again.

"This I take."

"A luck piece?" The doctor was busy with the bills, stacking them into a tidy pile. "By all means retain it then; a man can never have too much luck. And now, I dislike speeding the parting guest, but the power of the Siege is limited. And the proper moment is all important. This way, please."

He might have been ushering one into a dentist's office, or to a board meeting, Simon thought. And perhaps he was a fool to follow.

The rain had stopped, but it was still dark in the square box of yard behind the old house. Petronius pushed a switch and a light fanned out from the back door. Three gray stones formed an arch which topped Simon's head by a few scant inches. And before that lay a fourth stone, as unpolished, unshaped and angular as the others. Beyond that arch was a wooden fence, high, unpainted, rotted with age, grimed with city dirt, and a foot or two of sour slum soil, nothing else.

Simon stood for a long moment, inwardly sneering at his half-belief of a few moments earlier. Now was the time for Sammy to appear and Petronius to earn his real fee.

But the doctor had taken his stand to one side of the clock on the ground. He indicated it with a forefinger.

"The Siege Perilous. If you will just take your seat there, Colonel—it is almost time."

A grin, without humor, to underline his own folly,

twisted Simon's thin-lipped mouth, as he straddled the stone and then stood for an instant partly under that arch before he sat down. There was a rounded depression to fit his hips. Curiously, with a sense of foreboding, he put out his hands. Yes, there were two other, smaller hollows to hold his palms, as Petronius had promised.

Nothing happened. The wooden fence, the strip of musty. earth remained. He was about to stand up when—

"Now!" Petronius' voice fluted in a word which was half call.

There was a swirling within the stone arch, a melting.

Simon looked out across a stretch of moorland which lay under a gray dawn sky. A fresh wind laden with a strange, invigorating scent fingered his hair. Something within him straightened like a leashed hound to trace that wind to its source, run across that moorland.

"Your world, Colonel, and I wish you the best of it!"

He nodded absently, no longer interested in the little man who called to him. This might be an illusion, but it drew him as nothing else ever had in his life. Without a word of farewell Simon arose and strode beneath the arch.

There was an instant of extreme panic—such fear as he had never imagined could exist, worse than any physical pain—as if the universe had been wrenched brutally apart and he had been spilled out into an awful nothingness. Then he sprawled face down on thick wiry turf.

II

MOOR HUNT

The dawn light did not mean sun to come, for there was a thick mist filling the air. Simon got to his feet and glanced back over his shoulder. Two rough pillars of reddish rock stood there, between them no city yard but a stretch of the same gray-green moor running on and on into a wall of fog. Petronius had been right: this was no world he knew.

He was shivering. Though he had brought his top coat with him, he did not have his hat, and the moisture plastered his hair to his skull, trickled from scalp to neck and cheek. He needed shelter—some goal. Slowly Simon made a complete turn. No building showed within the rim of the horizon. With a shrug he chose to walk straight away from the rock pillars; one direction was as good as another.

As he plodded across the soggy turf the sky grew lighter, the mist lifted, and the character of the land changed slowly. There were more outcrops of the red stone, the rolling ground held more sharp rises and descents. Before him, how many miles away he could not judge, a broken line cut the sky, suggesting heights to come. And the meal he had treated himself to was many hours in the past He twisted a leaf from a bush, chewed it absently, finding the flavor pungent but not unpleasant. Then he heard the noise of the hunt.

A horn called in a series of ascending notes, to be answered by a yapping and a single muffled shout. Simon began to trot. When he came out on the lip of a ravine he was certain that the clamor came from the other side of that cut, and was heading in his direction. With the caution of past commando training, he went to earth between two boulders.

The woman was the first to break from the cover of the scrub brush on the opposite bank. She sprinted, her long legs holding to the steady, dogged pace of one who has had a long chase behind, an even more distant goal ahead. At the edge of the narrow valley she hesitated to look back.

Against the grayish-green of the vegetation her slim ivory body, hardly concealed by the tatters which were her only covering, seemed to be spotlighted by the wan light of the dawn. With an impatient gesture she pushed back strands of her long black hair, ran her hands across her face. Then she began to work her way along the crest of the slope, hunting for a path down.

The horn pealed and the yapping answered it. She started convulsively and Simon half arose out of his hiding place as he suddenly realized that in that grim hunt she must be the quarry.

He dropped to one knee again as she jerked one of her rags free from a thorn bush. The force of that impatient tug sent her skidding over the rim. Even then she did not scream, but her hands grabbed for a bush as she went forward, and its branches held. As she struggled for footing the hounds burst into view.

They were thin, white animals, their lanky bodies turning with almost boneless fluidity as they came to the edge of the valley wall. With sharp noses pointed down at the woman, they gave triumphant tongue in wailing howls.

The woman writhed, flinging out her legs in a frenzied fight to reach some toehold on a narrow ledge to her right, a ledge which might afford her a path to the valley floor. Perhaps she might have made it had the hunters not arrived.

They were on horseback, and he who wore the horn cord over his shoulder remained in the saddle, while his companion dismounted and walked briskly to look over, kicking and slapping the hounds from his path. When he saw the woman his hand went to a holster at his belt.

Seeing him in turn the woman stopped her vain efforts to reach the ledge, hanging from her bush, her blank face, impassive, up to his. He grinned as he unsheathed his weapon, obviously savoring the helplessness of his prey.

Then the slug from Simon's gun caught him dead center. With a scream he tottered forward and fell into the gully.

Before echo of shot and scream had died away, the other huntsman took cover, which told Simon a little of the caliber of those he faced. And the hounds went mad, racing wildly up and down, filling the air with their yapping.

But the woman made a last effort and found foothold on the ledge. She sped down that path to the floor of the gully, taking cover among the rocks and brush which choked it. Simon saw a flash in the air. Point deep in the earth, not two inches away from where he had crouched to make his shot, a small dart quivered back and forth and then stood still. The other hunter had given battle.

Ten years ago Simon had played such games almost daily, relished them. And, he discovered, some actions once learned by muscles and body are not quickly forgotten. He wriggled into denser cover to wait. The hounds were tiring, several had flung themselves down, to lie panting. It was now a matter of patience, and Simon had that in abundance. He saw that tremor of vegetation and fired for the second time—to be answered by a cry.

A few moments later, alerted by a crackling of brush, he crept to the edge of the valley, and so came face to face with the woman. Those dark eyes, set at a provocative slant in her triangular face, searched his with a keen intentness Simon found a little disconcerting. Then, as his hand closed about her shoulder to draw her into deeper cover, he gained a sharp impression of danger, of a desperate need to keep moving across the moor. There was only safety beyond the edge of the moor, back in the direction from which he had come.

So strong was that warning that Simon found himself crawling back among the rocks before getting to his feet and running, matching his stride to hers, the yammering of the hounds growing fainter behind them.

Although she must have already been running for weary miles, his companion held to a pace which he had to stretch to match. At last they came to a place where the moor began to give way to boggy ponds edged with waist-high weeds. It was then that a down wind brought them again the faint call of a horn. And at that echo the woman laughed, glancing at Simon as if to ask him to share some jest. She indicated the bog patches with a gesture which suggested that here lay their safety.

About a quarter of a mile before them a mist curled and curdled, thickening, spreading to cut across their path, and Simon studied it. In such a curtain they might be safe, but also they might be lost. And, oddly enough, that mist appeared to rise from a single source.

The woman raised her right arm. From a broad metal

band about her wrist shot a flash of light, aimed at the
mist. She waved with her other hand for him to be still,
and Simon squinted into that curtain, almost certain he
saw dark shapes moving about there.

A shout, the words of the cry incomprehensible, but
the tone of challenge unmistakable, came from ahead.
His companion answered that with a lilting sentence or
two. But when the reply came she staggered. Then she
drew herself together and looked to Simon, putting out
her hand in half-appeal. He caught it, enfolding it in his
own warm fist, guessing they must have been refused
aid.

"What now?" he asked. She might not be able to
understand the words but he was certain she knew their
meaning.

Delicately she licked a finger tip and held it into that
wind rising to whip her hair back from a face on which a
purple bruise swelled at jawline and dark shadows
deepened the hollows beneath her high cheekbones.
Then, still hand in hand with Simon, she pulled to the
left; wading out into evil-smelling pools where green
scum was broken by their passing and clung in slimy
patches to her legs and his sodden slacks.

So they made their way about the edge of the bog,
and that fog which sealed its interior traveled on a
parallel course with them, walling them out. Simon's
hunger was a gnawing ache, his soaked shoes rubbed
blisters on his feet. But the sounds of the horn were lost.
Perhaps their present path had baffled the hounds.

His guide fought her way through a reed thicket and
brought them out on a ridge of higher ground where
there was a road of sorts, hardened by usage, but no
wider than a footpath. With it to follow they made
better time.

It must have been late afternoon, though in that gray neutral light hours could not be marked, when the road began to climb. Ahead were the escarpments of the red rock, rising almost as a crudely constructed wall, pierced by a gap which cradled the road.

They were almost to this barrier when their luck failed. Out of the grass beside the trail burst a small dark animal to run between the woman's feet, throwing her off balance, sprawling on the beaten clay. She uttered her first sound, a cry of pain, and caught at her right ankle. Simon hastened to push her hands aside and used knowledge learned on the battlefield to assess the damage. Not a break, but under his manipulation she caught her breath sharply, and it was plain she could not go on. Then, once more, came the call of the horn.

"This tears it!" Simon said to himself rather than to the woman. He ran ahead to the gap. The trace of road wound on to a river in a plain, with no cover. Save for the rock pinnacles which guarded the pass, there was no other break in the flat surface of the ground for miles. He turned to the escarpment and examined it with attention. Dropping his coat, he kicked off his soggy shoes and tested handholds. Seconds later he reached a ledge which could be seen from road level only as a shadow. But its width promised shelter and it would have to do for their stand.

When Simon descended the woman came creeping toward him on her hands and knees. With his strength and determination added to hers they gained that shallow refuge, crouching so closely together in that pocket of wind-worn rock that he could feel the warmth of her hurried breath on his cheek as he turned his head to watch their back trail.

Simon also became aware of her trembling, half-clothed body as shudders shook her from head to foot when the wind licked at them. Clumsily he wrapped his coat, damp as it was, about her and saw her smile, though the natural curve of her lips was distorted by a torn lip marked by a recent blow. She was not beautiful, he decided; she was far too thin, too pale, too worn. In fact, though her body was frankly revealed by the disarray of her rags, he was conscious of no male interest at all. And as that thought crossed his mind Simon was also aware that she did in some way understand his appraisal and that it amused her.

She hitched forward to the edge of the hollow so that they were shoulder to shoulder, and now she pulled back the sleeve of his coat, resting her wrist, with its wide bracelet, on her knee. From time to time she rubbed her fingers across an oval crystal set in that band.

Through the keening of the wind they could hear the horn, the reply of the hounds. Simon drew his automatic. His companion's fingers flashed from the bracelet to touch the weapon briefly, as if by that she could divine the nature of the arm. Then she nodded as those white dots which were hounds came from the trees down the road. Four riders followed and Simon studied them.

The open method of their approach argued that they did not expect trouble. Perhaps they did not yet know the fate of their two comrades by the ravine; they might believe that they still trailed one fugitive instead of two. He hoped that that was the truth.

Metal helmets with ragged crests covered their heads and curious eye-pieces were snapped down to mask the upper halves of their faces. They wore garments which seemed to be both shirt and jacket laced from waist to throat. The belts about their waists were a good twenty inches wide and supported bolstered sidearms, as well as sheathed knives, and various pouches and accouterments he could not identify. Their breeches were tight-fitting and their boots arose in high peaks on the outside of the leg. The whole effect was a uniform one, for all were cut alike of a blue-green stuff, and a common symbol was on the right breast of the shirt jackets.

The lean, snake-headed hounds swirled up the road and dashed to the foot of the rock, some standing on hindlegs to paw at the surface below the ledge. Simon, remembering that silent dart, shot first.

With a cough the leader of the hunters reeled and slipped from his saddle, his boot wedging in the stirrups so that the racing horse jerked a limp body along the road. There was a shout as Simon snapped a second shot. A man caught at his arm as he took to cover, while the horse, still dragging the dead man, bore through the gap and down into the river plain.

The hounds ceased to cry. Panting, they flung themselves down at the foot of the pinnacle, their eyes like sparks of yellow fire. Simon studied them with a growing discomfort. He knew war dogs, had seen them used as camp guards. These were large beasts and they were killers, that was to be read in their stance as they watched and waited. He could pick them off one by one, but he dared not waste his ammunition.

Although the day had been so lowering, he knew that night would be worse with its full darkness, and it was coming fast. The wind sweeping wetly from the bogs was searching out their shelter with its chill.

Simon moved and one of the hounds jumped to alert, putting its forepaws on the rock and lifting a moaning howl of threat. Firm fingers closed about Simon's upper arm, drawing him back, to his former position. Again through touch he received a message. As hopeless as their case appeared, the woman was not daunted. He gathered that she was waiting for something.

Could they hope to climb to the top of the escarpment? In the dusk he caught the shake of her unkempt head as if she had read that thought.

Once again the hounds were quiet, lying at the foot of the crag, their attention for the prey above. Somewhere—Simon strained to see through the dusk—somewhere their masters must be on the move, planning to close in about the fugitives. He knew his skill as a marksman, but conditions were now rapidly changing to the others' favor.

He nursed the automatic tensely, alert to the slightest sound. The woman stirred with a bitten-off exclamation, a gasp of breath. He did not need the urgent tug at his arm to make him look at her.

In the dusky quarter light a shadow moved up the end of the ledge. And she snatched his gun, gaining it by surprise, to bring down its butt with a vicious deadliness upon that creeping thing.

There was a thin squeal cut sharply in the middle. Simon grabbed the weapon and only when it was back safely in his grasp, did he look at that broken backed, squirming creature. Needle teeth, white and curved in a flat head, a narrow head mounted on a furred body, red eyes alive with something which startled him—intelligence in an animal's skull! It was dying, but still it wriggled to reach the woman, a faint hissing trilling between those fangs, malignant purpose in every line of its broken body.

With squeamish distaste Simon lashed out with his

foot, catching the thing on its side, sending it over to plop among the hounds.

He saw them scatter, separate and draw back as if he had tossed a live grenade into the gathering. Above their complaint he heard a more heartening sound, the laughter of the woman beside him. And he saw her eyes were alight with triumph. She nodded and laughed again as he leaned forward to survey that pool of shadow which now lapped about the base of the pinnicle, concealing the body of the thing.

Had it been another form of hunter loosed upon them by the hidden men below? Yet the uneasiness, the swift departure of the dogs that now milled yards away, seemed to argue otherwise. If they coursed with the dead creature it was not by choice. Accepting this as just another of the mysteries he had walked into—of his own free will—Simon prepared for a night on sentry-go. If the silent attack of the small animal had been some move on the part of the besiegers, they might now come into the open to follow it up.

But, as the darkness thickened, there were no more sounds from below which Simon could interpret as attack. Again the hounds lay down in a half circle about the foot of the pinnacle, dimly visible because of their white hides. Once more Tregarth thought of climbing to the top of the outcrop—they might even cross it if the woman's lameness abated.

When it was almost totally dark she moved. Her fingers rested for a moment on his wrist and then slipped down to lay cool in his palm. Through his own watchfulness, through his listening for any sound, a picture formed in his mind. Knife—she wanted a knife! He loosened her hold and took out his pen knife, to have it snatched from him eagerly.

What followed Simon did not understand, but he had

sense enough not to interfere. The cloudy crystal strapped to her wrist gave off a faint graveside radiance. By that he watched the point of the knife stab into the ball of her thumb. A drop of blood gathered on the skin, was rubbed across the crystal, so for a moment the thick liquid obscured the scrap of light.

Then up from that oval shone a brighter glow, a shaft of flame. Again his companion laughed, the low chuckle of satisfaction. Within seconds the crystal was dim once again. She laid her hand across his gun and he read in that gesture another message. The weapon was no longer necessary, aid would come.

The swampland wind with its puffs of rottenness moaned around and between the tongues of rock. She was shivering again and he put his arm about her hunched shoulders drawing her to him so that the warmth of their bodies could be joined. Along the arch of the sky flashed a jagged sword of purple lightning.

III

SIMON TAKES SERVICE

Another vivid bolt of lightning rent the sky, just above the pinnacle. And that was the opening shot of such a wild battle of sky, earth, wind and storm as Simon had never seen before. He had crawled over battlefields under the lash of manmade terrors of war, but this was worse somehow—perhaps because he knew that there was no control over those flashes, gusts, blasts.

The rock shook and pitched under them as they clung as frightened little animals to each other, closing their eyes to the shock of each strike. There was a continuous roar of sound, not the normal rumble of thunder, but the throb of a giant drum beaten to a rhythm which sang angrily in one's blood and set the brain to spinning dizzily. The woman's face was pressed tight against him and Simon enfolded her shaking body as he would the last promise of safety in a reeling world.

It went on and on, beat, crash, lick of light, beat, wind—but as yet no rain. A tremor in the rock under them began to echo the thud of the thunderblasts.

A final spectacular blast left Simon both deaf and blind for a space. But as the seconds lengthened into minutes and there was nothing more, when even the wind appeared to have exhausted itself, sinking into small, fitful puffs, he raised his head.

The stench of burned animal matter poisoned the air. A wavering glow not too far away marked a brush fire.

But the blessed quiet held and the woman stirred in his arms, pushing free. Once again he had an impression of confidence, a confidence mixed with triumph, some game had come to a victorious end and to the woman's satisfaction.

He longed for a light with which to survey the scene below. Had the hunter or hound survived the storm? Orange-red light lapped out from the fire toward the escarpment. Against the foot of the pinnacle lay a tangle of stiff white bodies. There was a dead horse in the road, a man's arm resting on its neck.

The woman pushed forward, searching with eager eyes. Then, before Simon could stop her, she had swung over the ledge and he followed, alert for attack, but seeing only the bodies in the firelight.

Warmth of flame reached them and it was good. His companion held out both arms to the glow. Simon skirted the dead hounds, scorched and twisted by the bolt which had killed them. He came to the dead horse with the idea of taking its rider's weapons. Then he saw the fingers in the animal's coarse mane move.

The hunter must be mortally injured, and certainly Simon had little feeling for him since that harrying chase across the moor and bog. But neither could he leave a helpless man so trapped. He struggled with the weight of the dead mount, got that broken body free where the light of the fire could show him who and what he had rescued.

Those strained, bloodstained, harshly marked features held no sign of life, yet the broken chest rose and fell laboriously and he moaned now and then. Simon could not have named his race. The close-cropped hair was very fair, silver-white almost. He had a boldly hooked nose between wide cheek bones, an odd combination. And Simon guessed that he was young though there was little of the unformed boy in that drawn face.

Still on its cord about his shoulder was a dented horn. And the rich ornamentation of his habit, the gem-set brooch at his throat, suggested that he was no common soldier. Simon, unable to do anything for those extensive hurts, turned his attention to the wide belt and its arms.

The knife he tucked into his own belt. The strange sidearm he took from its holster to examine carefully. It had a barrel, and something which could only be a trigger. But in his hand the balance felt wrong, the grip awkwardly shaped. He pushed it inside his shirt.

He was about to loosen the next item, a narrow cylinder, when a white hand flashed across his shoulder and took it.

The hunter stirred as if that touch, rather than Simon's handling, had reached his dazed brain. His eyes opened, feral eyes, with a gleam of light within their depths such as a beast's holds in the darkness. And there was that in those eyes which made Simon recoil.

He had met men who were dangerous, men who wanted his death and who would go about the business of securing it with a businesslike dispatch. He had stood face to face with men in whom some trait of character worked upon him until he hated them on sight. But never before had he seen any such emotion as lay at the back of those shining green eyes in the battered face of the hunter.

But Simon realized that those eyes were not turned upon him. The woman stood there, a little crookedly for she favored her injured ankle, turning over in her hands the rod she had stripped from the hunter's belt. Almost Simon expected to see in her expression some answer to that burning, corrosive rage with which the wounded man faced her.

She was watching the hunter steadily, without any sign of emotion. The man's mouth worked, twisted. He raised his head with a tortured, visible effort which racked his whole body and spat at her. Then his head cracked back against the roadway and he lay still as if that last gesture of detestation had drained all his reserves of energy. And in the light of the now dying fire his face went queerly slack, his mouth fell open. Simon did not need to note the end of that laboring rise and fall of the crushed chest to know that he was dead.

"Alizon—" The woman shaped the word carefully, looking to Simon and then to the body. Stopping she indicated the emblem on the dead man's jacket. "Alizon."

"Alizon," Simon echoed as he got to his feet, having no desire to plunder farther.

Now she swung to face the gap through which the road ran on into the river plain.

"Estcarp—" Once more that careful pronouncement of a name, but her finger indicated the river plain. "Estcarp." She repeated that, but now touched her own breast.

And, as if by that name she had evoked an answer, there was a shrilling pipe from the other side of the gap. No demanding call such as the hunter's horns had given, but rather a whistling such as a man might make between his teeth as he waited for action. The woman replied with a shouted sentence which was taken up by the wind, echoed from the sides of the rock barrier.

Simon heard the thud of hooves, the jangle of metal against metal. But since his companion faced the gap welcomingly, he was content to wait before going into action. Only his hand closed about the automatic in his pocket and its blunt muzzle pointed to that space between the pinnacles.

They came one at a time, those horsemen. Skimming between the peaks, the first two fanning out, weapons ready. When they sighted the woman they called eagerly; plainly they were friends. The fourth man rode straight ahead to where Simon and the woman waited. His mount was tall, heavy through the barrel as if the animal had been selected to carry weight. But the figure in the high peaked saddle was so short of stature Simon thought him a young boy—until he swung to earth.

In the light of the fire his body glistened, and points of glitter sparkled on helm, belt, throat and wrist. Short he was, but his breadth of shoulder made that lack of height the more apparent, for his arms and chest were those intended for a man a third again his size. He wore armor of some sort with the apparent texture of chainmail, yet it clothed him so snugly that it might have been wrought of cloth, yielding to every movement of his limbs with the pliability of woven stuff. His helmet was crested with the representation of a bird, wings outstretched. Or was it a real bird charmed to unnatural immobility? For the eyes which glinted in its upheld head appeared to watch Simon with a sullen ferocity. The smooth metal cap on which it perched ended in a kind of scarf of the mail, looped about the wearer's neck and throat. He tugged at this impatiently as he walked forward, freeing his face from its half veiling. And Simon saw that he had not been so wrong in his first guess after all. The hawk-helmed warrior was young.

Young, yes, but also tough. His attention was divided between the woman and Simon, and he asked her a question as he surveyed Tregarth measuringly. She answered with a rush of words, her hand sketching some sign in the air between Simon and the warrior. Seeing that, the newcomer touched his helm in what was clearly a salute to the outlander. But it was the woman who commanded the situation.

Pointing to the warrior she continued her language lesson: "Koris."

It could be nothing but a personal name Simon decided quickly. He jerked his thumb at his own chest:

"Tregarth, Simon Tregarth." He waited for her to name herself.

But she only repeated what he had said. "Tregarth, Simon Tregarth," as if to set the syllables deep in her mind. When she did not answer otherwise he made his own demand.

"Who?" he pointed straight at her.

The warrior Koris started, his hand going to the sidearm at his belt. And the woman frowned, before her expression became so remote and cold that Simon knew he had blundered badly.

"Sorry," he spread his hands in gesture which he hoped she would take for apology. In some way he had offended, but it was through ignorance. And the woman must have understood that, for she made some explanation to the young officer, though he did not look at Simon with any great friendliness during the hours which followed.

Koris, showing a deference which did not match the woman's ragged clothing, but did accord with her air of command, mounted her behind him on the big black horse. Simon rode behind one of the other guardsmen, linking his fingers in the rider's belt and clinging tight, as they headed back into the river plain at a pace which even the dark of the night did not keep from approaching a gallop.

A long time later Simon lay still in a nest of bed coverings and stared with unseeing eyes up at the curve of the carved wood canopy overhead. Save for those wide open eyes he might have been deemed as suddenly asleep as he had been minutes earlier. But an old talent for passing from sleep into instant alertness had not been lost with his entrance into this new world. And now he was busy sorting out impressions, classifying knowledge, trying to add one fact to another to piece together a concrete picture of what lay about him beyond the confines of the massive bed, the stone walls of the room.

Estcarp was more than the river plain; it was a series of forts, stubborn defensive holds along a road marking a frontier. Forts where they had changed horses, had fed, and then swept on again, driven by some need for haste Simon had not understood. And at last it was a city of round towers, green-gray as the soil in which they were rooted under the pale sun of a new day, towers to guard, a wall to encircle, and then other buildings of a tall, proud-walking race with dark eyes and hair as black as his own, a race with the carriage of rulers and an odd weight of years upon them.

But by the time they had entered that Estcarp Simon had been so bemused by fatigue, so dulled by the demands of his own aching body, that there were only snatches of pictures to be remembered. And overlaying them all the sensation of age, of a past so ancient that the towers and the walls could have been part of the mountain bones of this world. He had walked old cities in Europe, seen roadways which had known the tramp of Roman legions. Yet the alien aura of age resting here was far more overpowering, and Simon fought against it when he marshalled his facts.

He was quartered in the middle pile of the city, a massive stone structure which had both the solemnity of a temple and the safety-promise of a fort. He could just barely remember the squat officer, Koris, bringing him to this room, pointing to the bed. And then— nothing.

Or was it nothing?

Simon's brows drew together in a faint frown. Koris, this room, the bed— Yet now as he stared up into the mingled pattern of intricate carving arching over him, he found things there which were familiar, oddly familiar, as if the symbols woven back and forth had a meaning which he would unravel at any moment now.

Estcarp—old, old, a country and a city, and a way of life! Simon tensed. How had he known that? Yet it was true, as real as the bed on which his saddle-sore body rested, as the carvings over him. The woman who had been hunted—she was of this race, of Estcarp—just as the dead hunter by the barrier had been of another and hostile people.

The Guardsmen in the frontier posts were all of the same mold, tall, dark, aloof in manner. Only Koris, with his misshapen body, had differed from the men he led. Yet Koris' orders were obeyed; only the woman who rode behind him had appeared to have more authority.

Simon blinked, his hands moved beneath the covers, and he sat up, his eyes on the curtains to his left. Soft as it had been, he had caught that whisper of footfall, and he was not surprised when the rings of the curtains clicked, and the thick blue fabric parted, so that he looked at the very man who had been in his thoughts.

Freed of his armor Koris was even more of a physical oddity. His too-wide shoulders, those dangling, over-long arms overweighed the rest of him. He was not tall and his narrow waist, his slender legs were doubly small in contrast to the upper part of his body. But set on those shoulders was the head of the man Koris might have been had nature not played such a cruel trick. Under a thick cap of wheat-yellow hair was the face of a boy who had only recently come to manhood, but also the face of one who had had no pleasure in that development. Strikingly handsome, apart from those shoulders, jarring with them, the head of a hero partnered to the body of an ape!

Simon slid his legs down the mound of the high bed and stood up, sorry at that moment that he must force the other to look up to him. But Koris had moved back with the quickness of a cat and perched on a broad stone ledge running beneath a slit window, so that his eyes were still on a level with Tregarth's. He gestured with a grace foreign to his long arm to a nearby chest, indicating a pile of clothing there.

Those were not the tweeds he had crawled out of before seeking bed, Simon noted. But he also saw something else, a subtle reassurance of his present status there. His automatic, the other contents of his pocket, had been laid out with scrupulous neatness to one side of that new clothing. He was no prisoner, whatever other standing he might have in that hold.

He pulled on breeches of soft leather, resembling those Koris now wore. Supple as a glove, they were colored a dark blue. And with them were a pair of calf-high boots of a silvery-gray substance he thought might be reptile hide. Having dressed so far he turned to the other and made gestures of washing.

For the first time a ghost of smile touched the Guardsman's well-cut mouth and he pointed to an alcove. Medieval the hold of Estcarp might be superficially, Simon discovered, but the dwellers therein had some modern views on sanitation. He found himself introduced to water which flowed, warm, from a wall pipe when a simple lever was turned, to a jar of cream, faintly fragrant, which applied and then wiped off erased all itch of beard. And with his discoveries came a language lesson, until he had a growing vocabulary of words Koris patiently repeated until Simon had them right.

The officer's attitude was one of studied neutrality. He neither made friendly overtures, save for his language instructions, nor accepted Simon's attempts at more personal conversation. In fact, as Tregarth pulled on a garment intended to serve as both shirt and jacket, Koris shifted halfway around on the window ledge to stare out into the day sky.

Simon weighed the automatic in his hand. The Estcarpian officer appeared to be indifferent as to whether this stranger went armed or not. At length Tregarth slipped it into his belt above his lean and now empty middle, and signed that he was ready to go.

The room gave on a corridor and that, within a few paces, upon a stair down. Simon's impression of immeasurable age was confirmed by the hollows worn in those same stone steps, a groove running along the left wall where fingers must have passed for eons. Light came palely from globes set far above their heads in metal baskets, but the nature of that light remained a mystery.

A wider hall lay at the foot and men passed there. Some in the scaled mail were guards on duty, others had the easier dress Simon now wore. They saluted Koris and eyed his companion with a somber curiosity he found vaguely disconcerting, but none of them spoke. Koris touched Tregarth's arm, motioned to a curtained doorway, holding back a loop of the cloth in a way which suggested an order.

Beyond stretched another hall. But here the bare stone of the walls were covered with hangings bearing the patterns of the same symbols he had seen on the bed canopy, half familiar, half alien. A sentry stood to attention at the far end of that way, raising the hilt of his sword to his lips. Koris looped back a second curtain, but this time he waved Simon by him.

The room seemed larger than it was because of the vault of the ceiling which pointed up far overhead. Here the light globes were stronger, and their beams, while not reaching into those lofty shadows, did show clearly the gathering below.

There were two women awaiting him—the first he had seen within the pile of the keep. But he had to look a second time to recognize in the one standing, her right hand on the back of a tall chair which held her companion, the woman who had fled before the hunters of Alizon. That hair which had hung in lank soaked strings about her then was coiled rather severely into a silver net, and she was covered primly from throat to ankle by a robe of a similar misty color. Her only ornament was an oval of the same cloudy crystal such as she had worn then in a wrist band, but this hung from a chain so that the stone rested between the small mounds of her breasts.

"Simon Tregarth!" It was the seated woman who summoned him, so his eyes passed to her, and he found that he could not take them away again.

She had the same triangular face, the same seeking eyes, the same black coils of netted hair. But the power which emanated from her was like a blow. He could not have told her age, in some ways she might have seen the first stones of Estcarp laid one upon another. But to him she seemed ageless. Her hand flashed up and she tossed a ball toward him, a ball seemingly of the same cloudy crystal as the gem she and her lieutenant wore as jewels.

Simon caught it. Against his flesh it was not cold as he had expected, but warm. And as he instinctively cupped it in both hands, her own closed over her jewel, a gesture echoed by her companion.

Tregarth could never afterwards explain, even to himself, what followed. In some weird fashion he pictured in his mind the series of actions which had brought him to the world of Estcarp, sensing as he did so that those two silent women saw what he had seen and in a measure shared his emotions. When he had done that a current of information flowed in his direction.

He stood in the main fortress of a threatened, perhaps a doomed land. The age-old land of Estcarp was menaced from the north and from the south, and also from the sea to the west. Only because they were the heirs of age-old knowledge were the dark people of her fields, her towns and cities, able to hold back the press. Theirs might be a losing cause, but they would go down fighting to the last blow of sword from the last living Guardsman, the last blasting weapon man or woman could lay hand upon.

And that same hunger which had drawn Simon under the rough arch in Petronius' yard into this land, was alive and avid in him once more. They made no appeal to him, their pride was unbending. But he gave his allegiance to the woman who had questioned him, chose sides in that moment with a rush of a boy's openhearted enthusiasm. Without a spoken word passing between them, Simon took service in Estcarp.

IV

THE CALL OUT OF SULCARKEEP

Simon raised the heavy tankard to his lips. Over the rim of the vessel he watched the scene alertly. On his first acquaintance he had thought the people of Estcarp somber, overshadowed by a crushing weight of years, the last remnants of a dying race who had forgotten all but dreams of the past. But during the past weeks he had learned bit by bit how surface and superficial that judgment had been. Now in the mess of the Guards his attention flickered from face to face, reappraising, not for the first time, these men with whom he shared a daily round of duties and leisure.

To be sure their weapons were strange. He had had to learn the swing of a sword for use in close melee, but their dart guns were enough like his automatic to cause him little trouble. He could never match Koris as a warrior—his respect for that young man's skill was unbounded. However Simon knew the tactics of other armies, other wars, well enough to make suggestions even that aloof commander came to appreciate.

Simon had wondered how he would be received among the Guards—after all they were making a stand against high odds and to them any stranger might represent an enemy, a breach in the wall of defense. Only he had not reckoned with the ways of Estcarp. Alone in the nations of this continent, Estcarp was willing to welcome one coming with a story as wild as his own. Because the power of that ancient holding was founded upon—magic!

Tregarth rolled the wine about his tongue before he swallowed, considering objectively the matter of magic. That word could mean sleight-of-hand-tricks, it could cover superstitious Mumbo-Jumbo—or it could stand for something far more powerful. Will, imagination and faith were the weapons of magic as Estcarp used it. Of course, they had certain methods of focusing or intensifying that will, imagination, and faith. But the end result was that they were extremely open-minded about things which could not be seen, felt, or given visible existence.

And the hatred and fear of their neighbors was founded upon just that basis—magic. To Alizon in the north, Karsten in the south, the power of the Witches of Estcarp was evil. "You shall not suffer a witch to live." How many times had that been mouthed in his own world as a curse against innocent and guilty alike, and with far less cause.

For the matriarchate of Estcarp did have powers beyond any human explanation, and they used them ruthlessly when necessary. He had helped to bring a witch out of Alizon where she had ventured to be eyes and ears for her people.

A witch— Simon drank again. Not every woman of Estcarp had the Power. It was a talent which skipped willfully from family to family, generation to generation. Those who tested out as children were brought to the central city for their schooling and became dedicated to their order. Even their names were gone, for to give another one's name was to give a part of one's identity, so that thereafter the receiver had power over

the giver. Simon could understand now the enormity of
his request when he had asked the name of the woman
in whose company he had fled over the moor.

Also the Power was not steady. To use it past a
certain point wore hardly upon the witch. Nor could it
always be summoned at will. Sometimes it was apt to
fail at some crucial moment. So, in spite of her witches
and her learnings, Estcarp had also her mail-clad
Guards, her lines of forts along her borders, her swords
loose in many sheaths.

"Sa . . ." The stool beside him was jerked back
from the table as a newcomer swung leg across to sit.
"It is hot for the season." A helm banged down on the
board and a long arm swept out to reach the jug of wine.

The hawk on the discarded helm stared at Simon
glassily, its beautifully wrought metallic plumage resembling true feathers. Koris drank while questions
were shot at him from about the table, as men might aim
darts for more deadly purpose. There was discipline in
the forces of Estcarp but off duty there was no caste and
the men about that board were avid for news. Their
commander banged his tankard down with some force
and answered briskly:

"You'll hear the muster horn before the hour of gate
closing, in my opinion. That was Magnis Osberic who
prayed safe passage from the west road. And he had a
tail in full war gear. It is to my mind that Gorm makes
trouble."

His words fell into a silence at the end. All of them,
now including Simon, knew what Gorm meant to the
Guards' Captain. For rightfully the lordship of Gorm
should have rested in Koris' powerful hands. His personal tragedy had not begun there, but it had ended on
that island when, wounded and alone, he had drifted
from its shore, face down in a leaking fishing boat.

Hilder, Lord Defender of Gorm, had been storm-stayed on those moors which were a no man's land between Alizon and the plains of Estcarp. There, separated from his men, he had fallen from a floundered horse and broken an arm, to blunder on in a half daze of pain and fever into the lands of the Tormen, that strange race who held the bogs against all comers, allowing no encroachment upon their soggy domain by any race or man.

Why Hilder had not been slain or driven forth again remained ever a mystery. But his story was untold even after he returned to Gorm some months later, healed again of body and bearing with him a new-made wife. And the men of Gorm—more straightly, the women of Gorm—would have none of that marriage, whispering that it had been forced upon their lord in return for his life. For the woman he had brought with him was misshapen of body, stranger yet of mind, being of the true blood of Tor. She bore him Koris in due time, and then she was gone. Perhaps she died, perhaps she fled again to her kin. Hilder must have known, but he never spoke of her again, and Gorm was so glad to be rid of such a liege lady that there were no questions asked.

Only Koris remained, with the head of a Gorm noble and the body of a bog loper, as he was never allowed to forget. And in time when Hilder took a second wife, Orna, the well-dowered daughter of a far-sailing sea master, Gorm again whispered and hoped. So they were only too willing to accept the second son Uryan, who, it was plain to see, had not a drop of suspect outland blood in the veins of his straight young body.

In time Hilder died. But he was a long time in dying and those who whispered had a chance to make ready against that day. Those who thought to use Orna and

Uryan for their purposes were mistaken, for the Lady
Orna, of trading stock and shrewd, was no easily befooled female of the inner courts. Uryan was still a
child, and she would be his regent—though there were
those who would say no to that unless she made a
display of strength.

She was not a fool when she played one lord of Gorm
against another, weakening each and keeping her own
forces intact. But she was the worst befooled mortal in
the world when she turned elsewhere for support. For it
was Orna who brought black ruin to Gorm when she
secretly summoned the fleet of Kolder to back her rule.

Kolder lay over the rim of the sea world, just where
you could find only one man in ten thousand among the
seafarers who could tell you. For honest men, or human
men, kept aloof from that grim port and did not tie at its
quays. It was accepted everywhere that those of Kolder
were not as other men, and it was damnation to have
any contact with them.

The death day of Hilder was followed by a night of
red terror. And only one of Koris' superhuman strength
could have broken from the net cast for him. Then there
was only death, for when the Kolder came to Gorm,
Gorm ceased to be. If any now lived there who had
known life under Hilder, they had no hope. For Kolder
was now Gorm, yes, and more than just the island of
Gorm, for within the year stark towers had risen in
another place on the coast and a city called Yle had
come into being. Though no man of Estcarp went to
Yle—willingly.

This Yle lay like a spreading stain of foulness between Estcarp and their one strong ally to the west—
the sea wanderers of Sulcarkeep. These fighter-traders
who knew wild places and different lands had built their
stronghold by Estcarp favor on a finger of land which

pointed into the sea, their road to encircle the world. Master Traders were the seamen of Sulcarkeep, but also they were fighting men who walked unchallenged in a thousand ports. No trooper of Alizon or shieldman of Karsten spoke to a Sulcarman except in a mild voice, and they were esteemed as swordbrothers by the Guardsmen of Estcarp.

"Magnis Osberic is not one to ride forth with the summoning arrow unless he must have already manned his walls," remarked Tunston, senior under officer who kept the forces of Estcarp to the mark. He arose and stretched. "We'd best see to our gear. If Sulcarkeep cries aid, then we loosen swords."

Koris gave only a preoccupied nod to that. He had dipped finger into his tankard and was drawing lines on the scrubbed board before him, chewing absentmindedly the while at a flat-sized hunk of brown bread. Those lines made sense to Simon, looking over the other's hunched shoulder, for they duplicated maps he had seen in the muster room of the city keep.

That finger which ended with Sulcarkeep on its tip formed one arm to encircle a wide bay, so that across the expanse of water the city of the traders faced— although many miles lay between them—Aliz, the main port of Alizon. In the confines of the bay itself was cupped the island of Gorm. And on that Koris carefully made the dot to signify Sippar, the main city.

Strangely enough Yle did not lie on the bayside section of the peninsula coast, but on the southwest portion of the shoreline, facing the open sea. Then there was a sweep of broken line southward, extending well into the Duchy of Karsten, all rock cliff with no safe anchorage for any ship. The bay of Gorm had been of old Estcarp's best outlet to the western ocean.

The Guards' Captain studied his work for a long

instant or two and then with an impatient exclamation, rubbed his hand across it, smearing the lines.

"There is only one road to Sulcarkeep?" asked Simon. With Yle to the south and Gorm to the north, parties from each Kolder post could easily slice in two a peninsula road without greatly bestirring themselves.

Koris laughed. "There is one road, as old as the ages. Our ancestors did not foresee Kolder in Gorm—who in their sane minds could? To make safe that road," he put his thumb on the dot he had made for Sippar and pressed it against the age-hardened wood as if he were remorselessly crushing an insect, "we would have to do so here. You cure a disease by treating its source, not the fever, the wasting which are the signs of its residence in the body. And in this case," he looked bleakly up at Tregarth, "we have no knowledge upon which to work."

"A spy—"

Again the Guards' officer laughed. "Twenty men have gone forth from Estcarp to Gorm. Men who suffered shape-changing without knowing whether they would ever again look upon their own faces in a mirror, but suffering that gladly, men who were fortified with every spell the learning here could summon for their arming. And there has come back out of Sippar—nothing! For these Kolder are not as other men and we know nothing of their devices of detection, save that they appear to be infallible. At last the Guardian forbade any further such ventures, since the drain of Power was too great to have only failure always as an answer. I, myself, have tried to go, but they had set a boundary spell which I cannot break. To land on Gorm would mean my death, and I can serve Estcarp better alive. No, we shall not tear out this sore until Sippar falls, and not yet have we any hopes of bringing that about.''

"But if Sulcarkeep is threatened?''

Koris reached for his helm. "Then, friend Simon, we ride! For this is the strangeness of the Kolder: when they fight upon their own land or their own ships, the victory is always theirs. But when they assail clean territory where their shadow has not yet fallen, then there is still a chance to blood them, to swing swords which bite deep. And with the Sulcarmen the war ravens feed well. I would mark my Kolders when and while I can.''

"I ride with you.'' That was a statement more than a question. Simon had been content to wait, to learn. He had set himself to school with the patience he had so painfully learned in the past seven years, knowing that until he mastered the skills which meant life or death here he could not hope for independence. And once or twice in the night watches he wondered whether the vaunted Power of Estcarp had not been used to bring about his acceptance of the status quo without question or rebellion. If so, that spell was wearing thin now; he was determined to see more of this world than just the city, and he knew that either he rode now with the Guard or he would go alone.

The Captain studied him. "We go for no quick foray.''

Simon remained seated, knowing the other's dislike of being towered over and willing to propitiate him by that costless courtesy.

"When have I seemed to you one who expects only easy victories!'' he got a caustic bite into that.

"See that you depend upon the darts then. As a swordsman you are still scarcely better than a stall keeper of Karsten!''

Simon did not fire at that jibe, knowing that it was only too true. As a marksman with the dart guns he could match the best in the hold and come off a shade the winner. Wrestling and unarmed combat to which he brought the tricks of Judo, had given him a reputation with the men now reaching to the border forts. But in sword use he was still hardly better than the gawky recruits with only boy-down to be scrubbed from their cheeks. And he swung a mace which Koris handled with cat-ease as if it were a shoulder-breaking burden.

"Dart gun it is," he returned readily. "But still I ride."

"So be it. But first we see whether or no any of us are to take the road."

That was decided in the conclave into which the officers under Koris, the witches on duty in the hold, were summoned. Though Simon had no official standing in that company, he ventured to follow the Captain and was not refused entrance, taking his place on the ledge of one of the window embrasures to study the company with speculation.

The Guardian who ruled the keep and Estcarp beyond, the woman without a name who had questioned him on his first coming, presided. And behind her chair stood that witch who had fled before the hounds of Alizon. There were five more of the covenanted ones, ageless—in a way sexless—but all keen-eyed and watchful. He would far rather fight with them behind him, than standing in opposition, Simon decided. Never had he known any like them, or seen such power of personality.

Yet facing them now was a man who tended to dwarf his surroundings. In any other company he might well have dominated the scene. The men of Estcarp were lean and tall, but this was a bronze bull of a man beside whom they were boys not yet come to their full growth. The armor plate which hooped his chest could have furnished close to two shields for the Guard, his shoulders and arms were a match for Koris' but the rest of his body was in keeping.

His chin was shaven, but on his broad upper lip a mustache bristled, stretching out across his weathered cheeks. And eyebrows furnished a second bar of hair on the upper part of his face. The helm on his head was surmounted with the skillfully modeled head of a bear, its muzzle wrinkled in a warning snarl. And a huge bearhide, tanned and lined with saffron yellow cloth, formed his cloak, gold-clawed forepaws clasped together under his square chin.

"We of Sulcarkeep keep traders' peace." Manifestly he was trying to tutor his voice to a tone more in keeping with the small chamber, but it boomed through the room. "And we keep it with our blades, if the need arises. But against wizards of the night of what use is good steel? I do not quarrel with the old learning," he addressed the Guardian directly, as if they faced each other across a trading counter. "To each man his own gods and powers, and never has Estcarp pushed upon others their own beliefs. But Kolder does not so. It laps out and its enemies are gone! I tell you, lady, our world dies, unless we rise to stem a tide together."

"And have you, Master Trader," asked the woman, "ever seen a man born of woman who can control the tides?"

"Control them, no, ride them, yes! That is my magic." He thumped his corselet with a gesture which might have been theatrical, save that for him it was right. "But there is no riding with Kolder, and now

they plan to strike at Sulcarkeep! Let the stupid wits of
Alizon think to hold aloof, they shall be served in turn
as Gorm was. But Sulcarmen man their walls—they
fight! And when our port goes, those sea tides sweep
close to you, lady. Rumor says that you have the magic
of wind and storm, as well as those spells which twist a
man's shape and wits. Can your magic stand against
Kolder?''

Her hands went to the jewel on her breast and she
smoothed it.

"It is the truth I speak now, Magnis Osberic—I do
not know. Kolder is unknown, we have not been able to
breach its walls. For the rest—I agree. The time has
come when we must take a stand. Captain,'' she hailed
Koris, ''what is your thought upon the matter?''

His handsome face did not lose its bitter shadow, but
his eyes were alight.

"I say that while we can use swords, then let us!
With your permission, Estcarp will ride to Sulcarkeep.''

"The swords of Estcarp shall ride, if that is your
decision, Captain, for yours is the way of arms and you
speak accordingly. But also shall that other Power ride
in company, so what force we have shall be given.''

She made no summoning gesture, but the witch who
had spied in Alizon moved from behind the chair to
stand upon the Guardian's right hand. And her dark,
slanted eyes moved over the company until they found
Simon sitting apart. Had a shadow of a smile, gone in
an instant, spread from her eyes to her lips? He could
not have sworn to it, but he thought that was so. He did
not understand why, but in that moment Simon was
aware of a very fragile thread spun between them, and
he did not know whether he chafed against the thinnest
of bonds or not.

When they rode out of the city in the midafternoon Simon discovered by some chance his mount matched pace with hers. As the men of the Guard she wore mail, the scarfed helmet. There was no outward difference between her and the rest, for a sword hung at her hip, and the same sidearm at her belt as Simon carried.

"So, man of war from another world," her voice was low and he thought it for his hearing alone, "we travel the same train once again."

Something in her serene composure irked him. "Let us hope this time to hunt instead of being hunted."

"To each his day," she sounded indifferent. "I was betrayed in Alizon, and unarmed."

"And now you ride with sword and gun."

She glanced down at her own equipment and laughed. "Yes, Simon Tregarth, with sword and gun—and other things. But you are right in one thought, we hasten to a dark meeting."

"Foretelling, lady?" His impatience ripened. For that moment he was an unbeliever. It was far easier to trust in steel which fitted into the hand than in hints, looks, feelings.

"Foretelling, Simon." Her narrow eyes regarded him still with that shadow smile somewhere in their depths. "I am laying no geas, nor quest upon you, outland man. But this I know: our two strands of life stuff have been caught up together by the Hand of the Over Guardian. What we wish and what will come of it may be two very different things. This I shall say, not only to you, but to all this company—beware the place where rocks arch high and the scream of the sea eagle sounds!"

Simon forced an answering smile. "Believe me, lady, in this land I watch as if I had eyes set around my head in a circlet. This is not my first raiding party."

"As has been known. Else you would not ride with the Hawk," she pointed with a lift of her chin to Koris. "Were you not of the proper metal he would have none of you. Koris is a warrior bred, and a leader born—to Estcarp's gain!"

"And you foresee this danger at Sulcarkeep?" he pressed.

She shook her head. "You have heard how it is with the Gift. Bits and patches are granted us—never the whole pattern. But there are no city walls in my mind picture. And I think it lies closer than the sea rim. Loose your dart gun, Simon, or bare those knowledgeable fists of yours." She was amused again, but her laughter did not jeer—rather it was the open good humor of comradeship. He knew that he must accept her on her own proffered terms.

V

DEMON BATTLE

The troop from Estcarp pushed the pace but they had still a day's journey before them when they rode out of the last of the frontier posts and headed along the curve of the seaport highway. They had changed mounts regularly at the series of Guard installations and spent the night at the last fort, keeping to a steady trot that ate up the miles.

Although the Sulcarmen did not ride with the same ease as the Guard, they clung grimly to saddles which seemed too small for their bulk—Magnis Osberic not being unique in his stature—and kept up, riding with the fixed purpose of men to whom time itself was a threatening enemy.

But the morning was bright, and patches of purple flowering bush caught radiance from the sun. The air carried the promise of salt waves ahead and Simon knew a lift of heart which he had thought lost long ago. He did not realize that he was humming until a familiar husky voice cut from his left.

"Birds sing before the hawk strikes."

He met that mockery good-naturedly. "I refuse to listen to the croaking of ill—it is too fine a day."

She plucked at the mail scarf wreathing her shoulders and throat, as if its supple folds were a kind of imprisonment. "The sea—it is in the wind here—" Her gaze roamed ahead where the road rippled to the horizon. "We have a portion of the sea in our veins, we of Estcarp. That is why Sulcar blood can mingle with ours, as it has oftimes. Someday I would take to the sea as a venture. There is a pull in the very surge of the waves as they retreat from the shore."

Her words were a singing murmur, but Simon was suddenly alert, the tune he had hummed dried in his throat. He might not have the gifts of the Estcarp witches, but deep within him something crawled, stirred into life, and before he reasoned it through, his hand flashed up in a signal from his own past as he reined in his horse.

"Yes!" Her hand was flung to echo his and the men behind them halted. Koris' head whipped about: he made his own signal and the whole company came to a stop.

The Captain passed the lead momentarily to Tunston and rode back. They had their flankers out; nothing could be charged to lack of vigilance.

"What is it?" Koris demanded.

"We are running into something." Simon surveyed the terrain ahead, laying innocently open under the sun. Nothing moved except a bird spiralling high. The wind had died so that even its puffs did not disturb the patches of brush. Yet he would stake all his experience and judgment upon the fact that before them a trap was waiting to snap jaws.

Koris' surprise was fleeting. He had already glanced from Simon to the witch. She sat forward in the saddle, her nostrils expanded as she breathed deeply. She might have been trying the scent as does a hound. Dropping the reins she moved her fingers in certain signs, and then she nodded sharply with complete conviction.

"He is right. There is a blank space ahead, one I can not penetrate. It may be a force barrier—or hide an attack."

"But how did he—the gift is not his!" Koris' protest was quick and harsh. He flashed a glance at Simon which the other could not read, but it was not of confidence. Then he issued orders, spurring forward himself to lead one of those circling sweeps which were intended to draw an overanxious enemy into the open.

Simon drew his dart gun. How had he known—how did he know they were advancing into danger? He had had traces of such foreknowledge in the past—as on the night he had met Petronius—but never had it been so sharp and clear, with a strength which increased as he rode.

The witch kept beside him, just behind the first line of Guards, and now she chanted. From inside her mail shirt she had brought out that clouded jewel which was both a weapon and the badge of her calling. Then she held it above her head at arm's length and cried aloud some command which was not in the tongue Simon had painstakingly learned.

There came into view a natural formation of rocks pointing into the sky as fangs from some giant jawbone, and the road ran between two which met in the semblance of an arch. About the foot of the standing stones was a mass of brush, dead and brown, or living and green, to form a screen.

From the gem a spearpoint of light struck upon the tallest of those toothstones, and from that juncture of beam and rock spread a curling mist which thickened into a cottony fog, blanketing out the pillars and the vegetation.

Out of that clot of gray-white stuff burst the attack, a

wave of armed and armored men coming forward at a run in utter silence. Their helms were head-enveloping and visored, giving them the unearthly look of beaked birds of prey. And the fact that they advanced without any calls or orders along their ranks added to the weirdness of the sudden sortie.

"Sul . . . Sul . . . Sul . . .!" The sea rovers had their swords out, and swung them in time to that thunderous shout as they drew into a line which sharpened into a wedge, Magnis Osberic forming its point.

The Guard raised no shout, nor did Koris issue any orders. But marksmen picked their men and shot, swordsmen rode ahead, their blades ready. And they had the advantage of being mounted, while the silent enemy ran afoot.

Simon had studied the body armor of Estcarp and knew where the weak points existed. Whether the same was true of Kolder armor he could not tell. But he aimed for the armpit of one man who was striking at the first Guard to reach the cresting wave of the enemy forces. The Kolder spun around and crashed, his pointed visor digging into the earth.

"Sul . . . Sul . . . Sul . . .!" The war shouts of the Sulcarmen were a surf roar as the two bands of fighters met, mingled, and swirled in a vicious hand to hand combat. In the first few moments of the melee Simon was aware of nothing but his own part in the affair, the necessity for finding a mark. And then he began to note the quality of the men they battled.

For the Kolder force made no attempt at self-preservation. Man after man went blindly to his death because he did not turn from attack to defense in time. There was no dodging, no raising of shields or blade to ward off blows. The foot soldiers fought with a dull ferocity, but it was almost mechanical. Clockwork toys, Simon thought, wound up and set marching.

Yet these were supposed to be the most formidable foemen known to this world! And now they were being cut down easily, as a child might push over a line of toy soldiers.

Simon lowered his gun. Something within him revolted against picking off the blind fighters. He spurred his mount to the right in time to see one of the beaked heads turn in his direction. The Kolder came forward at a brisk trot. But he did not engage Simon as the other had expected. Instead he leaped tigerishly at the rider just beyond—the witch.

Her mastery of her horse saved her from the full force of that dash and her sword swung down. But the blow was not clean, catching on the pointed visor of the Kolder and so being deflected over his shoulder.

Blind as he might be in some respects the fellow was well schooled in blade work. The blue length of steel in his hand flashed in and out, in its passing sweeping aside the witch's weapon, tearing it from her hand. Then he cast aside his own weapon and his mail-backed glove grabbed for her belt, tearing her from the saddle in spite of her struggles, with an ease which Koris might have displayed.

Simon was on him now and that curious fault which was losing his comrades their battle possessed this Kolder as well. The witch was fighting so desperately in his hold that Simon dared not use his sword. He drew his foot from the stirrups as he urged his horse closer, and kicked out with all the force he could put behind that blow.

The toe of his boot met the back of the Kolder's round helmet, and the impact of that meeting numbed

Simon's foot. The man lost his balance and sprawled forward, bearing the witch with him. Simon swung from the saddle, stumbling, with fear that his jarred leg would give under him. His groping hands slid over the Kolder's plated shoulder, but he was able to pull the fellow away from the gasping woman and send him over on his back, where he lay beetle-wise, his hands and legs still moving feebly, the blankness of his beaked visor pointing up.

Shedding her mailed gloves the woman knelt by the Kolder, busy with the buckles of his helm. Simon caught at her shoulder.

"Mount!" He ordered, drawing his own horse forward for her.

She shook her head, intent upon what she was doing. The stubborn strap gave and she wrenched off the helm. Simon did not know what he had expected to see. His imagination, more vivid than he would admit, had conjured up several mental pictures of the hated aliens—but none of them matched this face.

"Herlwin!"

The hawk crown helmet of Koris cut between Simon and that face as the Captain of the Guard knelt beside the witch, his hands going out to the fallen man's shoulders as if to draw him into the embrace of close friends.

Eyes as green-blue as the Captain's, in a face as regularly handsome, opened, but they did not focus either on the man who called, or the other two bending over him. It was the witch who loosened Koris' grip. She cupped the man's chin, holding still his rolling head, peering into those unseeing eyes. Then she loosed him and pulled away, wiping her hands vigorously on the coarse grass. Koris watched her.

"Herlwin?" It was more a question addressed to the witch than an appeal to the man in Kolder's trappings.

"Kill!" She ordered between set teeth. Koris' hand went out to the sword he had dropped on the grass.

"You can't!" Simon protested. The fellow was harmless now, knocked partly unconscious by the blow. They could not just run him through in cold blood. The woman's gaze crossed his, steel cold. Then she pointed to that head, rolling back and forth again.

"Look, outworld man!" She jerked him down beside her.

With an odd reluctance Simon did as she had done, took the man's head between his hands. And on that moment of contact he nearly recoiled. There was no human warmth in that flesh; it did not have the chill of metal nor of stone, but of some unclean, flabby stuff, firm as it looked to the eye. When he stared down into those unblinking eyes, he sensed rather than saw a complete nothingness which could not be the result of any blow, no matter how hard or straightly delivered. What lay there was not anything he had ever chanced upon before—an insane man still has the cloak of humanity, a mutilated or mangled body could awaken pity to soften horror. Here was the negation of all which was right. a thing so loathsomely apart from the world that Simon could not believe it was meant to see sun or walk upon wholesome earth.

As the witch had done before him, he scrubbed his hands on the grass trying to rub from them the contamination he felt. He scrambled to his feet and turned his back as Koris swung the sword. Whatever the Captain struck was dead already—long dead—and damned.

There were only dead men to mark the Kolder force, and two slain Guardsmen, one Sulcar corpse being lashed across his horse. The attack had been so strikingly inept that Simon could only wonder why it had been made. He fell in step with the Captain and discovered that he was in search of knowledge.

"Unhelm them!" The order passed from one group of Guardsmen to the next. And beneath each of those beak helms they saw the same pale faces with heads of cropped blond hair, those features which argued they were akin to Koris.

"Midir!" he paused beside another body. A hand twitched, there was the rattle of death in the man's throat. "Kill!" The Captain's order was dispassionate, and it was obeyed with quick efficiency.

He looked upon every one of the fallen, and three more times he ordered the death stroke. A small muscle twitched at the corner of his well-cut mouth, and what lay in his eyes was far from the nothingness which had been mirrored in the enemies'. The Captain, having made the rounds of the bodies, came back to Magnis and the Witch.

"They are all of Gorm!"

"They *were* of Gorm," the woman corrected him. "Gorm died when it opened its sea gates to Kolder. Those who lie here are not the men you remember, Koris. They have not been men for a long time—a long, long time! They are hands and feet, fighting machines to serve their masters, but true life they did not have. When the Power drove them out of hiding they could only obey the one order they had been given—find and kill. Kolder can well use these things they have made to fight for them, to wear down our strength before they aim their greater blows."

That lip twitch pulled the Captain's mouth into something which curved but in no way resembled a smile.

"So in a measure do they betray a weakness of their

own. Can it be that they lack manpower?'' Then he corrected himself, slamming his sword back into its sheath with a small rasp of sound. "But who knows what lies in a Kolder mind—if they can do this, then perhaps they have other surprises.''

Simon was well in the van as they rode on from that trampled strip of field where they had met the forces of Kolder. He had not been able to aid in the final task the witch urged on them, nor did he like to think now of those bodies left headless. It was hard to accept what he knew to be true.

"Dead men do not fight!'' He did not realize he had protested that aloud until Koris answered him.

"Herlwin was like one born in the sea. I have watched him hunt the spear fish with only a knife for his defense. Midir was a recruit in the bodyguard, still stumbling over his feet when the assembly trumpet blew on the day Kolder came to Gorm. Both of them I knew well. Yet those things which lie behind us, they were neither Herlwin nor Midir.''

"A man is three things.'' It was the witch who spoke now. "He is a body to act, a mind to think, a spirit to feel. Or are men constructed differently in your world, Simon? I can not think so, for you act, you think, and you feel! Kill the body and you free the spirit; kill the mind and ofttimes the body must live on in sorry bondage for a space, which is a thing to arouse man's compassion. But kill the spirit and allow the body, and perhaps the mind to live—'' her voice shook, "that is a sin beyond all comprehension of our kind. And that is what has happened to these men of Gorm. What walks in their guise is not meant for earthborn life to see! Only an unholy meddling with things utterly forbidden could produce such a death.''

"And you cry aloud the manner of our deaths, lady,

should Kolder come into Sulcarkeep as it did to Gorm.'' The Master Trader pushed his heavy-boned mount up level with them.

"We have bested them here, but what if they muster legions of these half-dead to assault our walls? There are only a few men within the keep, for this is the trading season and nine-tenths of our ships are at sea. We needs must spread thinly in the fortress. A man may clip heads with a will, but his arm tires at the business. And if the enemy keeps coming they can overwhelm us by sheer weight of numbers. For they have no fear for themselves and will go forward where one of us might have a second thought, or a third!''

Neither Koris nor the witch had a ready answer for that. Only Simon's first sight of the trading port, hours later, was in a manner reassuring. Seamen though the Sulcarmen might be by first choice, they were also builders, using every natural advantage of the point they had selected as an asset in the erection of the keep. From the land side it was mainly wall with watch towers and firing slits in plenty. And it was only when Magnis Osberic escorted them within that they saw the full strength of the place.

Two arms of rock curved out to the sea—a crab's open claws—and between them was the harbor. But each of those claws had been reinforced with blocks of masonry, walls, watch points, miniature forts, connected to the main body with a maze of underground ways. Wherever possible the outer walls ran down straight to the pound of the waves, providing no possible hold for climbers.

"It would seem," Simon commented, "that this Sulcarkeep was built with the thought of war in mind."

Magnis Osberic laughed shortly. "Master Tregarth,

the Peace of the Highways may hold for our blood within Estcarp, and to a measure within Alizon and Karsten—providing we clink gold in the hearing of the right ears. But elsewhere in the world we show swords along with our trade goods, and this is the heart of our kingdom. Down in those warehouses lies our life blood—for the goods that we barter is the flow of our life. To loot Sulcarkeep is the dream of every lordling and every pirate in this world!

"The Kolder may be the demon spawn rumor names them, but they do not disdain the good things of this earth. They would like to paddle their paws in our takings as well as the next. That is why we also have a last defense here—if Sulcarkeep falls her conquerors will not profit!" He brought his big fist down upon the parapet before them in a giant's crushing blow. "Sulcarkeep was built in my great-grandfather's day to provide all our race with a safe port in time of storm—storm of war as well as storm of wind and wave. And it would seem that we now need it."

"Three ships in the harbor," Koris had been counting. "A cargo bottom and two armed runners."

"The cargo is for Karsten in the dawning. Since it carries the Duke's bargainings it can go under his flag and her crew need not stand to arms in the port faring," remarked Osberic.

" 'Tis tongued about that the Duke is to wed. But there is a necklet of Samian fashioning lying in a chest down there intended for the white neck of Aldis. It would appear that Yvian may put the bracelet on some other's wrist, but he intends not to wear it on his own."

The witch shrugged and Koris appeared far more interested in the ships than in any gossip concerning the neighboring court. "And the runners?" he prompted.

"Those remain for a space." The Master Trader was evasive. "They shall patrol. I am better pleased to know what approaches from the sea."

A bomber might reduce the outer shell of Sulcarkeep to rubble in a run or two; heavy artillery could breach its massive walls within hours, Simon decided, as he continued on the inspection round with Koris. But there were a warren of passages and chambers in the rock beneath the foundations of the buildings, some giving on the sea—those having barred doors; unless the Kolder had weapons beyond any arms he had seen in this world, the traders would appear to be unnecessarily nervous. One could think that, until one remembered the empty-eyed foemen from Gorm.

He also noted that while there were guardrooms in plenty and well-filled racks of weapons, stands of the heavy mace-axes, there were few men, widely spread through those rooms, patrols stretched over area of wall. Sulcarkeep was prepared to equip and house thousands of men and a scant hundred or so stood to arms there.

The three of them, Koris, the witch, and Simon drew together on a sea tower where the evening wind strove against their mail.

"I dare not strip Estcarp," Koris spoke angrily, as if in reply to some argument neither of his companions heard, "to center all our manpower here. Such foolishness would be open invitation to Alizon or the Duchy to invade north and south. Osberic has an outer shell which I do not believe even the jaws of the Kolder can crack, but the meat within it is missing. He waited too long; with all his men in port he might hold, yes. With only this handful, I doubt it."

"You doubt, Koris, but you will fight," the woman

said. There was neither encouragement nor discouragement in her tone. "Because that is what must be done. And it may well be that this hold will break the Kolder's jaws. But Kolder does come—that Magnis has foreseen truly."

The Captain looked at her eagerly. "You have a foretelling for us, lady?"

She shook her head. "Expect nothing from me that I can not give, Captain. When we rode into that ambush I could see nothing but a blank ahead. By that very negative sign I recognized the Kolder. But better than that I cannot do. And you, Simon?"

He started. "I? But I have no pretense to your Power—" he began and then added more honestly, "I can say nothing—except as a soldier I think this is an able fort, and now I feel as one trapped within it." He had added that last almost without thinking, but he knew it for the truth.

"But that we shall not say to Osberic," Koris decided. Together they continued to watch the harbor as the sun set, and more and more the city beneath lost the form of a refuge and took on the outline of a cage.

VI

FOG DOOM

It began a little after midnight—that creeping line across the sea, blotting out both stars and waves, sending before it a chill which was born of neither wind nor rain, but which bit insidiously into a man's bones, slimed his mail with oily beads, tasted salty and yet faintly corrupt upon his lips.

The line of light globes which followed each curve of the claw fortifications was caught. One by one those pools of light were muffled into vague smears of yellow. To watch that creeping was to watch a world being blotted out inch by inch, foot by foot.

Simon strode back and forth across the small sentry platform on the central watch tower. Half the claw fortifications were swallowed, lost. One of the slim raiders in the harbor was sliced in two by that curtain. It resembled no natural fog he had ever seen, unlike the famous blackouts of London, the poisoned industrial smogs of his own world. The way it crept in from the west as a steady curtain suggested only one thing—a screen behind which an attack might be gathering.

Deadened and hollow he caught the clamor of the wall alarms, those brazen gongs stationed every so many feet along the claws. Attack! He reached the door of the tower and met the witch.

"They're attacking!"

"Not yet. Those are storm calls, to guide any ship which might be seeking port."

"A Kolder ship!"

"Perhaps so. But you cannot overturn the customs of centuries in an hour. In fog Sulcarkeep's gongs serve seamen, only Osberic's orders can mute them."

"Then such fogs as this one *are* known?"

"Fogs are known. Such as this—that is another matter."

She brushed past him to come out into the open, facing seaward as he had done moments earlier, studying the fast disappearing harbor.

"We of the Power have a certain measure of control over the natural elements, though like all else that is subject to failure or success beyond our forereckoning. It is in the providence of any of my sisterhood to produce a mist which will not only confuse the eyes of the unwary, but also their minds—for a space. But this is different."

"It is natural?" Simon persisted, sure somehow that it was not. Though why he was so certain of that he could not explain.

"When a potter creates a vase he lays clay upon the wheel and molds it with the skill of his hands to match the plan which is in his brain. Clay is a product of the earth, but that which changes its shape is the product of intelligence and training. It is in my mind that someone—or something—has gathered up that which is a part of the sea, of the air, and has molded it into another shape to serve a purpose."

"And what do you in return, lady?" Koris had come out behind them. He strode straight to the parapet and slapped his hands down upon the water-pearled stone. "We are like to be blind men in this!"

She did not look away from the fog, watching it with the intentness of a laboratory assistant engaged in a crucial experiment.

"Blindness they may seek, but blindness can enfold two ways. If they will play at illusion—then let them be countered with their own trick!"

"Fight fog with fog?" the Captain commanded.

"You do not fight one trick with the same. They are calling upon air and water. Therefore we must use water and air in return, but in another fashion." She tapped her thumbnail against her teeth. "Yes, that might be a confusing move," she murmured as she swung around. "We must get down to the harbor level. Ask of Magnis a supply of wood, dry chips will be excellent. But, if he has them not, get knives that we may cut them. Also some cloth. And bring it to the center quay."

The choked clamor of the gongs echoed hollowly across the heart of the harbor as the small knot of Sulcarmen and Guards came out on the quay. An armload of board lengths appeared and the witch took the smallest. Her hands plied the knife clumsily as she strove to whittle out the rude outline of a boat, pointed at bow, rounded at stern. Simon took it from her, peeling off the white strips easily, the others following his example as the woman approved.

They had a fleet of ten, of twenty, of thirty chip boats, palm-size, each fitted with a stick mast and a cloth sail the witch tied into place. She went down on her knees before that line, and, stooping very low, blew carefully into each of the tiny sails, pressed her finger for a moment on the prow of each of the whittled chips.

"Wind and water, wind and water," she singsonged. "Wind to hasten, water to bear, sea to carry, fog to ensnare!"

Swiftly her hands moved, tossing one and another of the crude representations of a sea fleet out into the water of the harbor. The fog was almost upon them, but it was still not too thick for Simon to miss an amazing sight. The tiny boats had formed into a wedge shaped line pointing straight for the now hidden sea. And, as the first dipped across the line of the fog curtain it was no hastily chipped toy, but a swift, gleaming ship, finer than the slim raiders Osberic had displayed with pride.

The witch caught at Simon's dangling wrist to draw herself to her feet again. "Do not believe all that you see, out-world man. We deal in illusion, we of the Power. But let us hope that this illusion will be as effective as their fog, frightening off any invaders."

"They can't be real ships!" Stubbornly he protested the evidence of his eyes.

"We depend too strongly upon our outer senses. If one can befool the eyes, the fingers, the nose—then the magic is concrete for a space. Tell me, Simon, should you be planning to enter this harbor for attack and then saw out of the fog about your ships a fleet you had not suspected was there, would you not think twice of offering battle? I have only tried to buy us time, for illusion breaks when it is put to any real test. A Kolder ship which would try to lock sides and board one of that fleet could prove it to be what it is. But sometimes time bought is a precious thing."

She was in a measure right. At least, if the enemy had planned to use the blanket of mist to cover an attack on the harbor, they did not follow through. There was no invasion alarm that night, neither was there any lifting of the thick cover over the city as the hour of dawn passed.

The masters of the three ships in the harbor waited upon Osberic for orders, and he could give none, save to wait out the life of the fog. Simon made the rounds of the Guards in Koris' wake, and sometimes it was necessary for one man to link fingers in the other's belt lest they lose touch, upon the outer stations of the sea wall. Orders were given that the gongs continue to beat at regular intervals, not now for the protection of those at sea, but merely that one sentry post keep in touch with the next. And men turned strained, drawn faces, half drew weapons as their reliefs came upon them, until one shouted the pass word or some identification ahead lest he be spitted upon the steel of a jumpy outpost.

"At this rate," Tregarth commented as he sidestepped one rush from a Sulcarman they came upon suddenly, and so saved himself from a crippling blow, if not worse, "they will not need to send any attack force, for we shall be flying out upon each other. Let a man seem to wear a beaked helm in this murk and he will speedily be short a head."

"So I have thought," the Captain answered shortly. "They play with illusion, too, born of our nerves and fears. But what answer can we give except what we had already done?"

"Anyone with good ears could pick up our pass words." Simon determined to face the worst. "A whole section of wall could fall to their control, post by post."

"Can we even be sure that this *is* an attack?" counter-questioned the other bitterly. "Outworlder, if you can give better orders here, then do so and I shall accept them gladly! I am a man of war, and the ways of war I know—or thought I knew—well. Also I believed that I knew the ways of wizards, since I serve Estcarp with a whole heart. But this is something I have never met before; I can only do my best."

"And never have I seen this manner of fighting either," Simon admitted readily. "It would baffle anyone. But this I think now—they will not come by sea."

"Because that is the way we look to have them creep upon us?" Koris caught him up quickly. "I do not think that the keep can be assaulted from land. These searovers have built shrewdly. It would need siege machinery such as would take weeks to assemble."

"Sea and land—which leaves?"

"Earth and air," Koris replied. "Earth! Those under passages!"

"But we cannot spread men too thinly to watch all the underground ways."

Koris' sea-green eyes glowed with the same feral battle light Simon had seen in them at their first meeting.

"There is a watch which can be put upon them, needing no men. A trick I know. Let us get to Magnis." He began to run, the point of his sheathed sword clinking now and again against the stone walls as he rounded the turns in the keep corridors.

Basins were lined up on a table, of all sizes and several shapes, but they were uniformly of copper and the balls Koris was carefully apportioning, one to a bowl, were also of metal. One of the bowl and ball combination, installed in the portion of wall overhanging an underground way, would betray any attempt to force the door far below by the oscilation of ball within basin.

Earth was safeguarded as best they could. Which left—the air. Was it because he was familiar with air warfare that Simon found himself listening, watching, at the cost of a crick in the neck, the murk encasing the towers of the port? Yet a civilization which depended upon the relatively primitive dart guns, the sword, the shield, and a mailed body for offense and defence—no matter what subtle tricks of the mind they called in bolstering aids—could not produce airborne attack as well.

Thanks to Koris' device of the bowls they had a few moments of warning when the Kolder thrust came. But from all five points where the bowls had been placed that alarm arose at nearly the same instant. The halls leading to each doorway had been stuffed during frenzied hours of labor with all the burnable stuff in the warehouses of the port. Mats of sheep wool and cowhair soaked in oil and tar, which the shipwrights used for the calking, were woven in around torn bales of fine fabrics, bags of dried grain and seeds, and oil and wine poured in rivulets to soak into these giant plugs.

When the bowls warned, torches were applied and other portals closed, sealing off from the central core those flame-filled ways.

"Let them run their cold dog noses into that!" Magnis Osberic thumped his war ax exultingly on the table in the central hall of the main keep. For the first time since the fog had imprisoned his domain the Master Trader appeared to lose his air of harassment. As a seafarer he hated and feared fog, be it born of nature or the meddling of powers. With a chance for direct action, he was all force and drive again.

"Ahhhhhh!" Across the hubbub in the hall that scream cut like a sword slice. Torture of body was not all of it, for only some supreme fear could have torn it from a human throat.

Magnis, his bull's head lowering as if he would charge the enemy, Koris, sword ready, a little crouched so that his dwarfish body gathered strength from the earth, the rest of the men in that chamber were frozen for a long second.

Perhaps because during all this period of waiting he had been half expecting it, Simon identified the source first, and sped for the stair which, three floors higher, gave upon the sentry go of the roof.

He did not reach that level. Screams and cries from above, the clash of metal against metal was warning enough. Slowing his pace, Simon drew his gun. And it was good he was cautious for he was midway to the second level when a body rolled down, missing him by a scant inch. It was a Sulcarman, his throat a ragged wound still pumping blood to spatter wall and stair. Simon looked up into a wild confusion.

Two Guardsmen and three of the seafarers still fought, their backs against the wall on the landing of the next level, keeping at bay invaders who attacked with the single-minded ferocity their kin had displayed at the road ambush. Simon snapped a shot, and then another. But a wave of beaked helms poured unceasingly from above. He could only guess that in some way the enemy had come by air and now held the top floors of the keep.

There was no time to speculate upon their method of getting there—it was enough that they had managed to break through. Two more of the seafarers, one of the Guard were down. The dead and wounded, friends and foe alike were disregarded by the beaked helms. Bodies slipped downstairs—they could not be stopped there. The plug must come below.

Simon leaped for the first landing, kicking open the two doors fronting on it. The furniture favored by Sulcar was heavy stuff. But the smaller pieces could be moved. In that moment Simon summoned up strength he did not know he possessed, jerking and pushing articles out to choke the stairwell.

A beaked head faced him through the upraised legs of a chair used to top his efforts, and a sword point struck for his face. Simon crashed the chair over on that helm. There was a smarting cut on his cheek but the attacker was not a part of the barricade.

"Sul! Sul!"

Simon was elbowed to one side and he saw Magnis' face, as red as its tawny bristle of mustache, loom up as the trader chopped down, smashed up at the first wave of invaders to reach the stair barrier and claw at the stuff which formed it.

Aim, fire, aim again. Throw away an empty dart clip, reload to fire anew. Straddle a Guardsman down moaning, until the man could be dragged back into whatever safety anyone could find in the keep now. Fire—Fire!

Somehow Simon had come back into the hall, then the party of which he was one were on another stairway, selling each flight dearly as they descended. There was a thin smoke here—tendrils of fog? No, for when it wreathed them its acrid bite stung nose and throat setting them coughing. Aim—fire—grab dart packs from the belt of a fallen Guardsman who could no longer use any weapon.

The steps were behind now. Men shouted hoarsely, and the smoke was worse. Simon smeared his hand across his watering eyes and pulled at the throat scarf of his helmet. His breath came in shallow gasps.

Blindly he followed after his companions. Doors of five-inch thickness swung after them, were barred and locked. One . . . two . . . three . . . four of such barriers. Then they stumbled into a room facing an installation housed in a casing taller than the giant of a man who leaned against it, dull-eyed. The Guardsmen and the seafarers who had made it rimmed the room, leaving the strange machine to the master of the city.

Magnis Osberic had lost his bear-crested helm, his fur cloak was a tattered string trailing from one shoulder. His ax lay across the top of the casing, and from its blade a red line dripped sluggishly to the stone pavement. The ruddiness of his coloring had faded, leaving his skin with a withered look. His eyes were wide, staring at men and not seeing them—Simon guessed that the man was in a state of shock.

"Gone!" He picked up the ax, slipped its long half back and forth in his rope-caloused hand. "From the air like winged demons! No man can fight against demons." Then he laughed softly, warmly, as a man might laugh when he took a willing woman into his arms. "But there is also an answer to demons. Sulcarkeep shall not serve that spawn for a nesting place!"

His bull head lowered for the charge once more, swung slowly as he singled out the Estcarp men from among his own followers. "You have fought well, you of the witch blood. But this last is no doom laid upon you. We shall loose the energy which feeds the city powers and blast the port. Get you forth that you may perhaps settle the accounting in a way those air-flying wizards can understand. Be sure we shall take with us such a number of them that they shall have thinned ranks against that day! Go your way, witch men, and leave us of Sulcarkeep to *our* final reckoning!"

Urged by his eyes and his voice, as if he had caught each of them in a bear's grip and thrust them away from him and his, the remnant of the Guard gathered together. Koris was still with them, his hawk helm lacking a wing. And the witch, her face serene, but her lips moving as she walked quietly across the chamber. Twenty more men and Simon.

As one the Guards drew to attention, their stained swords swinging up in salute to those they left. Magnis grunted.

"Pretty, pretty, witchmen. But this is no time for parade. Get out!"

They filed through a small door he indicated, Koris through last to slam and bar it. At a dead run they took that passage. Luckily there were globe lights set in the roof at intervals and the floor was smooth, for the need for haste burned in them.

The sound of sea and surf grew stronger and they came out in a cave where small boats swung at anchor.

"Down!" Simon was pushed aboard with others, and Koris' hand slapped between his shoulders, sending him face down. Men landed on him and about him, pinning him flat to the rocking bottom. There was the slam of another door—or was it a deck shutting over them? Light was gone and with it air. Simon lay quiet, having no idea of what would happen next.

Under him the boat moved, men's bodies rolled, he was kicked, prodded, and he buried his face in the crook of his arm. The craft which held them swung about and his stomach fought against that motion. He had never been too good a sailor. Mainly occupied with his fight against sickness, he was not prepared for a blast which seemed to end the world with one blow of sound and pressure.

They were still rolling in the waves, but when Simon lifted his head he gulped clean air. He wriggled and strove, paying no attention to the grunts and protests of those about him. No more fog was his first dazed thought—and then—it was day! The sky, the sea about them, the coast behind were clear and bright.

But when did the sun rise from the shore, leap up in sky-touching flames from a land base? He had been deafened by the blast, but not blinded. They were heading out to sea, leaving the source of that heat and light behind them.

One . . . two . . . three cockshells of boats he counted. There were no sails, they must be motored in some way. A man sat erect in the stern of theirs, his shoulders identifying him. Koris held that tiller. They were free of the inferno which had been the port of Sulcarkeep, but where did they head?

Fog gone, and the fire on shore giving them light. But the waves which swept them along were not born of any calm sea. Perhaps the shock of that blast with which Magnis had destroyed the keep had been communicated to the ocean. For a wind drove down upon them as if a hand strove to press them beneath the surface, and those on board the featherweight ships began to realize that they had gained perhaps only a few minutes of life rather than full escape.

PART II:
VENTURE OF VERLAINE

I

AX MARRIAGE

The sea was dull and gray, the color of an ax blade which would never take on a sheen no matter how much one polished, or a steel mirror misted by moisture one could not rub away. And above it the sky was as flat, until it was hard to distinguish the meeting line between air and water.

Loyse huddled on the ledge beneath the arrow-split window. She dreaded the depths, for this turret, bulging roundly from its parent wall, hung directly over the wicked, surf-collared rocks of the shoreline, and she had no head for heights. Yet she was often drawn to this very seat because when one stared straight out into the emptiness, which was seldom troubled save by a diving bird, one could see freedom.

Her hands, long fingered, narrow of palm, pressed flat against the stone on either side of the window as she did lean forward an inch or so, making herself eye what she feared, as she made herself do many things her body, her mind shrank from. To be Fulk's daughter one must grow an inner casing of ice and iron which no blow to the flesh, no taunt to the spirit could crack. And she had been intent upon that fashioning of an interior citadel for more than half the years of her short life.

There had been many women at Verlaine, for Fulk was a man of lusty appetite. And Loyse had watched them come and go from her babyhood, cold-eyed and measuring herself. To none had he given wifehood, by none had he sired other offspring—which was Fulk's great dissatisfaction and so far her own gain. For Verlaine was not Fulk's by blood, but by his one and only marriage with her mother, and only as long as Loyse lived could he continue to hold it and its rich rights of pillage and wreckage, ashore and afield. There were kinsmen of her mother's in Karsten who would be quick enough to claim lordship here were she to die.

But, had Fulk sired a son by any of the willing—and unwilling—women he had brought to the huge bed in the lord's chamber, then he could have claimed more than just his own life tenancy for the male heir under the new laws of the Duke. By the old customs motherright was for inheritance; now one took a father's holding, and only in cases where there was no male heir did the old law prevail.

Loyse cherished her tiny thread of power and safety, held to it as her one hope. Let Fulk be chopped down in one of his border raids, let him be sought out by some vengeful male of a family despoiled, and she and Verlaine would be free together! Ah, then they would see what a woman could do! They would learn that she had not been moping in secret all these years as most of them believed.

She drew back from the ledge, walked across the room. It was chill with the breath of the sea, gloomy with lack of sun. But she was used to cold and dusk, some of both were a fast part of her now.

Beyond the curtained bed she came to stand in front of a mirror. It was no soft lady's looking glass, but a shield, diamond-shaped, polished through patient hours until it gave back to the room a slightly distorted reflection. And to stand so, facing squarely what it told her, was another part of Loyse's strict self-dicipline.

She was small, but that was the only feminine characteristic she shared with the blowsy women who satisfied her father's men, or with the richer fare he kept for his own enjoyment. Her body was as straight and slender as a boy's, with only shadow curves to hint she was not a lad. The hair which lay in braids across her shoulders, and then fell below waist level, was thick enough. But it was lank and of so pale a yellow that except in direct sunlight it was white as a beldame's, while lashes and brows of the same colorless tint made her face seem strangely blank and without intelligence. The skin pulled tightly across the fine bones of her face and chest was smooth and also lacking in any real color. Even the line of her lips was of the palest rose. She was a bleached thing, grown in the dark, but a vitality within her was as strong as the supple blade a wise swordsman chooses over the heavier hacking weapon of the inexperienced.

Suddenly her hands flew together, gripped tightly for an instant. Then she as quickly snapped them apart and to her sides, though under her hanging sleeves they were still balled into fists, nails biting palms. Loyse did not turn to the door, nor give any other outward hint that she had heard that rattling of the latch. She knew just how far she dared go in her subtle defiance of Fulk, and from that limit she never retreated. Sometimes she thought despairingly her father never recognized her rebellion at all.

The door slammed back against the wall. Verlaine's lord always treated any barrier as if he were storming an enemy fortress. And he tramped in now with the tread of a man who has just lifted the city keys from the sword point of a vanquished commander.

If Loyse was the colorless creature of the dark, Fulk

was lord of sun and flamboyant light. His good body was beginning to show traces of his rough living, but he was still more than handsome, his red-gold head carried with the arrogance of a prince, his well-cut features only a little blurred. Most of Verlaine worshipped their lord. He had an openhanded if uneven generosity when he was pleased, and his vices were all ones which his men understood and shared.

Loyse caught his reflection in the mirror, brave, bright, turning her even more into a night taper. But she did not face about.

"Greetings, Lord Fulk." Her voice was toneless.

"Lord Fulk, is it? Is that the way you speak to your father, wench? Come show a little more than ice in your veins for once, girl!"

His hand slid under one of the braids on her shoulder, and he forced her around, gripping with strength which would leave her bruised for a week. He did it deliberately, she knew, but she would give no sign of feeling.

"Here I come with news as would send any proper wench leaping with joy, and you turn me that cold fish face of yours with no pleasure," he contemplated jovially. But that which looked out of his eyes was not born of good humor.

"You have not yet voiced this news, my lord."

His fingers kneaded into her flesh as if seeking to find and crush the bones hidden there.

"To be sure I have not! Yet it is news as will set any maid's heart to pounding in her. Wedding and bedding, my girl, wedding and bedding!"

Purposely Loyse chose, but with a fear she had not known before, to misunderstand him.

"You take a lady for Verlaine, my lord? Fortune grant you a fair face for such an occurrence."

His grip on her did not loosen, and now he shook her, with the outward appearance of one playfully admonishing, but with a force which brought pain.

"You may be a wry-faced nothing of a woman, but you are not stupid of wit, no matter how you may think to befool others. You should be properly a female at your age. At least you will now have a lord to make trial of that. And I'd advise you not to play your tricks with him. By all accounts he likes his bedfellows biddable!"

What she had long feared most had come upon her and it brought with it a betrayal of feeling she could not bite back in time.

"A wedding needs free consent—" She stopped then, knowing shame for her momentary breaking.

He was laughing, relishing having torn that protest out of her. His hand moved across her shoulder to vise upon the back of her neck in a pinch which brought an involuntary gasp out of her. Then, as one moves a lifeless puppet, he whirled her about, pushing her face toward the mirror shield, holding her helpless there while he pelted her with words he believed would hurt worse than any beating his hands could inflict.

"Look upon that curdled mass of nothing you call a face! Do you think any man could set his lips to it without closing his eyes and wishing himself elsewhere? Be glad, wench, that you have something besides your face and that bone of a body to lure a suitor. You'll consent freely to anyone who'll take you. And be glad you have a father who can make a bargain as good as I have for you. Yes, girl, you'd better crawl on those stiff knees of yours and thank any gods you have that Fulk looks after his own."

His words were a mutter of thunder; she saw no reflection in the mirror, save certain misty horrors of her own imagining. Which one of the brutes who rode in Fulk's train would she be thrown to—for some advantage for his lord?

"Karsten himself—" There was a sort of wonder underlying Fulk's rising exultation. "Karsten, mind you, and this lump of unbaked dough squeaks of consent! You *are* lacking in wits!" He released her with a sudden push which sent her flying against the shield and the metal rang against the wall. She fought for her balance, kept her feet, and turned to face him.

"The Duke!" That she could not believe. Why should the ruler of the duchy ask for the daughter of a shore baron, old and proud as her maternal lineage might be?

"Yes, the Duke!" Fulk seated himself on the end of the bed, swinging his booted feet. "Talk of fortune! Some good providence winked at your birth, my girl. Karsten's herald rode in this morning with an offer of ax marriage for you."

"Why?"

Fulk's feet stopped moving. He did not scowl, but his face was sober.

"There are a bristle of reasons like darts at his back!" He held up his hands and began to tell off the fingers of one with the forefinger of the other.

"Item: The Duke, for all his might, was a rider of mercenaries before he set his seal on Karsten, and I doubt if he can rightly name his dam, let alone his sire. He crushed those of the lords who tried to face him down. But that was a good half-score of years ago and he no longer wants to ride in mail and smoke rebels out of their castles. Having won his duchy he wishes now some easy years in which to enjoy it. A wife taken from the ranks of those he opposed is a gift offering for peace. And while Verlaine may not be the richest hold in Karsten, yet the blood of its lords is very high—was not that often made very plain to me when I came a-wooing? And I was no blank shield, but the younger son of Farthom in the northern hills.'' His lips twisted as if he remembered certain slights out of the past.

"And since you are the heiress of Verlaine you are very suitable.''

Loyse laughed. "It cannot be true, lord, that I am the only marriageable maid of gentle birth in all Karsten.''

"How right. And he could do very well elsewhere. But as I have said, my dearest of daughters, you have certain other advantages. Verlaine is a coast holding with age-old rights, and the Duke has ambitions which run in more peaceful lines now than sword conquest. What say you, Loyse, if there was to be a port here to attract the northern trade?''

"And what would Sulcarkeep be doing while such a port came into being? Those who swear by Sul are jealous of their holdings.''

"Those who swear by Sul may soon be able to swear by nothing at all,'' he returned with a calm certainty which carried a note of conviction. "They have troublesome neighbors who are growing more trouble-some yet. And Estcarp, where they might look for aid, is a hollow shell eaten out by its preoccupation with witchery. One push and the whole land will fall into the filthy dust which should have buried it long ago.''

"So, for my blood and a plan for a port, Lord Yvian offers marriage,'' she persisted, unable yet to believe that this was true. "Yet is the mighty lord free to send his ax hither for a wedding? I am a maid close kept in a hold far from Kars, yet have I heard of a certain Aldis who issues orders, to have them promptly obeyed by all who wear the Duke's sign.''

"Yvian will have Aldis, and, yes, half a hundred of her ilk, and it is no concern of yours, girl. Give him a son—if your thin blood can form a man, the which I doubt! Give him a son and hold up your head at the high table, but trouble him not with any mewling calls upon him for more than company courtesy. Be glad for your honors and if you are wise you'll speak Aldis and the others fair in their time. Yvian is not said to be a patient or easily forgiving man." He slid down the slope of the bed and stood up, ready to be gone. But before he went he detached a small key from the chain at his belt and tossed it to her.

"For all your ghost face, girl, you'll not go to your wedding without your due or gauds. I'll send Bettris to you; she has an eye for pretties and can help you pull out enough for robes. And veils for your face, you'll need them! And keep an eye to Bettris, don't let her take more than she can carry in her two hands—for herself."

Loyse caught up the key so eagerly that he laughed. "So that much of you is female—you want gauds as much as any wench. Give us another storm or two and we can make up what you drag out of the storehouse anyway."

He strode out, leaving the door wide open. As Loyse followed him to shut it once again, she treasured that key tight in her hand. For months, years, she had schemed to get that same bit of metal into her holding. Now she had been given it openly and none would dispute her rummaging for what she truly wanted in the storehouse of Verlaine.

Rights of wreckage and plunder over wave and shore! Since Verlaine Keep had risen on the heights between two treacherous capes, the sea had brought its lords a rich harvest. And the storehouse of the pile was indeed a treasure room, only opened upon its lord's orders. Fulk must believe that he had far the best of the bargain with Yvian to allow her unsupervised plundering there. For the company of Bettris she did not fear. Fulk's latest bedfellow was as greedy as she was fair, and she would not cast any eye on Loyse's choices, given a chance to hunt on her own.

She tossed the key from right hand to left, and for the first time a thin smile curved her pale lips. Well might Fulk be surprised at her choices from the treasure of Verlaine! Also he might be astounded at other things she knew about these walls which he accepted as such safe barriers. Her gaze flickered for a moment to the one where the shield mirror hung.

There was a hurried rap at her door. Loyse smiled again, this time with contempt. It had not taken Bettris long to act upon Fulk's orders. But at least the woman dared not intrude upon her lover's daughter uninvited. Loyse went to the door.

"The Lord Fulk—" began the girl who stood without, her plump beauty as full and vivid as Fulk's virility.

Loyse held up the key. "I have it." She named no name, gave no title to the other, but glanced at those well-rounded shoulders bursting out of the robe which strained over every luxuriant curve the other advertised. Behind Bettris were two of the serving men, a chest between them. Loyse raised her eyebrows and the other laughed nervously.

"Lord Fulk would have you select your bride-clothes, lady. He said there was no need to be timid in the storehouse."

"The Lord Fulk is generous," returned Loyse tonelessly. "Shall we go?"

The women avoided the great hall and the outer

chambers of the hold, for the treasure room lay at the foot of the tower in which were the private quarters of the family. For that Loyse was glad; she kept well away from the central life of her father's house. And when they came at last to the door opened by the key she bore, she was very pleased that only Bettris dared follow her within. The serving men pushed the chest in after them and left.

Three globes set in the ceiling gave light to show chests and boxes, bales and bags. Bettris smoothed the robe over her hips in the gesture of a keeper of a market stall settling down to a spate of bargaining. Her dark eyes darted from pile to pile, and Loyse, putting the key into her belt purse, added fuel to that avid hunger.

"I do not think that the Lord Fulk would deny you some selections for yourself. In fact he said as much to me. But I would warn you to be discreet and not too greedy."

Those plump hands fluttered from hips to full, only half-covered breasts. Loyse crossed to a table cutting down the center of the room, lifted the lid of a casket resting there. Even she blinked at the massed wealth within. She had not truly realized until that moment that Verlaine's rapine over the years had yielded so well. From a tangle of chains and necklets she freed a great brooch, gaudy with red stones and much chasing, a bauble not to her taste, but one which in a manner matched the over-blown comeliness of her companion.

"Such a piece as this," she suggested and held it out.

Bettris' hands crooked to hold it, then she snatched them back. The point of her tongue showed between her wet red lips as she glanced from the brooch to Loyse and back again. Conquering her repugnance, the girl held the massive gem-set thing to the deep V-throat of the other's robe, mastering the impulse to jerk back when she felt the softness of Bettris' flesh.

"It becomes you, take it!" In spite of her wish Loyse' words were a sharp order. But the bait was taken. With attention only for the gems, the woman moved to the table, and Loyse was, for that moment and perhaps others, free to do as she pleased.

She knew what to look for, but how it might be stored she was unsure. Slowly the girl moved between piles of goods. Some were stained with salt rime and from one or two came a faint exotic scent. Having put a small barrier of boxes between herself and Bettris, she chanced upon a chest which looked promising.

Loyse's fragile appearance was deceiving. Just as she had disciplined her emotions and her mind against this day, so had she trained her body. The lid was heavy, but she had it up. And knew by the smell of oil, the sight of the discolored cloths on top, she was hot on the scent. She pawed aside those cloths gingerly, fearing to stain her hands and so reveal the nature of her search. Then she lifted out a shirt of mail, holding it to measure against her shoulders. Too large—perhaps she could find nothing fitted to her slight frame.

She delved deeper. A second shirt—a third—this must have been part of the stock in trade of a master smith. At the bottom was one which must have been made to order for the stripling son of some overlord. For against her it needed very little change at all. The rest were bundled back into the chest while she folded her find as small as possible.

Bettris was trapped by the casket of jewels and Loyse did not doubt that more than one piece from that coffer was now hidden about her person. But it gave her a chance to make her own raids, moving almost openly now between the box she had brought with her and her sources of supply, adding lengths of silk and velvet, a cape of fur, as topping concealment.

To please Bettris and forestall suspicion, Loyse chose from the jewelry also and then summoned the men to carry the chest back to her chamber. She was afraid Bettris might urge unpacking on her, but the bribe had worked well, the woman was in a fever to examine her own spoils privately and did not linger.

In a fury of speed, tempered by caution and the precision of careful foreplanning, Loyse set to work. Those hastily selected lengths of fabric, those packets of lace and embroidery, were dumped on her bed. Then she was on her knees clearing the coffer where her present wardrobe lay. Some things were long ready, fashioned long ago. But here were all the rest. With a care she had not granted the fine stuffs Loyse placed together the dower she intended to take from Verlaine, on her back, in her purse, in the saddle bags which were all she dared carry.

Mail shirt, leather underclothing, weapons, helm, gold trade tokens, a handful of jewels. Over those she threw once more her own garments, patting them smooth, with the care of a good housekeeper. She was breathing a little fast, but she had the coffer closed and was spreading out the other loot when she heard that tread outside—Fulk returning for his key.

Impulsively she caught up a veil bordered in silver thread, a dew hung cobweb of a thing, and pulled it about her head and shoulders, seeing that it became her vilely, but generous enough now that her purpose was gained to allow her father his chance for a jeer or two. With it on she stepped once more to pose before the shield mirror.

II

SEA WRACK

The very circumstances which she hoped would set her free worked against Loyse during the next few days. For while Yvian of Karsten did not ride himself to Verlaine either to inspect the bride he had bargained for or the heritage which would come with her, he sent a train proper enough to do her honor. And she was called upon to be on show, so that underneath her outer shell she seethed with impatience and growing desperation.

At last she pinned her hopes to the wedding feast, for then, if ever, there would be muddled heads within the keep. Fulk wanted to impress the Duke's lords with his lavish open-handedness. He would produce the liquid treasures of the hold and it would be her best chance to follow her plans.

The storm struck first, such a wild blast of wind and raging sea water as Loyse, familiar with that coast since her birth, had never seen before. For the spray reached high enough to spatter the windows of her tower room with its salt foam. And Bettris, and the maid Fulk had sent to help with the sewing of her robes, shivered and shrank with each bat of the wind's fist ringing through the stones of the walls.

Bettris stood up, a roll of fine green silk tumbling to the floor, her dark eyes wide. Her fingers moved in the sacred sign of her forgotten village childhood.

"Witch storm," her voice came small, overridden by the scream of the gale until Loyse heard only a thin whisper.

"This is not Estcarp," Loyse matched a length of embroidery to satin and set even stitches. "We do not have power over wind and wave. And Estcarp does not move beyond her own borders. It is a storm, that is all. And if you wish to please Lord Fulk you will not tremble at sea storms for Verlaine knows them often. How else," she paused to draw a new length of thread through a needle-eye, "do you think our treasure is gathered?"

Bettris turned on her, lips strained over her sharp little teeth in a vixen's snarl. "I am coast born, I have seen storms in plenty. Yes, I have coursed the shore with the gleaners afterwards. Which is more than you have ever deigned to do, my lady! But this is like no storm I have seen or heard tell of in all my life! There is evil in it, I tell you—great evil!"

"Evil for those who must trust to the waves." Loyse put down her sewing. She crossed to the windows, but there was nothing to be seen through the lace of spume which blotted out the dark of the day.

The maid made no pretense at work. She was drawn in upon her self close to the hearth where sea coral burned fitfully, rocking back and forth, her hands pressed against her breast as if she would ease some pain there. Loyse went to her. She had little of pity or interest in the wenches of the castle—from Bettris and her countless predecessors to the slatterns in the kitchen. Now against her own inclination she asked:

"You ail, wench?"

The girl was cleaner than most. Perhaps she had been ordered to tidy herself before being sent hither. Now the face she turned to Loyse drew the attention of Fulk's daughter. This was no village girl, no peasant dragged in to pleasure a retainer and then become a work drudge. Her face was a mask of fear which had been so long a part of her that it had shaped her as a potter shapes clay. Yet under that something else struggled.

Bettris laughed shrilly. " 'Tis no pain in her belly that eats at her, only memories. She was a sea wrack herself once. Weren't you, slut!" Her soft leather shoe struck the girl's haunch, nearly turning her into the fire.

"Leave her alone!" For the first time Loyse flashed her hidden fire. She had always kept aloof from the strand after a storm, since there was nothing she could do to dispute Fulk's rule—or rather Fulk's license there—she would not harrow herself with sights she could not forget.

Bettris simpered uneasily. With Loyse she was uncertain of her ground, so she did not rise to the challenge.

"Send the mewling idiot away. You will get no work from her as long as the storm rages—nor afterwards for a while. 'Tis a pity for she is clever with her needle, else she would have been sent to fatten the shore eels long ago."

Loyse went to the wide expanse of the bed where much of her gear had been spread about. There was a shawl there, plain in the welter of brilliant silks and fine fabrics. Catching it up she took it back to the fireside and threw it about the shuddering maid. Disregarding Bettris' amazement, Loyse dropped on her knees, put her hands to cover those of the girl, and looking into that drawn face, tried to will away from them both the grisly customs of Verlaine which had warped them in different ways.

Bettris pulled at her sleeve.

"How dare you?" Loyse blazed.

The other stood her ground, a sly grin now on her full lips. "The hour grows late, lady. Would Lord Fulk take it well that you nurse this slut when he meets with the Duke's lords to sign the marriage contract? Shall I tell him why you do not come?"

Loyse regarded her levelly. "I shall do my lord's bidding in this, as in other things, wench. Do not think to lesson *me!*"

She broke hold with the girl's hands reluctantly, saying:

"Stay here. No one shall come near you. Understand—no one!"

Did the other understand? She was rocking back and forth again, racked by old pain cut into her dulled mind even after the scars had faded from her body.

"I do not need you to robe me," Loyse turned on Bettris, and the other flushed. She could not face the younger girl down and she knew it.

"You would be the better for some knowledge of the kind of sorcery any woman knows, lady," she replied sharply "I could show you how to make a man look at you full faced as you pass. If you would but put a little dark stain upon your brows and lashes, some of the rose salve on your lips—" Her annoyance was forgotten, as her creative instinct aroused. She surveyed Loyse critically and impersonally and the other found herself listening in spite of her scorn for Bettris and all she represented. "Yes, if you would listen to me, lady, you could perhaps draw your lord's eyes away from that Aldis long enough for him to see another face. There are other ways, also, for the charming of a man." Her tongue tip worked along her lips. "There is much I could teach you, lady, which would give you weapons to use for yourself.'' She drew nearer, some of the glitter of the storm flashing in her eyes.

"Yvian has bargained for me as I stand," Loyse replied, rejecting Bettris' offer, all that Bettris stood for, "and so must be satisfied with what he gets!" And that is more true than Bettris can guess, she added silently.

The woman shrugged. "It is your life, lady. And before you are out of it, you shall discover that you cannot order it to your liking."

"Have I ever?" asked Loyse quietly. "Now go. As you have said, it grows late and I have much to do."

She sat through the ceremonies of the contract signing with her usual calm acceptance. The men the Duke had sent to fetch his bride to Kars were three very different types, and she found it interesting to study them.

Hunold was a comrade from Yvian's old mercenary days. He had a reputation as a soldier which reached even into such a backwater as Verlaine. Oddly enough his appearance did not match either his occupation, nor his reputation. Where Loyse had expected to see a man such as her father's seneschal—though perhaps slicked over with some polish—she found herself fronting a silk clad, drawling, languid courtier, who might never have felt the weight of mail on his back. His rounded chin, long lashed eyes, smooth cheeks, gave him a deceptive youth, as well as the seeming of untried softness. And Loyse, trying to match the man to the things she had heard concerning him, wondered and was a little afraid.

Siric, who represented the Temple of Fortune, who tomorrow would say the words while her hands rested on the war ax, thus making her as much Yvian's as if he clasped her in truth, was old. He had a red face and there was a swelling blue vein in the middle of his low forehead. As he listened or spoke in a soft mumble, he munched continually on small sweetmeats from a comfit box his servant kept ever in reach, and his yellow priest's robe strained over a paunch of notable dimensions.

The Lord Duarte was of the old nobility. But in turn he did not suit his role very well. Small and thin, with a twitching tic which pulled at his lower lip, the harassed air of a man constrained to some task he loathed, he spoke only when an answer was demanded of him. And alone of the three he paid some attention to Loyse. She discovered him watching her broodingly, but there was nothing in his manner which hinted of pity or promise of aid. It was rather that she was the symbol of trouble he would like to sweep from his path.

Loyse was grateful that custom allowed her to escape that night's feasting. Tomorrow she must sit through the start of the wedding banquet, but as soon as the wine began to pass—yes—then! Holding to that thought she hurried back to her room.

She had forgotten the sewing wench, and it was with a start that she saw a figure outlined against the window. The wind was dying now as if the worst of the storm had blown out. But there was another sound, the keening of one who has been hopelessly bereaved. And salt air bit at her from the opened pane.

Angry because of her own worries, tense over what was to come and to what she must nerve herself during the next twenty-four hours, Loyse sprang across the room and seized the swinging window frame, pulling at the girl that she might slam it shut. Though the wind had ceased, the clouds were still slashed by lightning.

And in one such revelation Loyse saw what the other must have watched for long moments.

Driving in upon the waiting fangs of the cape were ships: two . . . three of them. And such ships as dwarfed the coastwise traders she had seen pulled to their deaths there before by that treacherous on-shore current which enriched and damned Verlaine. These could only be part of a proud fleet of some great seafaring lord. Yet in the continued flashes of light which gave only seconds' viewing, Loyse could sight no activity on board any of the vessels, no attempts being made to ward off fate. They were ghost ships sailing on to their deaths and apparently their crews did not care.

The lights of the wreckers, of the shoreline scavengers, were already moving in clusters from the high gate of Verlaine. For a man on the spot might just conceal some rich picking for himself in the general confusion, though Fulk's weighty hand and a quick noose for those caught had cut down such thievery to a shadow. They would cast nets to bring in the flotsam, turn to tasks they had long practice in. And for any who went ashore still living! Loyse exerted her strength and dragged the girl away, shut and barred the window.

But to her surprise the face the other now turned to her was no longer troubled by ancient terrors. There was intelligence in the depths of the girl's dark eyes, excitement, a gathering strength.

She held her head slightly to one side as if she listened for some sound she must sort out of the brazen clamor of the storm. More and more it was apparent that whatever had been her place in the world before the sea brought her to Verlaine, she was no common soldier's wench.

"That which has been long in the building," the

girl's tone was remote, she spoke as if from the core of some experience Loyse could never know. "Choose, choose well. For this night is the fate of countries, as well as that of men, to be made and unmade!"

"Who are you?" Loyse demanded as the girl continued to change before her eyes. She was no monster, put on no shape of beast or bird as rumor whispered could be done by the witches of Estcarp. But that which had lain dormant, wounded almost to death, within her struggled once again for life, showed through her scarred body.

"Who am I? Nobody . . . nothing. But one comes who is greater than the I who once lived. Choose well, Loyse of Verlaine—and live. Choose ill—and die, as I have died, bit by bit, day by day."

"That fleet—" Loyse half turned to the windows. Could it possibly be that some invader, reckless enough to sacrifice his ships to win foothold on the cape and so a path to Verlaine, sailed out there? That was a mad thought. The ships were doomed; few if any of their crewmen could win the shore alive, and there they would find the men of Verlaine had prepared the grimmest of welcomes.

"Fleet?" echoed the girl. "There is no fleet—only life— or death. You have something of us within you, Loyse. Prove yourself now and win!"

"Something of you? Who are you—or what?"

"I am nobody and nothing. Ask me rather what I was, Loyse of Verlaine, before your people pulled me from the sea."

"What were you?" the other asked obediently as might a child at an elder's command.

"I was one of Estcarp, woman of the sea coast. Now do you understand? Yes, I had the Power—until it was reft from me in the hall below us here, while men laughed and cheered the deed. For the gift is ours— sealed to our women—only while our bodies remain inviolate. To Verlaine I was a female body and no more. So I lost what made me live and breathe—I lost myself.

"Can you understand what it means to lose yourself?" She studied Loyse. "Yes, I almost believe that you do, since you move now to protect what you have. My gift is gone, crushed out as one crushes out the last coal of an unwanted fire, but the ashes of it remains. So do I now know that one greater than I had ever hoped to be comes in on the drive of the storm. And she shall determine more than one of our futures!"

"A witch!" Loyse did not shrink; instead excitement flared. The power of the women of Estcarp was legendary. She had fed upon every tale which had come out of the north concerning them and their gifts. And she smarted now with the realization of opportunity lost. Why had she not known of this woman before—learned of her—

"Yes, a witch. So they name us when they understand us but little. But do not think to have anything of me now, Loyse. I am only the charred brands of a long quenched fire. Bend your will and wit to aid the other who comes."

"Will and wit!" Loyse laughed harshly. "Wit I have and will, but no power here, ever. Not one soldier will obey me, nor stay his hand at my bidding. Better appeal to Bettris. When my father is in humor with her, she has some slight recognition from his people."

"You have only to seize opportunity when it comes." The other allowed the shawl to slip from her shoulders, folded it neatly, and laid it on the bed as she passed it on her way to the door. "Take your opportunity and use it well, Loyse of Verlaine. And tonight sleep sound for your hour has not yet come."

She was out of the door before Loyse could move to stop her. And then the room was curiously empty, as if the girl had drawn after her some pulsing life which had watched and waited in shadowed corners.

Slowly Loyse put off her robe of ceremony, replaited her hair by touch, rather than with the aid of the mirror. Somehow she did not wish to look into that mirror now, for a pricking thought that something else might stand behind to peer over her shoulder lurked in her mind. Many foul deeds had been done in the great hall of Verlaine since Fulk became master there. But now she believed that perhaps the one which would bring him to judgment had been wrought with the woman of Estcarp for its victim.

And so intent was she upon her thoughts that she did not remember this was her wedding eve. For the first time since she had hidden them there, she did not bring out the garments resting at the bottom of her chest, to examine them and gloat over the promise they held.

Along the shore the wind whined, though it did not toss the spray mountain high as it had earlier. And those who sheltered, waiting for the harvest of waves and rocks were eager. The fleet which had looked so fine from the tower of Loyse's chamber, was even more imposing from the shore.

Hunold gripped his cloak tight at his throat and stared through the gloom. No ships of Karsten were those, and this wrecking could only serve the duchy. He was firm in the private belief that they were about to witness the last moments of an enemy raiding force. And it was equally good that he could keep an eye upon Fulk under these circumstances. Rumor had built very high the harvest of plunder Verlaine took. And when Yvian wedded that pale nothing of a wench, he could demand an accounting of all treasure in his wife's name. Yes, Fortune smiled when she set Hunold on the shore this night to watch, and list, and gather a report for the Duke.

Certain now that the doomed ships could not possibly claw off the cape, the wreckers from the hold boldly set out their lanterns along the strand. If fools from the vessels tried to come ashore at those beacons, so much the better, they would only save the plunderers the time and bother of hunting them down.

So it was that those beams, reaching out over the heaving of the waves, caught upon the first prow swinging inward. It loomed high, buoyed up by the combers, and there were shouts from the watchers, wagers hurriedly offered and accepted as to the place of its crashing. High it lifted and then slammed forward, the rocks under the forepart of its keel. Then—it was gone!

Those on the shore were men confronted by the impossible. At first some of the more imaginative were certain they sighted the wreckage of a broken-backed ship, sure that it was tossing near to their nets. But there was nothing but the froth of wind beaten water. No ship nor wreckage.

None of them stirred. At that moment they were held by their disbelief in the evidence of their own eyes. Another of the proud ships was coming. This one pointed to the patch of rock upon which Hunold stood with Fulk as straightly as if some unseen helmsman set that course. In it came stoutly. No men clung to its rigging, no living thing could be sighted on deck.

Once again the waves raised up their burden to smash

the vessel down upon the teeth of the reef. And this time it was so close to shore that Hunold thought a man could leap to where he himself stood from the deserted deck. Up and up the prow rose, its fantastically carved figurehead showing open jaws to the sky. Then down—the water swirling.

And it was gone!

Hunold threw out a hand, seized upon Fulk, only to see in the shocked paleness of the other's face the same incredulous terror. And when a third ship came in, boring straight for the reef, the men of Verlaine fled, some of them screaming in panic. Deserted lanterns lit a shore where nets trailed into foaming water empty of even one floating board.

Later a hand caught such a net, caught and held with a grip which was a last desperate clutch for life. A body rolled in the surf, but net held, and hand held. Then there was a long crawl for shore, until a beaten, half-dead swimmer lay prone on the sand and slept.

III

CAPTIVE WITCH

It was generally conceded among the commoners of Verlaine that the vanishing fleet they had gathered to plunder was an illusion sent by demons. And Fulk could not have flogged any man to the strand side the next morning. Nor did he try his leadership so high as to give such an order.

The affair of the marriage must still be pushed before any hint of this tale could get back to Kars and give a legitimate reason for refusing the heiress of Verlaine. To counter any superstitious fears which the three ducal agents might harbor, Fulk reluctantly took them to the treasurehouse, presenting each with a valuable souvenir, setting aside a gem-set sword as a token of his admiration for the Duke's battle prowess. But throughout he sweated under his tunic, and fought in himself a new tendency to inspect dark corners of staircase and corridor a little too intently.

He also noted that none of his guests made an allusion to the happenings on the reef, and wondered whether that was a good or bad sign. It was not until they were in his private council chamber an hour before the wedding that Hunold took from the front of his furred over robe a small object he set with some care in a patch of watery sunlight from the largest window.

Siric pushed his paunch against his knees and puffed

once or twice as he leaned forward curiously to inspect it.

"What is this, Lord Commander? What is this? Have you despoiled some village brat of his toy?"

Hunold balanced his find on the palm of his hand. Clumsily fashioned as it was, the shape of the carved chip was clear enough—that of a boat. And a broken stick stood for a mast.

"This, Reverend Voice," he returned softly, "is the mighty ship, or one of the mighty ships, we saw come in to their end just outside these walls last night. Yes, it is a toy, but such a toy as we do not play with hereabouts. And for the safety of Karsten I must ask of you, Lord Fulk, what dealing do you have with that spawn of the outer darkness—the witches of Estcarp?"

Fulk, stung, stared at the chip boat. His face paled, and then grew dark as the blood tide arose. But he fought furiously to control his temper. If he played ill now he would lose the whole game.

"Would I have sent the gleaners to the reefs, prepared to receive a chip fleet to loot it?" He managed a reasonable counterfeit of serenity. "I take it that you fished that from the sea this morning, Lord Commander? But what leads you to believe that it was a part of any Estcarp magic, or that the ships we saw were born of such trickery?"

"This was plucked from the sand this morning, yes," Hunold agreed. "And I know of old the illusions of the witches. To make it certain, we found something else on the shore this morning, my men and I, and this is a very great treasure, one to rival any you have shown us as being wave-brought to your keep. Marc, Jothen!" He raised his voice and two of the Duke's shieldmen came in, a roped prisoner between them, though they seemed uneasy to handle that captive.

"I give you part of the fleet," Hunold tossed the chip to Fulk. "And now, Lord Fulk, I show you one who had the making of it, if I mistake not, and I do not think that I do!"

Fulk was used to salt-stained captives dragged from the sea's maw and his dealing with such was swift, designed mostly to one end. Also once before he had handled the self-same problem and handled it well. Hunold might have shaken him for a space, only a very small space. He was fully confident again.

"So," he settled back in his seat with the smile of one watching the amusement of the less sophisticated, "you have taken you a witch." Boldly he surveyed the woman. She was a thin piece, but there was spirit in her—she would furnish good sport. Perhaps Hunold would like to undertake her taming. None of these witches were ever beauties, and this one was as washed out as if she had been fighting waves for a month. He studied the clothing covering her straight limbs more closely.

That was leather—garments such as one wore under mail! She had gone armed then. Fulk stirred. A mail clad witch and that phantom fleet! Was Estcarp on the move and did that move head toward Verlaine? Estcarp had several scores she might mark up against his hold, though hitherto no northerner appeared to be aware of his activities. Put that to the back of the mind to be considered later; now one must think of Hunold and what could be done to keep Karsten an ally.

Carefully he avoided meeting the captive's eyes. But he asserted a measure of his old superiority.

"Has it not yet come to common knowledge in Kars, Lord Commander, that these witches may bend a man to their will by the power of their eyes? I see your shieldmen have taken no precautions against such an attack.''

"It would seem you know something of these witches.''

Careful now, thought Fulk. This Hunold did not keep his place at Yvian's right hand through the weight of his sword arm alone. He must not be provoked too far, only shown that Verlaine was neither traitor nor dolt.

"Estcarp has yielded tribute to our cape before.'' Fulk smiled.

Hunold seeing that smile, shot an order at his men. "You, Marc, your cloak over her head!''

The woman had not moved, nor had she uttered any sound since they had brought her in. They might have been dealing with a soulless, mindless body. Perhaps she had been dazed by her close escape from the sea, rendered only half-conscious by some blow from a reef rock. However, none of the men within Verlaine would relax vigilance because their prisoner did not scream, or beg, or struggle uselessly. As the folds of the cloak settled about her head and shoulders Fulk leaned forward in his chair once more and spoke, his words aimed at her rather than the men he seemed to address— hoping to wring some response from her that he might judge her state of awareness.

"Have they not told you either, Lord Commander, how one disarms these witches? It is a very simple— and sometimes enjoyable—process.'' Deliberately he went into obscene detail.

Siric laughed, his hands curved to support his jerking paunch. Hunold smiled.

"You of Verlaine do indeed have your more subtle pleasures,'' he agreed.

Only the Lord Duarte remained quiet, his eyes bent upon the hands resting on his knees as he built and felled towers with his fingers. A slow, red-brown flush spread up his thin cheeks beneath the close-clipped old man's beard.

There was no movement from the half-shrouded figure, no sound of protest.

"Take her away," Fulk gave the order, a small test of power. "Give her to the seneschal; he will keep her safe against our further pleasure. For to all pleasures there are a proper season." He was now all the courteous host, secure in his position. "And now we have before us our Lord Duke's pleasure—the claiming of his bride."

Fulk waited. No one could have guessed the tension with which he listened for Hunold's next words. Until Loyse stood before the altar in the seldom-used chapel, her hands safely on the ax, the right words wheezed out by Siric, Hunold could cry off in his master's name. But once Loyse was Lady Duchess of Karsten, if only in name, then Fulk was free to move along a path of his own, one carefully foremapped and long anticipated.

"Yes, yes," Siric puffed and labored to his feet, his attention hastening to pull out the folds of his overcape. "The wedding—Must not keep the lady waiting, eh, Lord Duarte—young blood, impatient blood. Come, come, my lords—the wedding!" This was his part of the venture and for once that young, ice-eyed upstart of a soldier could have no leading role. Far more fit and proper for Lord Duarte of the oldest noble line in Karsten to bear the ax and stand proxy for their overlord. That had been his own wise suggestion, and Yvian had thanked him for it warmly before they had ridden out of Kars. Yes, Yvian would discover . . .

was discovering, that with the power of the Temple Brotherhood and the support of the old families, he would no longer have to listen to such rufflers as Hunold. Let this marriage be solemnized and Hunold's sun would approach its setting!

It was cold. Loyse sped along the balcony of the great hall which was the heart of the keep. She had stood while the toasts were drunk, but she had not given lip service to their pious sentiments for happiness in her new life—happiness! Loyse had no conception of that. She wanted only her freedom.

When she slammed her door behind her, put in place the three bars which could withstand even a battering ram, she went to work. Jewels were stripped from throat, head, ear, finger, and thrown into a heap. Her long furred robe kicked aside. Until at last she stood before the mirror on a shawl, too excited to feel the cold seeping from the walls about her, her unbraided hair heavy on her shoulders, falling in a curtain cloak to her bare flanks.

Lock by lock she slashed at it ruthlessly with her shears, letting the long strands fall to the shawl. First to neck length, and then more slowly and awkwardly, to the cropped head one might naturally expect to see beneath a mail coif and helm. The tricks she had disdained to use at Bettris' urging, she applied with careful concentration. A mixture of soot rubbed delicately into her pale brows, more used upon her short, thick lashes. She had been so intent upon the parts that she had not considered the whole. Now, stepping back a little from the shield mirror, she studied her reflection critically, more than a little startled at what she saw.

Her spirits soared; she was almost sure she could tramp into the great hall below and have Fulk unable to set name to her. The girl ran to the bed, began to dress in each garment she had prepared so well. Her weapon belt hitched smoothly around her waist and she was reaching for the saddle bags. But her hand moved slowly. Why was she so reluctant to see the last of Verlaine? She had walked through the ceremonies of the day hiding her purpose, holding it to her as a most precious possession. And she knew very well that the feast was the best screen she could hope to find to cover her flight. Loyse doubted if any sentry within or without the keep tonight would be overzealous on his guard duty—in addition she had a secret exit.

Yet something held her there, wasting important moments. And she had such a strong desire to return to the balcony overlooking the hall, to spy upon the feasters there, that she moved to the door without conscious volition.

What had the wench said? Someone was coming in on the wings of the storm—take your opportunity and use it well, Loyse of Verlaine! Well, this *was* her opportunity and she was prepared to use it with all the wisdom her life in Fulk's house had forced her to develop.

Yet when she moved it was not to her private ways, of which Fulk and his men knew nothing, but to that door. And even while she fought impulse and such senseless recklessness, her hand slid back the bars and she was in the hall, the heels of her boots clicking on the steps which would take her to the balcony.

Just as the heat of the keep's heart did not appear to rise to warm these upper regions, so did the noise below make only a clamor in which no voice, no stave of song, reached her as separate words. Men drank, they ate, and soon they would think of other amusements.

Loyse shivered, yet she still lingered, her gaze for the high table and those who sat there, as if it were necessary to keep some close check upon their movements.

Siric, who in the chapel of Verlaine had actually achieved a short measure of dignity—or perhaps it was his robes of office which had conferred that momentary presence upon his bloated body—was all belly once more, cramming into his mouth the contents of an endless line of dishes, though his tablemates had long since turned to their wine.

Bettris, who had no right to any seat there until Loyse had left—as well she knew—for Fulk capriciously insisted upon some observances of proper conduct, had been watching for her chance. Now, bedecked with that garish brooch from the treasure house, she leaned against the carved arm of her lover's high seat ready for his attention. But, Loyse noted, her awareness of the whole scene heightened because she was a spectator only, Bettris also gave a sidewise, calculating glance now and again to Lord Commander Hunold. Just as she allowed a curved and dimpled white shoulder, artfully framed in the deep wine of her robe, to accent that surreptitous bid for regard.

Lord Duarte sat huddled in upon himself, occupying less than two-thirds of his chair of state, staring into a goblet he held as if he read in its depths some message he would rather not know. The plain lines of his plum robe, the pinched meagerness of his old features, gave him the aspect of a mendicant in that lavish assembly, and he put on no pretense of one enjoying the festivities.

She must go—now! With leather and mail, and over it all the cloak of a traveler, making her a dusky shadow among many shadows past the discerning of winebleared eyes, she was safe for a space. And it was so cold, colder than when the rime of winter patterned walls, yet it was well into spring! Loyse took one step and then another before that voiceless order which had brought her there drove her back to the railing.

Hunold leaned forward to speak to her father. He was a well-favored man; Bettris' interest was to be expected. His fox face with a fox brush of hair was as vivid as Fulk's for virile coloring. He made a quick gesture with his hands and Fulk voiced one of his great roars of laughter, the faint echoes of it reaching to Loyse's ears.

But there was a sudden sharp dismay on Bettris' face. She caught at Fulk's oversleeve which lay across the chair arm, and her lips shaped some words Loyse could not guess. He did not even turn his head to look at her. His hand flailed up in a cuff to sweep her from his side, back from the table, so that she sprawled awkwardly into the dust behind their chairs.

Lord Duarte arose, putting down his goblet. His thin white hands with their ropy blue veins pulled at the wide fur collar of his robe, drawing it closer about his throat, as if he alone in that company felt the same chill which benumbed Loyse. He spoke slowly, and it was clear that he made some protest. Also, from the way he turned aside from the table, it was apparent that he did not expect any polite reply or agreement from his companions.

Hunold laughed and Fulk drummed his fist upon the table in a signal to the wine steward, as the oldest of the Duke's deputies made his way among the tables of the lesser men on the floor below the dais to climb the stairs leading to his own apartment.

There was a flurry at the outer door of the hall. Men

still fully armed and armored came in, and a path parted before them, leading to the dais. Some of the clamor died, fading as the guards tramped on, a prisoner in their midst. To Loyse it appeared that they hustled along a man, his hands bound behind his back. Though why they had also chosen to hide his head in a bag so that he staggered blindly in answer to their jerks at him, she could not guess.

Fulk threw out his arm, clearing a stretch of table between him and Hunold, sending flying Duarte's goblet so that its dregs of contents splashed Siric, whose hot protests neither man chose to heed. From a pocket the Lord of Verlaine brought a pair of wager discs, tossing them into the air and letting them spin on the board before they flattened so their uppermost legend might be read. He pushed them to Hunold, offering the right of first throw.

The Lord Commander gathered them up, examined them with a laughing remark, and then threw. Both men's heads bent and then Fulk took them up in turn to spin. Bettris, in spite of her rough rebuff, had crept forward, her eyes as fixed upon the spinning discs as were the men's. When they flattened, she resumed her grasp on Fulk's chair, as if the result of that throw had given her new courage, while Fulk laughed and made a mock salute to his guest.

Hunold arose from his seat and moved about the end of the table. Those about the prisoner widened their circle as he came down to front the blinded captive. He made no move to pull away the bag over the other's head, but his fingers caught at the stained leather jerkin, busy with the latches holding it. With a pull he ripped it open to the waist and there was a shout from the company.

The Lord Commander transferred his grip to the captive woman's shoulder as he faced the grins of the men. Then he displayed a strength surprising for his spare figure, and swung her over his shoulder, starting for the staircase. Fulk was not the only one to protest missing the planned amusement, but Hunold shook his head and went on.

Would Fulk follow? Loyse did not wait to see. How could she stand against Fulk—even against Hunold? And why out of all those who had been unwilling prey of Fulk and his men in the past should Loyse be moved to help this particular one? Though she fought against the knowledge that she must take a hand in this, her feet bore her on, constrained to act against her better judgment.

She sped to her own chamber once more, finding it far easier to run in her new guise than in the robes of her sex. Once more the triple door bars thudded into place, and she was shedding her cloak, paying no attention to the reflection in the mirror of a slight youth in mail. Then the reflection was distorted as the mirror became a door.

Only dark lay beyond. Loyse must depend upon her memory, upon the many explorations she had made since three years before when she had chanced upon this inner Verlaine which no one else within the pile seemed to suspect.

Steps; she counted aloud as she raced down them. One passage at the bottom, a sharp turn into a second. She brushed her hand along the wall as a guide as she hurried, trying to picture the proper ways to her goal.

Once more steps, upward this time. Then a round of light on one wall, marking one of the spy holes—this must give on an occupied room. Loyse stood on tiptoe to peer within. Yes, this was one of the state bedchambers.

Lord Duarte, looking even more shrunken and withered without his overrobe with its wide fur collar, passed about the foot of the bed and stood before the fire, his hands held out to the blaze, his small mouth working as he chewed upon some bitter word or thought he could not spit away.

Loyse went on. The next spyhole was dark, the room where Siric was housed no doubt. She quickened pace to reach the last where a second circle of gold showed light. So sure was she of this that she fumbled for the catch of the secret entrance without looking.

Mutterings—the sound of a scuffle. Loyse pushed her full weight on the concealed spring. But here there had been no careful oiling, no reason to keep it workable. It stuck. Loyse backed around and put her shoulder against it, bracing her hands flat against the wall on the other side of the narrow passage and then exerting her strength, saving herself from falling as it burst open by catching at the edges of the opening.

She whirled about, her sword out with the snap of one who had practiced in secret and steadily. Hunold's startled face fronted her from the bed where he fought to pin down his writhing victim. With the quick recovery and menace of a cat, he slid to the opposite side, abandoning his hold upon the woman, and sprang for the weapon belt hanging on the back of the nearest chair.

IV

THE INNER WAYS

Loyse had forgotten her new trappings and that Hunold might see in her another male come to spoil his sport. He had whipped out his dart gun, although she had sword in hand, his move being against age-old custom. But his aim wavered ever so slightly between the invader and the woman on the bed, who, in spite of her bound hands, was wriggling her way toward him across the rumpled covers.

Moved by instinct more than plan, Loyse seized upon the outer robe he had discarded and tossed it at him, thus perhaps saving her life. For the thick cloth folds deflected his aim and the dart quivered in the bed post and not in her breast.

With a spate of oaths Hunold kicked at the tangle of cloth and swung upon the woman. She made no move to escape. Rather now she stood facing him with an odd calm. Her lips parted and an oval object dropped from between them, to swing on a short length of chain still gripped in her teeth.

The Lord Commander did not move. Instead his eyes traveled from one side to the other beneath his half-closed lids, following the slow pendulous passage of that dull gem.

Loyse was around the foot of the bed now, only to pause at a scene which might have been part of a nightmare. The woman edged around, and Hunold, his eyes fast on the gem at her chin level moved after her. Now her bound arms were presented to Loyse, her body formed a partial barrier between girl and man.

Hunold's eyes went left to right, and back, then, as the jewel quieted, he stood very still. His mouth opened slackly. There were beads of moisture forming along the edge of his hair line.

That drive which had brought her there, moving her about as a playing piece in some other's game, still held Loyse. She drew the cutting edge of the sword across the cords binding the women's wrists, sawing through their cruel loops, freeing flesh which was ridged and purple. And when the last bit fell away the woman's arms dropped heavily to her sides as if they could not obey her will.

Hunold moved at last. The hand which gripped the dart gun circled, but slowly as if great pressure bent it. His skin glistened with sweat, a pendulous drop gathered upon his loose lower lip, spun a thread as it fell to his heaving chest.

His eyes were alive, fiery with hate and rising panic. Yet, still that hand continued to turn, and he could not tear his gaze away from the dull jewel. His shoulder quivered. Loyse across the few feet of space which separated them could sense the agony of his fruitless struggle. He no longer wanted to slay; he wanted only escape. But for the Lord Commander of Kars there was no escape.

The end of that barrel touched the soft, unweathered white of his upper breast where his throat met the arch of his chest. He was moaning, very faintly, as might a trapped animal, before the trigger clicked.

Coughing out a spume of blood, released from the

vise of will which had forced him to his death, Hunold
staggered forward. The woman slipped lithely aside,
pushing Loyse with her. He fell up against the bed and
collapsed half upon it, his head and shoulders down, his
knees upon the floor as one might kneel in petition, as
his hands tore spasmodically at the covers.

For the first time the woman looked directly at
Loyse. She made an effort to raise one of those puffed
and horribly swollen hands to her mouth, perhaps to
hold the stone. And when she could not, she sucked the
jewel back between her lips, nodding imperatively at
the opening in the wall.

Loyse was no longer so assured. All of her life she
had heard of the magic of Estcarp. But those had been
tales of far-off things which did not demand full belief
from the listener. The disappearance of the fleet along
the reef the night before had been described to her by
Bettris while she had been dressing for her bridal. But
she had been so absorbed by her plans and fears at that
moment that she had dismissed it all as a piece of great
exaggeration.

What she had seen here was something which tran-
scended all her ideas and she shrank from contact with
the witch, stumbling ahead into the cavity of the ways,
only wishing that she could or dared shut the other out
with a safe wall between them. But the woman came
readily after her with an agility which argued that she
still had reserves of energy in spite of the rough handling she had known.

Loyse had no desire to linger with Hunold's body.
Nor was she sure that Fulk, cheated of his sport, might
not burst in at any moment. But she snapped shut the
hidden panel with the greatest reluctance. And shivered
throughout her body as the other pawed at her with one

of those useless hands for a guide. She looped her fingers in the belt which still held the witch's ripped clothing to her body and drew her along.

They headed for her own chamber. There was so little time left. If Fulk followed the Lord Commander—if Hunold's body servant chanced into that room—or if for some reason her father would seek her out—! She must be out of Verlaine before dawn, witch or no witch! And setting her mind firm upon that, she towed the stranger along the dark ways.

Only, when she stood once more in the light, Loyse could not be as callous as her sense of urgency dictated. She found soft cloth to wash and bind the raw grooves cut in the other's wrists. And from her stores of clothing offered a selection to the other.

At last the witch mastered her body to the point where she was able to cup her hands beneath her pointed chin. She allowed the jewel to fall from her lips into that hold. Manifestly she did not want Loyse to touch it, nor would the girl have done so for less than her freedom.

"This about my neck please." For the first time the other spoke.

Loyse caught the jewel's chain, pulled open the catch and fastened it again beneath the ragged ends of hair which must have been cut as hastily and as inexpertly as her own—and perhaps for the same reason.

"Thank you, lady of Verlaine. And now, if you please," her voice was husky as if it rasped through a dry throat, "a drink of water."

Loyse held the cup to the other's mouth. "Thanks from you to me are hardly necessary," she returned with what boldness she could muster. "It would appear that you carry with you a weapon as potent as any steel!"

Over the rim of the cup the witch's eyes were smiling. Loyse, meeting that kindliness, lost some of her awe. But she was still young, awkward, unsure of herself, sensations she resented bitterly.

"It was a weapon I could not use until you distracted the attention of my would-be bedfellow, the noble Lord Commander. For it is one I dare not risk falling into other hands, even to save my own life. Enough of that—" She lifted her hands, examined the bandages about her wrists. Then she surveyed the disordered room, noting the shawl on the floor with its burden of sheared hair, the saddle bags on the coffer.

"It is not to your mind to travel to your bridegroom, my lady duchess?"

Perhaps it was the tone of her voice, perhaps it was her power compelling something within Loyse. But she answered directly with the truth.

"I am no duchess in Karsten, lady. Oh, they said the words over me this morning before Yvian's lords, and afterwards they paid me homage on their knees." She smiled faintly remembering what an ordeal that had been for Siric. "Yvian was none of my choosing. I welcome this wedding only to cover my escape."

"Yet you came to my aid," the other prompted, watching her with those great, dark eyes which measured until Loyse smarted under their gaze.

"Because I could not do otherwise!" she flared. "Something bound me here. Your sorcery, lady?"

"In a way, in a way. I appealed in my fashion to any within these walls who had the ability to hear me. It would appear that we share more than a common danger, lady of Verlaine, or," she smiled openly now, "seeing that you have changed your guise for this outfaring, lord of Verlaine."

"Call me Briant, a mercenary of blank shield,"

Loyse supplied, having prepared for that days ago.

"And where do you go, Briant? To seek employment in Kars? Or in the north? There will be a demand for blank shields in the north."

"Estcarp wars?"

"Say rather that war is carried to her. But that is another matter." She stood up. "One which can be discussed at length once we are without these walls. For I am sure you know a road out."

Loyse draped the saddle bags across her shoulder, drew the hood of her cloak over her uncrested helm. As she moved to turn off the light globes, the witch jerked at the shawl on the floor. Vexed at her own forgetfulness, the girl caught it and threw the strands of hair into the dying fire.

"That is well done," the other commanded. "Leave nothing which could be used to draw you back—hair has power." She glanced to the middle window.

"Does that give on the sea?"

"Yes."

"Then lay a false trail, Briant. Let Loyse of Verlaine die to cover it!"

It was the work of a moment to throw open that casement, to drop her fine bride robe just below. But it was the witch who bade her fasten a scrap of undergarment to the rough edge of the stone sill.

"With such open door to face them," she commanded, "I do not think they will seek too assiduously for other ways out of this chamber."

Back they went through the mirror door, and now their path led down through the dark where Loyse urged that they hug the wall to the right and take the descent slowly. Under their hands that wall grew moist, and dank smells of the sea, tainted with an ancient rottenness, were thick in the air. Down and down, and now the murmur of the waves came faintly thrumming through the wall. Loyse counted step after step.

"Here! Now there is the passage leading to the strange place."

"The strange place?"

"Yes, I do not like to linger there, but we shall have little choice. We must wait for the dawn light to guide us out."

She crept on, fighting the building reluctance within her. Three times had she come that way in the past, and each time she had carried on this silent warfare with her own body as the field of battle. Again she knew that rise of brooding apprehension, that threat out of the dark promising more and worse than just bodily harm. But still she shuffled on, her fingers hooked in her companion's belt, drawing her also.

Out of the blackness Loyse heard the heavy breathing, a catch of breath. And then the other spoke, in a faint whisper, as if there crouched near that which might overhear her words.

"This is a Place of Power."

"It is a strange place," Loyse repeated stubbornly. "I do not like it, but it holds our gate out of Verlaine."

Though they could not see, they sensed they had come out of the passage into a wider area. Loyse caught a glimpse of a bright point of light overhead—the beacon of a star hung far above some rock crevice.

But now there was another faint gleam which brightened suddenly, as if some muffling curtain had been withdrawn. It moved through the air well above ground level—a round gray spot. Loyse heard a sing-song chant, words she did not know. And that sound vibrated in the curiously charged air of the space. As the light grew stronger she knew that it came from the witch's jewel.

Her skin tingled, the air about them was charged with energy. Loyse knew an avid hunger—for what she could not have told. In her other visits to this place, the girl had been afraid and had made herself linger to control that fear. Now she left fear behind, this new sensation was one she could not put name to.

The witch, revealed in the light of the gem on her breast, was swaying from side to side, her face set and rapt. The stream of words still poured from her lips— petition, argument, protective incantation—Loyse could not have said which. Only the girl knew that they were both caught up in a vast wave of some energizing substance drawn from the sand and rock under their feet, from the walls about them, something which had remained asleep through long centuries to come instantly awake and aware now.

Why? What? Slowly Loyse made a complete turn, staring out into the gloom she could not pierce by eyepower. What lurked just beyond the faint pool of light the jewel granted them?

"We must go!" That came urgently from the witch. Her dark eyes were widely open, her hand moved clumsily to Loyse. "I cannot control forces greater than my own! This place is old, also it is apart from human kind and from the powers we know. Gods were worshiped here once, such gods as altars have not been raised to these thousand years. And there is a residue of their old magic rising! Where is your outer gate? We must try it while yet we can."

"The light of your jewel—" Loyse shut her own eyes, pulling forth her memory of this place, as earlier she had used her memory of the other wall-hidden ways. "There," she opened them again and pointed ahead.

Step by step the witch moved in that direction and the light went with and around her as Loyse had hoped. Steps wide and roughly hewn, rounded by ages of time, loomed to their right. They led Loyse knew to a flat block with certain sinister grooves which lay directly under a break in the roof, so that at intervals light from the sun, or from the moon, bathed it in gold or silver.

Around that platform fashioned of broad steps, they crept on to the far wall. The light of the jewel caught the fall of earth which lay below Loyse's gate. It would be risky to climb that tumble of stone and clay in this gloom, but she was impressed by the urgency of the witch.

The climb was as great a task as Loyse had feared. Though her companion made no complaint, she knew that to use those swollen hands must be torment. When and where she could the girl pushed and pulled the other, tensing together when the rubble shifted under their feet, threatening to plunge them both to the bottom once again. Then they were out, lying on coarse grass with the salt air about them, and a grayish glimmer in the sky telling them that the night was almost gone.

"Sea or land?" asked the witch. "Do you seek a boat along the shore, or do we trust to our two feet and head into the hills?"

Loyse sat up. "Neither," she replied crisply. "This lies at the end of the pastures between the hold and the sea. At this season the extra mounts are turned loose to range here until they are needed. And in a hut near the gate is the horse gear of the rangers. But that may be under guard."

The witch laughed. "One guard? Little enough to

stand between two determined women and their desire
this night, or rather this morning. Show me this hut
with the horse gear and I shall make you free of it with
no man the wiser thereafter.''

They went across the end of the pasture. The horses,
Loyse knew, would be close to the hut where block salt
had been set out two days before the storm. The jewel
had gone dead when they had emerged from the cavern
and they had to pick their way carefully.

A lantern burned over the door of the hut and Loyse
saw horses moving back and forth. The heavy war
chargers bred to carry an armored man in battle did not
interest her. But there were the rough coated, smaller
mounts kept for hunting in the hills, able to withstand
hardship and keep going far past the exhaustion point of
the costlier animals Fulk fancied for his own riding.

Out into the circle of the lantern light moved two
such ponies—almost as if her thought had called them.
They seemed uneasy, tossing their heads until their
ragged manes flopped on their necks, but they came.
Loyse put down the saddle bags, whistling softly. To
her delight the small horses came on, snuffling to one
another, their forelocks looping over their eyes, with
shaggy patches of their winter coats making them look
dappled in the dim light.

If they would only prove tractable once she had the
gear! She circled about them slowly and approached the
hut. There was no sign of the guard. Could he have
deserted his post for the feasting? It would be his death
if Fulk discovered it.

Loyse pushed inward on the door and it creaked.
Then she was peering into a place which smelt of horses
and oiled leather, yes, and of the strong drink the
village people brewed of honey and herbs, which was
enough to make even Fulk blink into sleep at the third

tankard. A jug rolled on its side, away from the touch of her boot, and sticky stuff dribbled sluggishly from its mouth. The guardian of the pastures lay on a truss of straw snoring lustily.

Two bridles, two of the riding pads used by hunters and swift riding messengers. They were easy to lift from pegs and ledge. Then she was back in the field and the door pulled to behind her.

The horses remained docile as she bridled them and slapped on the pads, cinching them as tightly as she could. But when both women were mounted and on the upper trail which was the only way out of Verlaine, her companion asked for the second time:

"Where do you ride, blank shield?"

"The mountains." Most of Loyse's concrete plans had dealt only with the mechanics of her escape from Verlaine. Beyond this point where she now rode, equipped, mounted, she had foreseen little. To be free and out of Verlaine had seemed so impossible a happening, so difficult an achievement that she had bent all her wits to the solving of that, with little thought of what would happen after she gained the mountain trails.

"You say Estcarp wars?" She had never really thought of venturing through the wild band of outlaw territory between Verlaine and the southern border of Estcarp, but with one of the witches of that land as a riding companion it might now be the best choice of all.

"Yes, Estcarp wars, blank shield. But have you thought of Kars, lady duchess? Would you look upon your realm in secret and see what manner of a future you have tossed away?

Loyse, startled, almost kneed her mount into a trot unsafe for the way they threaded.

"Kars?" she repeated blankly.

Something in that worked in her mind. Yes, she had no mind to be Yvian's lady duchess. But on the other hand Kars was the center of the southern lands and she might find a kinsman or two there if she needed help later. In so large a city a blank shield with money in his purse could lose himself. And should Fulk manage to discover something of her trail he would not think to search for her in Kars.

"Estcarp must wait yet awhile," the other was saying. "Trouble stirs through the land. And I would know more of it, and of those who do the stirring. Kars is a starting point."

She had been managed; Loyse knew that, but there was no feeling of outrage in her. It was rather that she had at long last found the end of a tangled cord, one which, if she dared to follow it through all its coils, would bring her where she had always wanted to be.

"We shall ride to Kars," she consented quietly.

PART III:
VENTURE OF KARSTEN

I

THE HOLE OF VOLT

Five men lay on the wave-beaten sand of the tiny cup of bay and one of them was dead, a great gash across his head. It was a hot day and shafts of sun struck full on their half-naked bodies. The smell of the sea and the stink of rotting weeds combined with the heat in a tropic exhalation.

Simon coughed, bracing his battered body up on his elbows. He was one great bruise and he was very nauseated. Slowly he crawled a little apart and was thoroughly sick, though there was little enough to be ejected from his shrunken stomach. The spasm shook him into full consciousness, and, when he could control his heaving, he sat up.

He could remember only parts of the immediate past. Their flight from Sulcarkeep had begun the nightmare. Magnis Osberic's destruction of the power projector, that core of energy supplying light and heat to the port, had not only blown up the small city but must have added to the fury of the storm which followed. And in that storm the small party of surviving Guards, trusting to the escape craft, had been scattered without hope of course keeping.

Three of those vessels had set out from the port, but their period of keeping together had lasted hardly beyond their last sight of the exploding city. And what had ensued had been sheer terror, for the craft had been whirled, pitched, and finally shattered on coastwise rock teeth in a period of time which had ceased to be marked in any orderly procession of hours and minutes.

Simon rushed his hands over his face. His lashes were matted with a glue of salt water and caught together, making it hard to open his eyes. Four men here— Then he sighted that half crushed head—three men, maybe, and the dead.

On one side was the sea, quiet enough now, washing the tangles of weed ripped loose and deposited on the shore. Fronting the water was a cliff face, broken, with handholds enough, Simon supposed. But he had not the slightest desire to essay that climb, or to move, for that matter. It was good just to sit and let the warmth of the sun drive out the bitter cold of storm and water.

"Saaa . . ."

One of the other figures on the strand stirred. A long arm swept the sand, pushing away a mass of weed. The man coughed, retched, and raised his head, to stare blearily about. Then the Captain of Estcarp caught sight of Simon and regarded him blankly, before his mouth moved in an effort at a grin.

Koris hunched up, his over-heavy shoulders and arms taking most of his weight as he crawled on hands and knees to a clear space of water-flattened sand.

"It is said on Gorm," he spoke rustily, his voice hardly more than a croak, "that a man born to feel the weight of the headsman's ax on his neck does not drown. And, since it has ofttimes been made clear to me that the ax is my fate—see how the oldsters are proven right once again!"

Painfully he moved on to the nearest of the still prone men, and rolled the limp body over, exposing a face which was grey-white under its weathering. The Guardsman's chest rose and fell with steady breath and he appeared to have no injuries.

"Jivin," Koris supplied a name, "an excellent riding master." He added the last thoughtfully, and Simon found himself laughing weakly, pressing his fists against his flat middle where strained muscles protested such usage.

"Naturally," he got out between those bursts of half-hysterical mirth, "that is an employment most needed now!"

But Koris had gone on to the next intact body. "Tunston!"

Dimly Simon was glad of that. He had developed, during his short period of life with the Guard in Estcarp, a very hearty respect for that under officer. Making himself move, he helped Koris draw the two still unconscious men above the noisome welter of tide drift. Then clawed his way to his feet with the aid of the rock wall.

"Water—" That sense of well-being which had held him for a short space after his own awakening was gone. Simon was thirsty, his whole body now one vast longing for water, inside and out, to drink and to lave the smarting salt from his tender skin.

Koris shuffled over to examine the wall. There were only two ways out of the cup which held them. To return to the sea and strive to swim around the encircling arms of rocks, or to climb the cliff. And every nerve within Simon revolted against any swimming, or return to the water from which he had so miraculously emerged.

"This is not too hard a path," Koris said. He was frowning a little. "Almost could I believe that once there were hand holds here and here.'' He stood on tiptoe, flattened against the rock, his long arms stretched full length over his head, his fingers fitting into small openings in the cliff wall. Muscles roped and knotted on his shoulders; he lifted one foot, inserted the toe of a boot into a crevice and began to climb.

Giving a last glance at the beach and the two men now well above the pull of the water, Simon followed. He discovered that the Captain was right. There were convenient hollows for fingers and toes, whether made by nature or man, and they led him up after Koris to a ledge some ten feet above the level of the beach.

There was no mistaking the artificial nature of that ledge for the marks of the tools which had shaped it were still visible. It slanted as a ramp, though steeply, toward the cliff top. Not an easy path for a man with a whirling head and a pair of weak and shaking legs, but infinitely better than he had dared to hope for.

Koris spoke again. ''Can you make it alone? I will see if I can get the others moving.''

Simon nodded, and then wished that he had not tried that particular form of agreement. He hugged the wall and waited for the world to stop an unpleasant sidewise spiral. Setting his teeth, he took the upgrade. Most of the journey he made on his hands and knees, until he came out under a curving hollow of roof. Nursing raw hands he peered into what could only be a cave. There was no other way up from here, and they would have to hope that the cave had another opening above.

''Simon!'' The shout from below was demanding, anxious.

He made himself crawl to the outer edge of the ledge and look down.

Koris stood there below, his head thrown far back as

he tried to see above. Tunston was on his feet, too, supporting Jivin. At Simon's feeble wave they went into action, somehow between them getting Jivin up the first climb to the ledge.

Simon remained where he was. He had no desire to enter the cave alone. And anyway his will appeared to be drained out of him, just as his body was drained of strength. But he had to back into it as Koris gained the level and faced about to draw up Jivin.

"There is some trick to this place," the Captain announced. "I could not see you from below until you waved. Someone has gone to great trouble to hide his doorway."

"Meaning this is highly important?" Simon waved to the cave mouth. "I do not care if it is a treasure house of kings as long as it gives us a chance of reaching water!"

"Water!" Jivin echoed that feebly. "Water, Captain?" he appealed to Koris trustfully.

"Not yet, comrade. There is still a road to ride."

They discovered that Simon's chosen method of hands and knees was necessary to enter the cave door. And Koris barely scraped through, tearing skin on shoulders and arms.

There was a passage beyond, but so little light reached this point that they crept with their hands on the walls, Simon tapping before him.

"Dead end!" His outstretched hands struck against solid rock facing them. But he had given his verdict too soon, for to his right was a faint glimmer of light and he discovered that the way made a right-angled turn.

Here one could see a measure of footing and they quickened pace. But disappointment waited at the end of the passage. For the light did not increase and when they came out into an open space, it was into twilight and not the bright sun of day.

The source of that light riveted Simon's attention and pulled him out of his preoccupation with his own aches and pains. Marching in a straight line across one wall were a series of perfectly round windows, not unlike ship's portholes. Why they had not sighted them from the strand, for it was apparent that they must be in the outer surface of the cliff, he could not understand. But the substance which made them filtered the light in cloudy beams.

There was light enough, however, to show them only too clearly the single occupant of that stone chamber. He sat at ease in a chair carved of the same stone as that on which it was based, his arms resting upon its broad side supports, his head fallen forward on his breast as if he slept.

It was only when Jivin drew breath in a sound close to a sob, that Simon guessed they stood in a tomb. And the dusty silence of the chamber closed about them, as if they had been shut into a coffer with no escape.

Because he was awed and ill at ease, Simon moved purposefully forward to the two blocks on which the chair rested staring up in defiance at the one who sat there. There was a thick coating of dust on the chair, sifting over the sitter. Yet Tregarth could see that this man—chieftain, priest, or king, or whatever he had been in his day of life—was not allied by race to Estcarp or to Gorm.

His parchment skin was dark, smooth, as if the artistry of the embalmer had turned it to sleek wood. The features of the half hidden face were marked by great force and vigor with a sweeping beak of nose dominating all the rest. His chin was small, sharply pointed, and the closed eyes were deep set. It was like seeing a humanoid creature whose far distant ancestors had been not primates but avian.

To add to this illusion his clothing, under its film of dust, was of some material which resembled feathers. A belt bound his slim waist and resting across both arms of his chair was an ax of such length of haft and size that Simon almost doubted the sleeper could ever have lifted it.

His hair had grown to a peak-crest, and binding it into an upright plume, was a gem-set circlet. Rings gleamed on those claw fingers resting on ax head and ax haft. And about chair, occupant, and that war ax there was such a suggestion of alien life as stopped Simon short before the first step of the dais.

"Volt!" Jivin's cry was close to a scream. Then his words became unintelligible to Simon as he gabbled something in another tongue which might have been a prayer.

"To think that legend is truth!" Koris had come to stand beside Tregarth. His eyes were as brilliant as they had been on the night they had fought their way out of Sulcarkeep.

"Volt? Truth?" echoed Simon and the man from Gorm answered impatiently.

"Volt of the Ax, Volt who throws thunders—Volt who is now a bogey to frighten children out of naughtiness! Estcarp is old, her knowledge comes from the days before man wrote his history, or whispered his legends. But Volt is older than Estcarp! He is of those who came before man, as man is today. And his kind died before man armed himself with stick and stone to strike back at the beasts. Only Volt lived on and knew the first men and they knew him—and his ax! For Volt in his loneliness took pity on man and with his ax hewed for them a path to follow to knowledge and lordship before he, too, went from among them.

"In some places they remembered Volt with thanksgiving, though they fear him for being what they could not understand. And in other places they hate with a great hate, for the wisdom of Volt warred against their deep desires. So do we remember Volt with prayers and with cursings, and he is both god and demon. Yet now we four can perceive that he *was* a living creature, and so in that akin to ourselves. Though perhaps one with other gifts according to the nature of his race.

"Ha, Volt!" Koris flung his long arm up in a salute. "I, Koris, who am Captain of Estcarp and its Guards, give to you greetings, and the message that the world has not changed greatly since you withdrew from it. Still we war, and peace sits only lightly, save that now our night may have come upon us out of Kolder. And, since I stand weaponless by reason of the sea, I beg of your arms! If by your favor we set our faces once more against Kolder, may it be with your ax swinging in the van!"

He climbed the first step, his hand went out confidently. Simon heard a choked cry from Jivin, a hissed breath from Tunston. But Koris was smiling as his fingers closed about the ax haft, and he drew the weapon carefully toward him. So alive did the seated figure seem that Simon half expected the ring laden claws to tighten, to snatch the giant's weapon back from the man who begged it from him. But it came easily, quickly into Koris' grasp, as if he who had held it all these generations had not only released it willingly, but had indeed pushed it to the Captain.

Simon expected the haft to crumble into rottenness when Koris drew it free. But the Captain swung it high, bringing it down in a stroke which halted only an inch or so above the stone of the step. In his hands the weapon was a living thing, supple and beautiful as only a fine arm could be.

"My gratitude for life, Volt!" he cried. "With this I shall carve out victories, for never before has such a weapon come into my hands. I am Koris, once of Gorm, Koris the ugly, the ill-fashioned. Yet, under your good wishing, oh, Volt, shall I be Koris the conqueror, and your name shall once more be great in this land!"

Perhaps it was the very timber of his voice which disturbed age-old currents of air; Simon held to that small measure of rational explanation for what followed. For the seated man, or man-like figure, appeared to nod once, twice, as if agreeing to Koris' exultant promises. Then that body, which had seemed so solid only seconds before, changed in front of their eyes, falling in upon itself.

Jivin buried his face in his hands and Simon bit back an exclamation. Volt—if Volt it had really been—was gone. There was dust in the chair and nothing else, save the ax in Koris' grip. Tunston, that unimaginative man spoke first, addressing his officer:

"His tour of duty was finished, Captain. Yours now begins. It was well done, to claim his weapon, And I think it shall bring us good fortune."

Koris was swinging the ax once more, making the curved blade pass in the air in an expert's drill. Simon turned away from the empty chair. Since his entrance into this world he had witnessed the magic of the witches and accepted it as part of this new life, now he accepted this in turn. But even the acquiring of the fabulous Ax of Volt would not bring them a drink of water nor the food they must have, and he said as much.

"That is also the truth," Tunston agreed. "If there is no other way out of here then we must return to the shore and try elsewhere."

Only there was another way, for the wall behind the great chair showed an archway choked with earth and rubble. And they set to work digging that out with their belt knives and their hands for tools. It was exhausting work, even for men who came to it fresh. And only Simon's new horror of the sea kept him at it. In the end they cleared a short passage, only to front a door.

Once its substance may have been some strong native wood. But no rot had eaten at it, rather it had been altered by the natural chemistry of the soil into a flint hard surface. Koris waved them back.

"This is my work."

Once more the Ax of Volt went up. Simon almost cried out, fearing to see the fine blade come to grief against that surface. There was a clang, and again the ax was raised, came down with full force of the Captain's mighty shoulders.

The door split, one part of it leaning outward. Koris stood aside and the three of them worried at that break. Now the brightness of full day light struck them, and the freshness of a good breeze beat the mustiness of the chamber away.

They manhandled the remnants of the door to allow passage and broke through a screen of dried creepers and brush out onto a hillside where the new grass of spring showed in vivid patches and some small yellow flowers bloomed like scattered goldpieces. They were on the top of the cliff and the slope of this side went down to a stream. Without a word Simon stumbled down to that which promised to lay the dust in his throat, ease the torture of his salted skin.

He raised dripping head and shoulders from the water some time later to find Koris missing. Though he was sure that the Captain had followed them out of the Hole of Volt.

"Koris?" he asked Tunston. The other was rubbing his face with handfuls of wet grass, sighing in content, while Jivin lay on his back beside the stream, his eyes closed.

"He goes to do what is to be done for his man below," Tunston answered remotely. "No Guardsman must be left to wind and wave while his officer can serve him otherwise."

Simon flushed. He had forgotten that battered body on the beach. Though he was of the Guard of Estcarp by his own will, he did not yet feel at one with them. Estcarp was too old, its men—and its witches—alien. Yet what had Petronius promised when he offered the escape? That the man who used it would be transported to a world which his spirit desired. He was a soldier and he had come into a world at war, yet it was not his way of fighting, and he still felt the homeless stranger.

He was remembering the woman with whom he had fled across the moors, unknowing then that she was a witch of Estcarp and all that implied. There had been times during that flight when they had had an unspoken comradeship. But afterwards that, too, was gone.

She had been on one of those other ships when they had broken out of Sulcarkeep. Had hers fared as badly on the merciless sea? He stirred, pricked by something he did not want to acknowledge, clinging fiercely to his role of onlooker. Rolling over on the grass he pillowed his head on his bent arm, relaxing by will as he had learned long ago, to sleep.

Simon awoke as quickly, senses alert. He could not have slept long for the sun was still fairly high. There was the smell of cooking in the air. In the lee of a rock a small fire burned where Tunston tended some small fish spitted on sharp twigs. Koris, his ax his bedfellow, slept, his boyish face showing more drawn and fined down with fatigue then when he was conscious. Jivin sprawled belly down beside the streamlet, fast proving that he was more than a master of horsemanship, as his hand emerged with another fish he had tickled into capture.

Tunston raised an eyebrow as Simon came up. "Take your pick," he indicated the fish. " 'Tis not mess fare, but it will serve for now."

Simon had reached for the nearest when Tunston's sudden tension brought his gaze to follow the other's. Circling over their heads in wide, gliding sweeps was a bird, black feathered for the most part save for a wide V of white on the breast.

"Falcon!" Tunston breathed that word as if it summed up a danger as great as a Kolder ambush.

II

FALCON'S EYRIE

The bird, with that art known to the predatory clans, hung over them on outspread wings. Simon saw enough of those bright red thongs or ribbons fluttering from about its feet to guess that it was not a wild creature.

"Captain!" Tunston edged over to shake Koris awake, and the other sat up, rubbing his fists across his eyes in a small boy gesture.

"Captain, the Falconers are out!"

Koris jerked his head sharply up and then got to his feet, shading his eyes against the sun, to watch the slow circles of the bird. He whistled a call which arose in clear notes. Those lazy circles ceased and Simon watched the miracle of speed and precision—the strike. For the bird came in to settle upon the haft of Volt's ax where the weapon lay half hidden in the grass of this tiny meadow. The curved beak opened and it gave a harsh cry.

The Captain knelt by the bird. Very carefully he picked up one of the trailing cords at its feet and a small metal pendant flashed in the sun. This he studied.

"Nalin. He must be one of the sentries. Go, winged warrior," Koris addressed the restless bird. "We be of one breed with your master and there is peace between us."

143

"A pity, Captain, that your words will not carry to the ears of this Nalin," commented Tunston. "The Falconers are apt to make sure of the borders first and ask questions later, if any invaders are left alive to ask them of."

"Just so, vagabond!"

The words came from immediately behind them. Almost as one, they whirled, to see only rocks and grass. Had it been the bird that spoke? Jivin eyed the hawk doubtfully, but Simon refused to accept that piece of magic or illusion. He fingered his only weapon, the knife which had been in his belt when he had made the shore.

Koris and Tunston showed no surprise. It was apparent they had expected some such challenge. The Captain spoke to the air about them, distinctly and slowly, as if his words must carry conviction to the unseen listener.

"I am Koris, Captain of Estcarp, driven upon this shore by storm. And these are of the Guards of Estcarp: Tunston, who is officer of the Great Keep, Jivin, and Simon Tregarth, an outlander who has taken service under the Guardian. By the Oath of Sword and Shield, Blood and Bread, I ask of you now the shelter given when two war not upon each other, but live commonly by the raised blade!"

The faint echo of his words rolled about them and was gone. Then once more the bird gave its screeching cry and arose. Tunston grinned wryly.

"Now I take it, we wait for either a guide or a dart in the back!"

"From an invisible enemy?" asked Simon.

Koris shrugged. "To every commander his own mysteries. And the Falconers have theirs in plenty. If they send the guide, we are indeed fortunate." He sniffed. "And there is no need to go hungry while we wait."

Simon gnawed at the fish, but he surveyed the small meadow cut by the stream. His companions appeared to be philosophical about the future, and he had no idea how that trick with the voice had been worked. But he had learned to use Koris as a measuring instrument when in a new situation. If the Guard Captain was willing to wait this out, then they might not have to face a fight after all. But on the other hand he would like to know more about his might-be hosts.

"Who are the Falconers?"

"As Volt," Koris' hand went to the ax, slipping in caress down its handle, "they are legend and history, but not so ancient.

"In the beginning they were mercenaries, come overseas in Sulcar ships from a land where they lost their holdings because of a barbarian invasion. For a space they served with the traders as caravan guards and marines. Sometimes they still hire out when in their first youth. But the majority did not care for the sea; they had a hunger for mountains eating into them, since they were heights born. So they came to the Guardian at Estcarp city and suggested a pact, offering to protect the southern border of the land in return for the right to settle in the mountains."

"There was wisdom in that!" Tunston broke in. "It was a pity the Guardian could not agree."

"Why couldn't she?" Simon wanted to know.

Koris smiled grimly. "Have you not dwelt long enough yet in Estcarp, Simon, not to know that it is a matriarchate? For the Power which has held it safe lies not first in the swords of its men, but in the hands of its women. And the holder of Power are in truth all women.

"On the other hand the Falconers have strange customs of their own, which are as dear to them as the mores of Estcarp are to the witches. They are a fighting order of males alone. Twice a year picked young men are sent to their separate villages of women, there to sire a new generation, as stallions are put out to pasture with the mares. But of affection, or liking, of equality between male and female, there is none recognized among the Falconers. And they do not admit that a woman exists save for the bearing of sons.

"Thus they were to Estcarp savages whose corrupt way of life revolted the civilized, and the Guardian swore that were they to settle within the country with the consent of the witches the Power would be affronted and depart. So were they told that not by the will of Estcarp could they hold her border. However they were granted leave to pass in peace through the country with what supplies they needed, to seek the mountains on their own. If there they wished to carve out a holding beyond the boundaries of Estcarp the witches would wish them well and not raise swords against them. So it has been for a hundred years or more."

"And I take it they were able to carve out their holding?"

"So well," Tunston answered Simon's question, "that three times have they beaten into the earth the hordes of Dukes of Karsten have sent against them. The very land they have chosen fights upon their side."

"You say that Estcarp did not offer them friendship," Simon pointed out. "What did it mean then when you spoke of the Oath of Sword and Shield, Blood and Bread? It sounded as if you *did* have some kind of an understanding."

Koris became very busy picking a small bone from his fish. Then he smiled and Tunston laughed openly. Only Jivin looked a little conscious, as if they spoke of things it was better not to mention.

"The Falconers are men—"

"And the Guards of Estcarp are also men?" Simon ventured.

Koris' grin spread, though Jivin was frowning now. "Do not misunderstand us, Simon. We have the greatest reverence for the Women of Power. But it is in the nature of their lives that they are apart from us, and the things which may move us. For, as you know, the Power departs from a witch if she becomes truly a woman. Therefore they are doubly jealous of their strength, having given up a part of their life to hold it. Also they are proud that they are women. To them the customs of the Falconers, which deny that pride as well as the Power, reducing a female to a body without intelligence or personality, are close to demon-inspired.

"We may not agree with the Falconers' customs, but as fighting men we Guards pay them respect, and when we have met with them in the past there was no feud between us. For the Guards of Estcarp and the Falconers have no quarrel. And," he tossed aside the spit from which he had worried the last bite of fish, "the day may be coming soon when the fact shall be an aid to us all."

"That is true!" Tunston spoke eagerly. "Karsten has warred upon them. And whether the Guardian wills it or not, if Karsten marches upon Estcarp the Falconers stand between. But we know that well and this past year the Guardian turned her attention elsewhere when the Big Snow struck and grain and cattle moved southward to Falconer villages."

"There were women and children hungry in those villages," Jivin said.

"Yes. But the supplies were ample and more than villagers ate," countered Tunston.

"The Falcon!" Jivin jerked a thumb skywards, and they saw that black and white bird sail through the air over their campsite. It proved this time to be the forescout of a small party of men who rode into view and sat watching the Guards.

The horses they bestrode were akin to ponies, rough-coated beasts that Simon judged were nimble footed enough on the narrow trails of the heights. And their saddles were simple pads. But each possessed a forked horn on which perched at ease one of the falcons, that of the leader offering a resting place to the bird that had guided them.

As did the Guards and the man of Sulcarkeep, they wore mail shirts and carried small, diamond-shaped shields on their shoulders. But their helms were shaped like the heads of the birds they trained. And, though he knew that human eyes surveyed him from behind the holes in those head coverings, Simon found the silent regard of that exotic gear more than a little disquieting.

"I am Koris, serving Estcarp."

Koris, the great ax across his forearm, stood up to face the silent four.

The man whose falcon had just returned to its perch held up his empty sword hand palm out in a gesture as universal and as old as time.

"Nalin of the outer heights," his voice rang hollow in the helm-mask.

"Between us there is peace. The Lord of Wings opens the Eyrie to the Captain of Estcarp."

Simon had doubts about those ponies carrying double. But when he mounted behind one of the Falconers he discovered that the small animal was as sure-footed on the slightest of trails as a burro and the addition of an extra rider appeared to be no inconvenience.

The trails of the Falconer's territory were certainly not laid to either entice or comfort the ordinary traveler. Simon kept his eyes open only by force of will as they footed along ledges and swung boots out over drops he had no desire to measure.

Now and again one of the birds soared aloft and ahead, questing out over the knife slash valleys which were a feature of the region, returning in time to its master. Simon longed to ask more concerning the curious arrangement between man and bird, for it seemed that the feathered scouts must have a way of reporting.

The party came down from one slope onto a road which was smooth as a highway. But they crossed that and bored up into the wilderness once more. Simon ventured to speak to the man behind whom he rode.

"I am new to this southern country—is that not a way through the mountains?"

"It is one of the traders' roads. We keep it open for them and so we both profit. You are this outlander, then, who has taken service with the Guards?"

"I am."

"The Guards are no blank shields. And their Captain rides to a fight and not from it. But it would seem that the sea has used you ill."

"No man may command storms," Simon returned evasively. "We live—for that we offer thanks."

"To that give thanks in addition that you were not driven farther south. The wreckers of Verlaine haul much from the sea. But they do not care for living men. Someday," his voice sharpened, "Verlaine may discover that none of her cliffs, nor her toothed reefs shall shelter her. When the Duke sets his seal upon that place then it will no longer be a small fire to plague travelers, but rather a raging furnace!''

"Verlaine is of Karsten?'' Simon asked. He was a gatherer of facts where and when he could, adding them piece by piece to his jigsaw of this world.

"Verlaine's daughter is to be wed to the Duke after the custom of these foreigners. For they believe that holding of land follows a female! Then by such a crooked right the Duke will claim Verlaine for its rich treasure seized out of storm seas, and perhaps enlarge the trap for the taking of all coastwise ships. Of old we have given our swords to the traders, though the sea is not our chosen battlefield, so shall we perhaps be summoned when Verlaine is cleansed.''

"You reckon the men of Sulcarkeep among those you would aid?''

The bird's head on the shoulders before him nodded vigorously. ''It was on Sulcar ships that we came out of blood, death and fire overseas, Guardsman! Sulcar has first claim upon us since that day.''

"It will no more!'' Simon did not know why he said that, and he regretted his loose tongue immediately.

"You bear some news, Guardsman? Our hawks quest far, but not as far as the northern capes. What has chanced to Sulcarkeep?''

Simon's hesitation was prolonged into no reply at all as one of the falcons hung above them, calling loudly.

"Loose me and slide off!'' his companion ordered sharply. Simon obeyed, and the four Guardsmen were left on the trail while the ponies forged ahead at a pace reckless for the country. Koris beckoned the others on.

"There is a sortie.'' He ran after the fast-disappearing ponies, the ax over his shoulder, his slender legs carrying him at a muscle-straining trot which Simon alone found it easy to equal.

There were shouts beyond and the telltale clash of metal meeting metal.

"Karsten forces?" panted Simon as he drew abreast of the Captain.

"I think not. There are outlaws in these wastes, and Nalin says they grow bolder. To my mind it is but a small part of all the rest. Alizon threatens to the north, the Kolder moves in upon the west, the outlaw bands grow restless, and Karsten stirs. Long have the wolves and the night birds longed to pick the bones of Estcarp. Though they would eventually quarrel over those bones among themselves. Some men live in the evening and go down into darkness defending the remnants of that they reverence."

"And this is the evening for Estcarp?" Simon found breath to ask.

"Who can say? Ah—outlaws they are!"

They looked down now upon a trade road. And here swirled a battle. The bird-helmeted horsemen dismounted as the level ground was too limited to give cavalry any advantage, to strike in as a well-trained fighting unit, cutting down those who had been enticed into the open. But there were snipers in hiding and they took toll by dart of the Falconers.

Koris leaped from ledge to trail, coming down in a pocket where two men crouched. Simon worked his way along a thread of path to a point where, with a well-aimed stone, he brought down one who was just shooting into the melee. It took only a moment to strip that body of gun and ammunition and turn the weapon against the comrades of its former owner.

Hawks flew screaming, stabbing at faces and eyes, raking with savage claws. Simon fired, took aim and fired again, marking his successes with dour satisfaction. A fraction of the bitterness of their defeat at Sulcarkeep oozed from him during those few wild moments while there was still active resistance around and below.

A squeal of horn cut the shrieks of the birds. Across the valley a rag of flag was waved vigorously and those of the outlaws who still kept their feet fell back, though they did not break and run until they reached cover where mounted men could not pursue. The day was slipping fast into evening and a host of shadows swallowed them up.

Hide from the men they might, but concealment from the hawks was another matter. The birds swirled over the rising ground, striking down, sometimes finding a quarry as screams of pain testified. Simon saw Koris on the road, ax still in hand, a dark stain on the blade of that weapon. He was talking eagerly with a Falconer, oblivious of those who walked from one body to the next, sometimes making sure of its status with a quick sword stroke. There was the same grim finality to this engagement as there had been after the ambush of those from Gorm. Simon busied himself with the buckling on of his new arms belt, taking care not to watch that particular activity.

The hawks were drifting back down the arch of the evening sky, coming in answer to the whistles of their masters. Two bodies in bird helms were lashed across the pads of nervous ponies, and other men rode bandaged, supported by their fellows. But the toll among the outlaw force had been far the greater.

Simon rode behind a Falconer again, not the same

man. And this one was not inclined to talk as he nursed a slashed arm across his breast and swore softly at every jolt.

Night came quickly in the mountains, the higher peaks shutting out the sun, enclosing growing pools of gloom. The track they took was a broader one and smooth as a highway when compared to their earlier trails. It brought them at last, up a stiff climb, to the home the Falconers had made for themselves in their exile. And it was such a keep as drew a whistle of astonishment out of Simon.

He had been truly impressed by the ancient walls of Estcarp with their air of having been wrought from the bones of the earth in the days of its birth. And Sulcarkeep, though it had been cloaked with the spume of that unnatural fog, had been indeed a mighty work. But this was a part of the cliffs, of the mountain. He could only believe that the makers had chanced upon a peak where there were a series of caves which had been enlarged and worked. For the Eyrie was not a castle, but a mountain itself converted into a fort.

They entered over a drawbridge spanning a chasm luckily hidden in the twilight, a drawbridge giving footing to only one horse at a time. Simon released his indrawn breath only when the pony he bestrode in company passed under the wicked points of a portculis into a gaping cave. He aided the wounded Falconer to the pavement and into the hands of one of his fellows, and then looked about for the Guardsmen, sighting Tunston's height and bare dark head before he saw the others.

Koris pushed his way to them, Jivin at his heels. For a space they seemed to be forgotten by their hosts. Horses were led away, and each man took his falcon

upon a padded glove before going into another passage.
But at last one of the bird heads swiveled in their
direction and a Falconer officer approached.

"The Lord of Wings would speak with you,
Guardsmen. Blood and Bread, Sword and Shield to our
service!"

Koris tossed his ax, caught it, and turned the blade
away from the other with ceremony. "Sword and
Shield, Blood and Bread, man of the hawks!"

III

A WITCH IN KARS

Simon sat up on the narrow bunk, knuckles pressed to his aching head. He had been dreaming, a vivid and terrifying dream of which he could recall only the terror. And then he awakened to find himself in the cell—like quarters of a Falconer with this fierce pain in his head. But more urgent than the pain was a sense of the need to obey some order—or was it to answer a plea?

The ache faded, but the urgency did not and he could not remain in bed. He dressed in the leather garments his hosts had provided and went out, guessing that it was close to morning.

They had been five days at the Eyrie and it was Koris' intention to ride north soon, heading to Estcarp through leagues of outlaw infested territory. Simon knew that it was in the Captain's mind to bind the Falconers to the cause of the northern nation. Once back in the northern capital he would bring his influence to work upon the prejudices of the witches, so that the tough fighting men of the bird helms might be enlisted in Estcarp's struggle.

The fall of Sulcarkeep had aroused the dour men of the mountains, and preparations for war buzzed in their redoubt. In the lower reaches of the strange fortress smiths toiled the night through and armorers wrought cunningly, while a handful of technicians worked on those tiny beads strung on the hawk jesses through which a high circling bird reported and recorded for his master. The secret of those was the most guarded of their nation, and Simon had only a hint that it was based on some mechanical contrivance.

Tregarth had been often brought up short in his estimation of these peoples by just some curious quirk such as this. Men who fought with sword and shield should not also produce intricate communication devices. Such odd leaps and gaps in knowledge and equipment was baffling. He could far more readily accept the "magic" of the witches than the eyes and ears, and when necessary, voices which were falcon borne.

The magic of the witches— Simon climbed stairs cut in one of the mountain burrows, came out upon a lookout post. There was no mist to mask a range of hills visible in the light of early morning. By some feat of engineering he could see straight through a far gap into that opcn land which he knew to be Karsten.

Karsten! He was so intent upon that keyhole into the duchy that he was not aware of the sentry on post there until the man spoke:

"You have a message, Guardsman?"

A message? Those words triggered something in Simon's mind. He experienced for an instant the return of pain to press above his eyes, that conviction there was something for him to do. This was foreknowledge of a kind, but not such as he had known on the road to Sulcarkeep. Now he was being summoned, not warned. Koris and the Guardsmen would ride north if they willed, but he must head south. Simon put down his last guard against this insidious thing, allowed himself to be swayed by it.

"Has any news come out of the south?" he demanded of the sentry.

"Ask that of the Lord of Wings, Guardsman." The man was suspicious after the training of his kind. Simon headed for the stairs.

"Be sure that I shall!"

Before he went to the Commander of the Falconers, he tracked down the Captain, finding Koris busied with preparations for taking the trail. He glanced up from his saddlebags to Simon, and then his hands stopped pulling at buckles and straps.

"What's to do?"

"Laugh if you will," Simon replied shortly. "My road lies to the south."

Koris sat down on the edge of a table and swung one booted foot slowly back and forth. "Why does Karsten draw you?"

"That is just it!" Simon struggled to put into words what compelled him against either inclination or sense. He had never been an articulate man and he was discovering it even harder here to explain himself. "I am drawn—"

The swinging foot was still. In that handsome, bitter face there was no readable expression. "Since when—and how has it come upon you?" That demand was quick and harsh, an officer desiring a report.

Simon spoke the truth. "There was a dream and then I awoke. When I looked just now through the gap into Karsten I knew that my road leads there."

"And the dream?"

"It was of danger, more I cannot remember."

Koris drove one fist into the palm of the other. "So be it! I wish you had more power or less. But if you are drawn, we ride south."

"We?"

"Tunston and Jivin shall carry our news to Estcarp. The Kolder cannot cut through the barrier of the Power yet awhile. And Tunston can rally the Guard as well as I. Look you, Simon, I am of Gorm and now it is Gorm which fights against the Guard, though it may be a Gorm which is dead and demon-inspired. I have served Estcarp to the best of my ability since the Guardian gave me refuge, and I shall continue to serve her. But it may be that the time has come that I can serve her best outside the ranks of her liege men instead of within them.

"How do I know . . ." his dark young eyes had shadow smudges under them, tired eyes, worn with a fatigue which was not of body, "how do I know that through me because I am of Gorm danger cannot strike at the very heart of Estcarp? We have seen what the Kolder have done to living men whom I knew well, what else that devil-haunted brood can accomplish what man may tell? They flew through the air to take Sulcarkeep."

"But that may be no fruit of magic," Simon cut in. "In my own world air flight is a common mode of travel. I wish I had had sight of how they came—it could tell us much!"

Koris laughed wryly. "Doubtless we shall be given numerous other occasions in the future to observe their methods. I say this to you, Simon, if you are drawn south, I believe it to be by intelligent purpose. And two swords, or rather," he corrected himself with a little smile, "one ax, and one dart gun, are of greater force than one gun alone. The very fact of this summoning is good hearing, for it must mean that she who went with us to Sulcarkeep still lives and now moves to further our cause."

"But how do you know it is she, or why?" Such a suspicion had been Simon's also, to have it confirmed by Koris carried conviction.

"How? Why? Those who have the Power can send it forth along certain lanes of mind, as these Falconers dispatch their birds through the reaches of the air. And if they meet any of their kind, then they call or warn. As to why—it is in my mind, Simon, that she who sends must be the lady you saved from the pack of Alizon, for she would be well able to communicate with one she knows.

"You are not blood of our blood, bone of our bone, Simon Tregarth, and it would seem in your world the Power lies not only in the hands of women. Did you not smell out that ambush on the shore road as well as any witch might do? Yes, I shall ride into Karsten on no more proof than you have given me at this hour, because I know the Power and because, Simon, I have fought beside you. Let me give Tunston his instructions and a message for the Guardian, and we shall go to cast in troubled waters for important fish."

They rode south well equipped with mail and weapons taken from vanquished enemies, blank shields signifying that they were wandering mercenaries open for hire. The Falconer border guard escorted them to the edge of the mountains and the traders' road to Kars.

With no more than that tenuous feeling as a guide Simon wondered at the wisdom of their venture. Only the pull was still on him night and day, though he had no more nightmares. And each morning found him impatient to take the highway once more.

Karsten had villages in plenty, growing larger and richer as the travelers penetrated into the black-earthed bottom lands along the wide rivers. And there were petty lordlings set up in fiefs who offered employment to the two from the north. Though Koris laughed to scorn the wages they suggested and thus increased the respect with which he and his ax were regarded, Simon said little, but was alert to everything about him, mapping the land in his head, and noting small customs and laws of behavior, while, between times when they journeyed alone, he pumped the Guard Captain for information.

The Duchy had once been a territory sparsely held by a race akin to the ancient blood of Estcarp. And now and then a proud-held dark head, a pale face with cleanly cut features, reminded Simon of the men of the north.

"The curse of the Power finished them here," Koris observed when Simon commented on this.

"The curse?"

The Captain shrugged. "It goes back to the nature of the Power. Those who use it do not breed. And so each year the women who will wed and bear grow fewer. A marriageable maid of Estcarp may choose among ten men, soon among twenty. Also there are childless homes in plenty.

"So it was here. Thus when the sturdier barbarians came overseas and settled along the coast they were not actively opposed. More and more land came to their hands. The old stock withdrew to the backlands. Then warlords arose among the newcomers in the course of time. So we have the Dukes, and this Duke last of all—who was a common man of a hired shield company and climbed by his wits and the strength of his sword arm to complete rule."

"And so will it go with Estcarp also?"

"Perhaps. Only there was a mingling of blood with the Sulcarman, who, alone, it seems, can mate with

Estcarp and have fruit of it. Thus in the north there was a stirring of the old blood and a renewing of vigor. However, Gorm may swallow us up before there has been a proving of anything. How is it, Simon; does this town we approach beckon you? It is Garthholm on the river, and beyond it lies only Kars.''

"Then we go to Kars," Simon answered wearily after a long moment. ''For the burden is still on me.''

Under his plain helm Koris' brows rose. ''Then it is indeed laid upon us to walk softly and watch over our shoulders the while. Though the blood of the Duke is not high and he is eyed sidewise by the nobles, yet his wits are far from blunt. There will be eyes and ears within Kars to mark the lowliest stranger and questions asked of blank shields. Especially if we do not strive to enlist at once under his banner.''

Simon gazed thoughtfully at the river barges swinging at anchor by the town quay.

"But he would not be inclined to enlist a maimed man. Also are there not doctors within Kars who would treat one injured in battle? A man, say, who ailed from a blow on the head so that his eyes no longer served him well?''

"Such a one as would be brought by a comrade to see the wise doctors of Kars?'' chuckled Koris. ''Yes, that is a fine tale, Simon. And who is this injured warrior?''

"I think that role is mine. It would cover any awkward mistakes which a keen witted eye-and-ear of the Duke would note.''

Koris nodded vigorously. ''We sell these ponies here. They label us too much as being from the mountains, and in Karsten mountains are suspect. Passage can be bought on one of the river boats. A good enough plan.''

It was the Captain who carried out the bargaining

over the ponies, and he was still counting the wedge-shaped bits of metal which served as payment tokens in the duchy as he joined Simon on the barge. Koris grinned as he slapped the handful into his belt purse.

"I have trader blood and today I proved it," he said. "Half again what I was prepared to take, enough to aid in any palm-greasing when we come to Kars, should that be needed. And provisions to keep us until that hour." He dumped the bag he carried on board along with the ax from which he had not been parted since he took it from the hands of Volt.

There were two days of lazy current gliding on the river. As it neared sunset on the second, and the walls and towers of Kars stood out boldly not too far ahead, Simon's hands went to his head. The pain once more shot above his eyes with the intensity of a blow. Then it was gone, leaving behind it a small vivid picture of an ill-paved lane, a wall, and a door deep set therein. That was their goal and it lay in Kars.

"This is it then, Simon?" The Captain's hand fell on his shoulder.

"It is." Simon closed his eyes to the sunset colors bending the river. Somewhere in that city he must find the lane, the wall, the door, and meet with the one who waited.

"A narrow lane, a wall, a door—"

Koris understood. "Little enough," he remarked. His gaze was for the city, as if by the force of his will he could hurl them across the space still separating the barge from the waiting wharf.

Soon enough they came up the quay to the arch in the city wall. Simon moved slowly in his chosen role, trying to walk with the timidity of a man who could not trust his sight. Yet his nerves were prickling, he was certain that once within the city he could find the lane. The thread which had drawn him across the duchy was now a tight cord of direction.

Koris talked for them at the gate and his explanation of Simon's disability, his plausible story—as well as a gift passed under hand to the sergeant of the guard—got them in. The Captain snorted as they passed down the street and turned the corner.

"Were that man in Estcarp I'd have the sign off his shield and his feet pointing on the road away before he had time to name me his name! It has been said that the Duke grows soft since he came into rule, but I would not have believed it so."

"Every man is said to have his price," Simon remarked.

"True enough. But a wise officer knows the price of the men under him and uses them accordingly. These arc mercenaries and can be bought in little things. But perhaps if the code still prevails, they will stand firm in battle for him who pays them. What is it?"

He asked that sharply for Simon had stopped, half swung around.

"We head wrong. It is to the east."

Koris studied the street ahead. "There is an alley four doors from here. You are sure?"

"I am sure."

Lest the sergeant of the gate be more astute than they judged him, they went at a slow pace, Simon being guided. The eastward alley led on into more streets. Simon sheltered in a doorway while Koris sniffed their back trail. In spite of his distinctive appearance the Captain knew how to take cover, and he came flitting back soon.

"If they have set any hound on us he is better than

Estcarp's best, and that I do not believe. So now let us get to earth before we are remarked to be remembered. East still it is?''

The dull pain in Simon's head ebbed and flowed, he could use it as a ''hot'' and ''cold'' guide in a strange fashion. Then a particularly bad blast brought him to the mouth of a curving lane and he stepped within. It was walled with blank backs of buildings and what windows looked out on it were dark and curtained.

They quickened pace and Simon shot a glance at each window as they passed, fearing to see a face there. Then he saw it—the door of his vision. He was breathing a little hard as he paused before it, not from the exertion of pace, but rather from the turmoil inside him. He raised his fist and rapped on the solid portal.

When there was no answer he was absurdly disappointed. Then he pushed, to encounter a barrier which must be backed with bars.

''You are sure this is it?'' Koris prodded.

''Yes!'' There was no outer latch, nothing he could seize upon to force it open. Yet what he wanted, what had brought him there, was on its other side.

Koris stepped back a pace or two, measuring the height of the wall with his eye.

''Were it closer to dark we could mount this. But such a move now might be noted.''

Simon threw away caution and pounded, his assault on the wood that of a drum. Koris caught at his arm.

''Would you rouse out the Duke's companies? Let us lay up in a tavern and come back at nightfall.''

''There is no need for that.''

Koris' ax lifted from his shoulder. Simon's hand was on his gun. The door showed a wedge of opening and that low, characterless voice had come through it to them.

A young man stood in that crevice between wood and brick. He was much shorter than Simon, less in inches even than Koris, and light of limb. The upper part of his face was overhung with the visor of a battle helm, and he wore mail without the badge of any lord.

From Simon he looked to the Captain, and the sight of Koris appeared oddly to reassure him, for he stepped back and motioned them within. They came into a garden with brittle stalks of winter-killed flowers in precise beds, past a dry fountain rimmed with the mark of ancient scum where a stone bird with only half a beak searched endlessly for a water reflection which no longer existed.

Thcn another door into a house, and there the stream of light was a banner of welcome. The young man pushed before them, having sped from the barring of the wall door. But another stood to bid them enter.

Simon had seen this woman in rags as she fled from a pack of hunting hounds. And he had seen her in council, wearing the sober robes of her chosen order. He had ridden beside her when she went girt in mail with the Guards. Now she wore scarlet and gold, with gems on her fingers and a jeweled net coifing her short hair.

"Simon!" She did not hold out her hands to him, offered no other greeting save the naming of his name, yet he was warmed and at peace. "And Koris." She voiced a gentle laughter which invited them both to share some private joke, and swept them the grand curtsy of a court lady. "Have you come, lords, to consult the Wise Woman of Kars?"

Koris grounded the half of his ax on the floor and

dropped the saddle bags which had been looped over his wide shoulder.

"We have come at your bidding, or rather your bidding to Simon. And what we do here is for your saying. Though it is good to know that you are safe, lady."

Simon only nodded. Once again he could not find the proper words to express feelings he shrank from defining too closely.

IV

LOVE POTION

Koris put down his goblet with a sigh. "First a bed such as no barracks ever boasted and then two meals like this. I have not tasted equal wine since I rode out of Estcarp. Nor have I feasted in such good company."

The witch clapped her hands lightly. "Koris the courtier! And Koris and Simon the patient. Neither of you have yet asked what we do in Kars, though you have been a night and part of a day under this roof."

"Under this roof," Simon repeated thoughtfully. "Is this perchance the Estcarp embassy?"

She smiled. "Now that is clever of you, Simon. But, no, we are not official. There *is* an Estcarp embassy in Kars, housing a lord with impeccable background and not a single smell of witchcraft about him. He dines with the Duke upon formal occasions and provides a splendid representation of respectability. This house is located in quite a different quarter. What we do here—"

When she paused Koris asked lightly:

"I gather our aid is needed or Simon would not have had that aching head of his. Do we kidnap Yvian for your pleasure, or merely split a few skulls here and there?"

The young man who moved quietly, spoke little, but was always there, whom the witch named Briant and yet had not explained to the Guardsmen, reached for a dish of pastry balls. Stripped of the mail and helm he had worn at their first meeting, he was a slender, almost frail youngster, far too young to be well-schooled in the use of the weapons he bore. Yet there was a firm set to his mouth and chin, a steady purpose in his eyes which argued that the woman from Estcarp had perhaps chosen wisely in her recruiting after all.

"How, Briant," she said to him now, "shall they bring us Yvian?" There was something approaching mischief in that inquiry.

He shrugged as he bit into the pastry. "If you wish to see him. I do not." And that faint emphasis on the "I" was lost on neither of the men.

"No, it is not the Duke we plan to entertain. It is another member of his household, the Lady Aldis."

Koris whistled. "Aldis! I would not think—"

"That we have any business with the Duke's leman? Ah, you make the mistake of your sex there, Koris. There is a reason I wish to know more of Aldis, and an excellent one to urge her to come."

"Those being?" prompted Simon.

"Her power within the duchy is founded upon Yvian's favor alone. While she holds him to her bed she has what she wants most, not gauds and robes, but influence. Men who wish to further some scheme must seek out Aldis as a passage to the Duke's ear, even if they are of the old nobility. As for women of rank— Aldis has repaid heavily many old slights.

"When she first climbed to Yvian's notice the gauds and glitter sufficed, but through the years her power has come to mean more. Without that she is no better than a wench in a dockside tavern, as well she knows."

"Does Yvian grow restive now?" Koris wanted to know.

"Yvian has wed."

Simon watched the hand at the pastry dish. This time it did not complete its mission, but went instead to the goblet before Briant's plate.

"We heard talk in the mountains of the wedding of Verlaine's heiress."

"Ax marriage," the witch explained. "He has not seen his new bride yet."

"And the present lady fears a competition. Is the lady of Verlaine then counted so beautiful?" Simon asked idly but he caught a sudden swift glance from Briant.

And it was the boy who answered. "She is not!" There was a note in that hot denial which baffled Simon with its bitter hurt. Who Briant was or where the witch had found him, they had no idea, but perhaps the boy had nursed a liking for the heiress and was disappointed by his loss.

The witch laughed. "That, too, may be a matter of opinion. But, yet, Simon, I think that Aldis does not lie easy of nights since she heard the decree read forth in Kars' market place—wondering how long Yvian will continue to reach for her. In this state of mind she is ripe for our purpose."

"I can see why the lady might seek aid," Simon conceded, "but why yours?"

She was reproachful. "Though I do not go under my true colors as a Woman of Power out of Estcarp, I have a small reputation in this city. It is not my first visit here. Men and women, especially women, are ever intrigued to hear of their futures. Two of Aldis' waiting

maids have come here in these past three days, armed
with false names and falser stories. When I named them
for what they are and told them a few facts, they went
scuttling back wry-faced to their mistress. She will
come soon enough, never fear."

"But why do you want her? If her influence with
Yvian is on the wane—" Koris shook his head. "I have
never pretended to an understanding of women, but
truly am I now in a maze. Gorm is our enemy—not
Karsten, at least, not actively."

"Gorm!" There was some emotion stirring behind
the smooth facade of her face. "Here also Gorm finds
roots."

"What!" Koris' hands slapped down hard on the
table between them. "How comes Gorm to the
duchy?"

"It is the other way around. Karsten goes to Gorm,
or a part of her manpower does." The witch, resting her
chin upon her clasped hands, her elbows on the board,
spoke earnestly.

"We saw at Sulcarkeep what the Kolder forces did to
the men of Gorm, using them for war weapons. But
Gorm is only a small island and when she was overrun
many of her men must have died in battle before they
could be . . . converted."

"That is true!" Koris' voice was savage. "They
could not have netted too many captives."

"Just so. And when Sulcarkeep fell Magnis Osberic
must have taken with him the major parts of the invading force with the destruction of the hold. In that he
served his people. Most of the trading fleet were at sea,
and it is the custom of the Sulcarmen to carry their
families with them on long voyages. Their haven on
this continent is gone, but their nation lives and they

can build again. Only, can the Kolder so easily replace the men *they* lost?''

''It must be that they lack manpower,'' Simon half questioned, his mind busy with the possibilities that suggested.

''Which may be true. Or for some other reason they cannot or will not face us openly themselves. We know so little concerning the Kolder, even when they squat before our door. Now they are buying men.''

''But slaves are chancy as fighting men,'' Simon pointed out. ''Put weapons in their hands and you ask for revolt.''

''Simon, Simon, have you forgotten what manner of men we flushed from ambush on the sea road? Ask yourself if they were ready for revolt. No, those who march to Kolder war drums have no will left in them. But this much is also true: for the past six months galleys have come to an island lying off the sea-mouth of Kars' river and prisoners from Karsten are transferred to those ships. Some are from the prisons of the Duke, other men are swept up on the streets and docks, friendless men, or ones not to be missed.

''Such dealings cannot be kept secret forever. A whisper here, a sentence there—piece by piece we have gathered it. Men sold to the Kolder for Kolder purposes. And if thus it happens in Karsten, why not in Alizon? Now I can better understand why my mission there failed and how I was so speedily uncovered. If the Kolder have certain powers—as we believe that they do—they could stalk me or any such as me, as the hounds hunted us by scent on the moors.

''It is our belief now that the Kolder on Gorm is gathering a force to the purpose of invading the mainland. Perhaps on that day Karsten and Alizon shall both discover that they provided the weapons for their own defeat. That is why I deal with Aldis, we must know more of this filthy traffic with Gorm and it could not exist without the Duke's knowledge and consent.''

Koris stirred restlessly. "Soldiers gossip also, lady. A round of wine shops made by a blank shield with tokens in his purse might bring us tidings in plenty.''

She looked dubious. "Yvian is far from stupid. He has his eyes and ears everywhere. Let one such as you appear in the wine shops you mention, Captain, and he shall hear of it.''

Koris did not appear worried. "Did not Koris of Gorm, a mercenary, lose his men and his reputation at Sulcarkeep? Doubt not that I shall have a good story to blat out if any should ask it of me. You,'' he nodded to Simon, "had best lie close lest the tale we told to get through the gates trips us up. But how about the youngling here?'' He grinned at Briant.

Somewhat to Simon's surprise the generally sober-faced youth smiled back timidly. Then he looked to the witch as if for permission. And, equally to Simon's astonishment, she gave it, with some of the same mischief she had shown earlier.

"Briant is no ruffler of the barracks, Koris. But he has been prisoned here long enough. And don't underrate his sword arm; I'll warrant he can and will amaze you—in several ways!''

Koris laughed. "That I do not doubt at all, lady, seeing that it is you who says it.'' He reached for the ax by his chair.

"You'd best leave that pretty toy here,'' she warned. "It, at least, will be remarked.'' She laid her hand on the shaft.

It was as if her fingers were frozen there. And for the

first time since their arrival Simon saw her shaken out of her calm.

"What do you carry, Koris?" her voice was a little shrill.

"Do you not know, lady? It came to me with the good will of one who made it sing. And I guard it with my life."

She snatched back her hand as if that touch had seared flesh and bone.

"Willingly it came?"

Koris fired to that doubt. "About such a matter I would speak only the truth. To me it came and only me will it serve."

"Then more than ever do I say take it not into the streets of Kars." That was half order, half plea.

"Show me then a safe place in which to set it," he countered, with openly displayed unwillingness.

She thought a moment, her finger rubbing at her lower lip. "So be it. But later you must give me the full tale, Captain. Bring it hither and I shall show you the safest place in this house."

Simon and Briant trailed after them into another room where the walls were hung with strips of a tapestry so ancient that only the vaguest hints of the original designs could be surmised. One of these she bypassed to come to a length of carved wall panel on which fabulous beasts leered and snarled in high relief. She pulled at this, to display a cupboard and Koris set the ax far to its back.

Just as Simon had been aware of the past centuries within Estcarp city, solid waves of time beating against a man with all the pressure of ages, as he had also known awe for the non-human in the Hole where Volt had held silent court for dust and shadows, so here there was also a kind of radiation from the walls, a tangible something in the air which made his skin creep.

Yet Koris was brisk about the business of storing his treasure and the witch shut the cupboard as might a housewife upon a broom. Briant had lingered in the doorway, his usual impassive self. Why did Simon feel this way? And he was so plagued by that that he stayed when the others left, making himself walk slowly to the center of the chamber.

There were only two pieces of furniture. One a highbacked chair of black wood which might have come from an audience hall. Facing it was a stool of the same somber coloring. And on the floor between the two an odd collection of articles Simon studied as if trying to find in them the solution to his riddle.

First there was a small clay brazier in which might burn a palm load of coals, no more. It stood on a length of board, polished smooth. And with it was an earthen bowl containing some gray-white meal, that was flanked by a squat bottle. Two seats and that strange collection of objects—yet there was something else here also.

He did not hear the witch's return and was startled out of his thoughts when she spoke.

"What are you, Simon?"

His eyes met hers. "You know. I told you the truth at Estcarp. And you must have your own ways of testing for falsehood."

"We have, and you spoke the truth. Yet I must ask you again, Simon—what are you? On the sea road you felt out that ambush before the Power warned me. Yet you are a man!" For the first time her self-possession was shaken. "You know what is done here—you feel it!"

"No. I only know that there is something here that I can not see—yet it exists." He gave her the truth once again.

"That is it!" She beat her fists together. "You should not feel such things, and yet you do! I play a part here. I do not always use the Power, that is, greater power than my own experience in reading men and women, in guessing shrewdly what lies within their hearts or are their desires. Three quarters of my gift is illusion; you have seen that at work. I summon no demons, toll nothing here from another world by my spells, which are said mainly to work upon the minds of those who watch for wonders. Yet there is the Power and sometimes it comes to my call. Then I can work what are indeed wonders. I can smell out disaster, though I may not always know what form it will take. So much can I do—and that much is real! I swear to it by my life!"

"That I believe," Simon returned. "For in my world, too, there were things which could not be explained with any sober logic."

"And you had your women to do such things?"

"No, it came to either sex there. I have had men under my command who had foreknowledge of disaster, of death, their own or others'. Also I have known houses, old places, in which something lurked which was not good to think about, something which could not be seen or felt any more than we can now see or feel what is with us here."

She watched him now with undisguised wonder. Then her hand moved in the air, sketching between them some sign. And that blazed for an instant in fire hanging in space.

"You saw that?" Was that an accusation or triumphant recognition? He did not have time to discover which, for, sounding through the house was the note of a gong.

"Aldis! And she will have guards with her!" The witch crossed the room to rip open that panel where Koris had stored the ax. "In with you," she ordered. "They will search the house as they always do, and it would be better if they do not know of your presence."

She allowed him no time for protest, and Simon found himself cramped into space much too small. Then the panel was slammed shut. Only it was more spyhole than cupboard, he discovered. There were openings among the carvings, which gave him air to breath and sight of the room.

It had all been done so swiftly that he had been swept along. Now he revolted and his hands went to that panel, determined to be out. Only to discover, too late, that there was no latch on his side and that he had been neatly put into safe keeping, along with Volt's ax, until the witch chose to have him out again.

His irritation rising, Simon pressed his forehead against the carven screen to gain as full sight as he could of the room. And he kept very still as the woman from Estcarp reentered, to be pushed aside by two soldiers who strode briskly about, flipping aside strips of tapestry.

The witch was laughing as she watched them. Then she spoke over her shoulder to one still lingering on the other side of the threshold:

"It seems that one's word is not accepted in Kars. Yet when has this house and those under its roof even been associated with ill dealings? Your hounds may find some dust, a spider web, or two—I confess that I am not a notable housewife, but naught else, lady. And they waste our time with their searching."

There was a faint jeer in that, enough to flick one on the raw. Simon appreciated her skill with words. She spoke as an adult humoring children, a little impatient to be about more important business. And subtly she invited that unseen other to join her in adulthood.

"Halsfric! Donnar!"

The men snapped to attention.

"Prowl through the rest of this burrow if you will, but leave us in private!"

They stood aside nimbly at the door as another woman came in. The witch closed the portal behind them before she turned to the newcomer, who dropped her hooded cloak to let it lie in a saffron pool on the floor.

"Welcome, Lady Aldis."

"Time is wasting, woman, as you pointed out." The words were harsh, but the voice in which they were spoken surrounded that bruskness with layers of velvet. Such a voice could well twist a man to her will through hearing it alone.

And the Duke's mistress had the form, not of the tavern wench to which the witch had compared her, over-ripe and full-curved, but of a young girl not fully awakened to her own potentialities, with small high breasts modestly covered, yet perfectly revealed by the fabric of her robe. A woman of contradictions— wanton and cool at one and the same time. Simon, studying her, could well understand how she had managed to hold sway over a proved lecher as long and successfully as she had.

"You told Firtha—" again that sharp note swathed in velvet.

"I told your Firtha just what I could do and what was necessary for the doing," the witch was as brisk as her client. "Does the bargain suit you?"

"It will suit me when it is proved successful and not before. Give me that which makes me secure in Kars and then claim your pay."

"You have a strange way of bargaining, lady. The advantages are all yours."

Aldis smiled. "Ah, but if you have the power you claim, Wise Woman, then you can blast as well as aid and I shall be easy meat for you. Tell me what I must do and be quick; I can trust those two outside only because I hold both their lives with my tongue. But there are other eyes and tongues in this city!"

"Give me your hand." The woman from Estcarp picked up the tiny bowl of meal. As Aldis extended her beringed hand, the other stabbed it with a needle drawn from her clothing, letting a drop or two of blood fall into the bowl. She added more moisture from the bottle, mixing it into a batter. And coaxed the charcoal in the tiny stove to a blaze.

"Sit down." She pointed to the stool. When the other was seated, she slapped the board across her knees, putting the stove upon it.

"Think on the one you want, keep him only in your mind, lady."

The batter of that cake was spread out above that handful of fire and the woman from Estcarp began to sing. Strangely enough that something which had so alerted Simon moments earlier, which had thickened and curdled about them in that second when she had traced the fiery sign in the air, was now ebbing from the room.

But in its way her singing wove a spell of its own, changing thought images, evoking another kind of response. Simon, realizing it for what it was, for what it could do, after an incredulous second or two, bit hard upon his lower lip. This—coming from the woman he thought he was beginning to know. Fit magic for Aldis and her like; for the cool cleanliness of Estcarp, no! And it was beginning to work upon him also. Simon screwed his fingers into his ears to close out that sultry heat which seeped from words in the air to the racing blood in his own body.

He took away that defense only when he saw the witch's lips ceased to move. Aldis' face was a delicate pink, her parted lips moist, her eyes fixed before her unseeingly, until the witch lifted from her knees the board and brazier. The woman from Estcarp took up the cake, crumbled it into a square of white cloth and held it out to her client.

"A pinch of this added to his food or drink." The life had gone from the witch's voice; she spoke as one drugged with fatigue.

Aldis whipped the package from her, thrust it into the breast of her gown. "Be sure I shall use it rightly!" She caught up her cloak, already on her way to the door. "I shall let you know how I fare."

"I shall know, lady, I shall know."

Aldis was gone and the witch stood, one hand on the back of the chair as if she needed its support. Her expression was one of weary distaste with a faint trace of shame, as if she had used ill means to gain a good end.

V

THREE TIMES HORNED

Koris' hands moved in steady rhythm, polishing the ax blade with slow strokes of a silken cloth. He had reclaimed his treasure the minute he returned, and now, perched on a window ledge, with it resting upon his knees, he talked.

". . . he burst in as if the Kolder were breathing upon his back and blurted it out to the sergeant who spewed up half the wine I had paid for and was like to choke loose his guts, while this fellow pawed at him and yammered about it. I'd stake a week's looting of Kars that there is a kernel of truth in it somewhere, though the story's a muddle."

Simon was watching the other two in that room. He did not expect the witch to reveal either surprise or the fact that she might already have heard such a tale. However, the youngster she had produced out of nowhere might be less well schooled, and his attitude proved Simon right. Briant was *too* well controlled. One better trained in the game of concealment *would* have displayed surprise.

"I take it," Simon cut through the Captain's report, "that such a story is not a muddle to you, lady." The wariness which had become a part of his relationship with her since that scene with Aldis hours earlier was the shield he raised against her. She might sense its presence, but she made no effort to break through it.

"Hunold is truly dead," her words were flat. "And he died in Verlaine. Also is the Lady Loyse gone from the earth. That much did your man have true, Captain," she spoke to Koris rather than to Simon. "That both these happenings were the result of an Estcarp raid is, of course, nonsense."

"That I knew, lady. It is not our manner of fighting. But is this story a cover for something else? We have asked no questions of you, but did the remainder of the Guards come ashore on the Verlaine reefs?"

She shook her head. "To the extent of my knowledge, Captain, you and those who were saved with you are the only survivors out of Sulcarkeep."

"Yet a report such as this will spread and be an excuse for an attack on Estcarp." Koris was frowning now. "Hunold stood high in Yvian's favor. I do not think the Duke will take his death calmly, especially if some mystery surrounds it."

"Fulk!" The name exploded out of Briant as if it were a dart shot from his side arm. "This is Fulk's way out!" His pale face had expression enough now. "But he would have to deal with Siric and Lord Duarte, too! I think that Fulk has been very busy. That shieldman had so many details of a raid, that he must have been acquainted with a direct report."

"A messenger from the sea just landed. I heard him babble that much," Koris supplied.

"From the sea!" The witch was on her feet, her scarlet and gold draperies stirring about her. "Fulk of Verlaine cannot be termed in any way a simpleton, but there is a swiftness of move here, a taking advantage of every chance happening which smacks of something more than just Fulk's desire to protect himself against Yvian's vengeance!"

There was a stormy darkness in her eyes as she regarded all three of them coldly. She might almost have been numbering them among hostile elements. "This I do not like. Oh, some tale from Verlaine might have been expected; Fulk needed a story to throw into Yvian's teeth lest the stones of his towers be rained down about his own ears. And he is perfectly capable of spitting both Siric and Durate to give added credence and cover his tracks. But the moves come too swiftly, too well fitting into a pattern! I would have sworn—"

She strode up and down the chamber, her scarlet skirts swirling about her. "We are mistresses of illusion, but I will take oath before the Power of Estcarp that that storm was no illusion! Unless the Kolder have mastered the forces of nature—" Now she stood very still, and her hands flew to her mouth as if to trap words already spoken. "If the Kolder have mastered—" her voice came as a whisper. "I can not believe that we have been moved hither and yon at their bidding! That I dare not believe! Yet—" She whirled about and came directly to Simon.

"Briant I know, and what he does and why, all that I know. And Koris I know, and what drives him and why. But you—man out of the mists of Tor, I do not know. If you are more than you seem, then perhaps we have brought our own doom upon us."

Koris stopped polishing the ax blade. The cloth fell to the floor as his hands closed about the haft. "He was accepted by the Guardian," he said neutrally, but his attention centered upon Simon with the impersonal appraisal of a duelist moving forward to meet a challenge.

"Yes!" The woman from Estcarp agreed to that.

"And it is impossible that what Kolder holds to its core cannot be uncovered by our methods. They could cloak it, but the very blankness of that cloak would make it suspect! There is one test yet." She plucked at the throat fastening of her robe and drew forth the dull jewel she had worn out of Estcarp. For a long moment she held it in her hands, gazing down into its heart, and then she slipped the chain from about her neck and held it out to Simon. "Take it!" she ordered.

Koris cried out and scrambled off the ledge. But Simon took it into his hand. At first touch the thing was as smooth and cold as any polished gem, then it began to warm, adding to that heat with every second. Yet the head did not burn, it had no effect upon his flesh. Only the stone itself came to life; trails of opalescent fire crawled across its surface.

"I knew!" Her husky half-whisper filled the room. "No, not Kolder! Not Kolder; Kolder could not hold without harm, fire the Power and take no hurt! Welcome, brother in power!" Again she sketched a symbol in the air which glowed as brightly as the gem before it faded. Then she took the stone from his hold and restored it to its hiding place beneath her robe.

"He is a *man*! Shape changing could not work so, nor is it possible to befool us in the barracks where he has lived," Koris spoke first. "And how does a *man* hold the Power?"

"He is a man out of our time and space. What chances in other worlds we cannot say. Now I will swear that he is not Kolder. So perhaps he is that which Kolder must face in the final battle. But now we must . . ."

Their preoccupation was sharply broken by the burr of a signal in the wall. Alert, Simon and Koris looked to the witch. Briant drew his gun. "The wall gate," he said.

"Yet it is the right signal, though the wrong time. Answer it, but be prepared."

He was already half out of the room. Koris and Simon sped after him to the garden door. As they reached outside, free from the deadening thickness of the walls of that unusual house, they heard a clamor from the town. Simon was plagued by a wisp of memory. There was a note in that far-off shouting which he had surely heard before. Koris looked startled.

"That is a mob! The snarl of a hunting mob."

And Simon, remembering a red horror out of his own past, nodded briskly. He poised the dart gun to welcome whoever stood without the wall gate.

There was no mistaking the race of the man who stumbled in to them. A bloody gash could not disguise Estcarp features. He fell forward and Koris caught him about the body. Then they were all nearly rocked from their feet as a blast of sound and displaced air beat in on them and the very ground moved under them.

The man in Koris' hold moved, smiled, tried to speak. Deafened momentarily they could not hear. Briant slammed shut the gate and set its locking bars. Together Simon and the Captain half carried, half supported the fugitive into the house.

He recovered enough to sketch a salute to the witch as they brought him to her. She measured some bluish liquid into a cup and held it to his lips as he drank.

"Lord Vortimer?"

He leaned back in the chair into which they had lowered him. "You just heard his passing, lady—in that thunder clap! With him went all of our blood

fortunate to reach the embassy in time. For the rest—
they are being hunted in the streets. Yvian has ordered
the three times horning for all of Estcarp or of the old
blood! He is like a man gone mad!''

"This too?'' She pressed her hands tight against her
temples as if she might so ease some almost intolerable
pain. "We have no time, no time at all?''

"Vortimer sent me to warn you. Do you choose to
follow him along the same path, lady?''

"Not yet.''

"Those who have been horned can be cut down
without question wherever they are found. And in Kars
today the cutting down does not come swiftly as a clean
death,'' he warned dispassionately. "I do not know
what hopes you may have of the Lady Aldis—''

The witch laughed. "Aldis is no hope at all, Vortgin.
Five of us . . .'' She turned the cup around and around
in her fingers and then looked directly to Simon.
"More depends upon this than just our lives alone.
There are those in the outer parts of Karsten of the old
blood, who, warned, might safely get through the
mountains to Estcarp, and so swell our ranks. Also
what we have learned here, patchy though it is, must be
taken back. I could not hope to summon power
enough—you will have to aid me, brother!''

"But I don't know how—I have no use of power,''
he protested.

"You can back me. It is our only hope.''

Koris came away from the window where he had
been peering into the garden.

"Shape changing?''

"It is the only way. And how long will it hold?'' she
shrugged.

Vortgin ran his tongue across his lips. "Set me

outside this cursed city and I'll rouse your countryside for you. I have kin in the backlands who'll move on my word!''

"Come!" She led the way to that tapestried room of magic. But just inside the door Koris halted.

"What I have been given I bear with me. Put on me no shape in which I cannot handle the gift of Volt."

"I would call you lack-witted," she flared back, "if I did not know the worth of that biter of yours. But it is not of human make and so may change shape also in illusion. We can only try. Now let us make ready, quickly!"

She pulled a strip of carpet from the floor as Simon and Koris shoved the chair and stool, bore the other things to the other end of the room. Stooping she traced lines with the jewel of power and those lines glowed faintly in the form of a five pointed star. A little defiantly Koris dropped his ax in the center of that.

The witch spoke to Simon. "Shapes are not changed in truth, but an illusion is created to bemuse those who would track us down. Let me draw upon your power to swell my own. Now," she glanced around and brought the small clay brazier to sit by the ax, puffing its coals into life, "we can do what is to be done. Make yourselves ready."

Koris caught Simon by the arm. "Strip—to the skin—the power does not work otherwise!" He was shedding his own jerkin. And Simon obeyed orders, both of them aiding Vortgin.

Smoke curled up from the brazier, filling the room with a reddish mist in which Koris' squat form, the fugitive's muscular body were half hidden.

"Take your stand upon the star points—one to each point," came the witch's order out of the murk. "But you, Simon—next to me."

He followed that voice, losing Koris and the other man in the fog. A white arm came out to him, a hand reached for and enfolded his. He could see under his feet the lines of a star point.

Someone was singing—at a far distance. Simon was lost in a cloud where he floated without being. Yet at the same time he was warm—not outwardly, but inwardly. And that warmth floated from his body, down his right arm. Simon thought that if he could watch it he would be able to see that flow—blood red, warm— being drained in a steady stream. Yet he saw nothing but the greyish mist, he only knew that his body still existed.

The singing grew louder. Once before he had heard such singing—then it had aroused his lusts, and urged him to satisfy appetites he had beaten under by force of will. Now it worked upon him in another way, and he no longer loathed it fiercely.

He had closed his eyes against the endless swirling of the mist, stood attuned to the singing so that each note throbbed within his body to be a part of him, made into flesh and bone from this time forth—yet also did that warm flood trickle out of him.

Then his hand fell limply back against his thigh. The drain had ceased and the singing was fading. Simon opened his eyes. Where the murk had been a solid wall it was now showing holes. And in one of them he caught sight of a brutish face, a beastly caricature of human. But in it sat Koris' sardonic eyes. And a little beyond was another with disease-eaten skin and a flat lid where an eye had once been.

He wearing the Captain's eyes glanced from Simon to his neighbor and grinned widely, displaying decayed and yellowed fangs. "A fair company we shall be!"

"Dress you!" snapped the witch from the disappearing murk. "This day you have come out of the stews of Kars to loot and kill. It is your kind who thrive upon hornings!"

They put on the gear they had brought into Kars, but not enough to go too well clad for the dregs of the city that they seemed. And Koris took up from the floor— not the Ax of Volt—but a rust incrusted pole set with hooks, the purpose of which Simon would rather not imagine.

There was no mirror to survey his new self, but he gathered that he was as disreputable as his companions. He had been expecting changes in the witch and Briant also—but not what he saw. The woman of Estcarp was a crone with filthy ropes of grayish hair about her hunched shoulders, her features underlined with ancient evil. And the youngster was her opposite. Simon stared in pure amazement, for he fronted a girl being laced into the scarlet and gold gown discarded by the witch.

Just as Briant had been pallid and colorless, here was rich beauty, more than properly displayed since her tiring maid did not bother to pull tight breast laces. Instead the crone quirked a finger at Simon.

"This is your loot, bold fellow. Hoist the pretty on your shoulder, an if you grow tired of your burden— well, these other rogues will lend a hand. Play your part well." She gave the seeming girl a shove between her shoulder blades which sent her stumbling into Simon's arms. He caught her up neatly, swinging her across his shoulder, while the witch surveyed them with the eye of a stage manager and then gave a tug to strip the bodice yet farther from those smooth young shoulders.

Inwardly Simon was astonished at the completeness of the illusion. He had thought it would be for the eyes only, but he was very conscious that he held what was also feminine to the touch. And he had to keep reminding himself that it was indeed Briant he so bore out of the house.

They found Kars harbored many such bands as theirs that day. And the sights they had to witness, the aid they could not give, ate into them during that journey to the wharves. There was a watch at the gates right enough, but as Simon approached, with his now moaning victim slung over his shoulder, his raffish fellows slinking behind him, as if to welcome the leavings of his feast, the witch scuttled ahead with a bag. She tripped and fell so that the brilliant contents of her looter's catchall rolled and spilled across the roadway.

Those on guard sprang into action, the officer kicking the crone out of his way. But one man had a slightly higher sense of duty, or perhaps he was more moved by Simon's supposed choice of pillage. For he swung a pike down in front of Tregarth and grinned at him over that barrier.

"You've got you a soft armload there, fishguts. Too good for you. Let a better man sample her first!"

Koris' pole with its rusty hooks snaked out, hooking his feet from under him. As he sprawled they darted through the gate and along the wharf, other guards in pursuit.

"In!" Briant was pulled out of Simon's grasp, thrown out into the flood of the river, the Captain following in a cleancut dive to come up beside the struggling red and gold clad body. Vortgin took off at a stumbling run. But Simon, seeing that Koris had Briant to hand, looked back for the witch.

There was a flurry down the wharf and a tangle of figures. Gun in hand he ran back, pausing for three snap shots, each taking out a man, dead or wounded. His rush brought him there in time to see that twisted gray-haired body lying still while a sword swung downward aimed at the scrawny throat.

Simon shot twice more. Then his fist struck flesh, crushed it against bone. Someone shrieked and fled as he scooped up the witch, finding her weight more than Briant's. Bearing her over his shoulder he staggered to the nearest barge, his lungs laboring as he dodged among the piled cargo on its deck, heading for the far rail and open water.

The woman in his arms came to life suddenly, pushing against him as if he were indeed a captor she might fight. And that overbalanced Simon so that they went over together, tumbling to strike the river with a force he had not expected. Simon swallowed water, choked, and struck out instinctively, if clumsily.

His head broke the surface and he stared about him for the witch, to see a wrinkled arm, hampered by water soaked rags cutting in a swimmer's stroke.

"Ho!"

The call came from a barge floating downstream and a rope flicked over its side. Simon and the witch gained the deck, only to have Koris wave them impatiently to the opposite rail into the river again, the craft serving as a screen between them and the city shore.

But here a small boat with Vortgin sitting therein, Briant leaning over the side being actively sick into the water, while he clutched his red robe about him as if indeed he had been the victim of rapine. As they scrambled down to this refuge, Koris pushed them away from the barge, using the point of his hook spear.

"I thought you lost that at the gate!"

Koris' ruffian face mirrored his astonishment at Simon's comment. "This I would never lose! Well, we have us a breathing space. They will believe us hiding on the barge. At least so we can hope. But it would be wise to head to the other shore as soon as this has drifted far enough from the wharves."

They agreed with the Captain's suggestion, but the minutes during which they remained wedded to the barge were very long ones. Briant straightened at last, but he kept his face turned from them as if heartily ashamed of the guise he wore. And the witch sat in the bow surveying the far shore with searching intensity.

They were lucky in that night was closing in. And Vortgin knew the surrounding country well. He would be able to guide them inland across the fields, avoiding houses and farms, until they had put enough distance between them and Kars to feel reasonably safe.

"Thrice horned—yes, that sentence he can enforce in Kars. For the city is his. But the old lords have ties with us, and where they lack such ties or sympathy, they may be moved by jealousy of Yvian. They may not actively aid us, but neither will they help the Duke's men cut us down. It will be largely a matter of their closing their eyes and ears, hearing and seeing naught."

"Yes, Karsten is now closed to us," the witch agreed with Vortgin. "And I would say to all of the old race that they should flee borderward, not leaving escape until too late. Perhaps the Falconers will aid in this matter. Aie . . . aie . . . our night comes!"

But Simon knew that she did not mean the physical night closing about their own small party.

VI

FALSE HAWK

They lay behind the winter pressed stack in the field, Simon, Koris, and Vortgin, wisps of the dank straw pulled over their bodies, watching what went on at the crossroads hamlet beyond. There were the brilliant blue-green surcoats of the Duke's men, four of them, well mounted for hard and far riding, and a fringe of the dull-robed villagers. With some ceremony the leader of the small force out of Kars brought his horse beneath the Pole of Proclamation and put a horn to his lips, its silver plating catching fire from the morning sun.

"One . . . two . . . three . . ." Koris counted those blasts aloud. They heard them clearly, all the countryside must have heard them, although what the Duke's men said to the assembly afterwards they caught only as a mumble.

Koris looked to Vortgin. "They spread it fast enough. You'd best be on your way, if any of your kin is to be warned at all."

Vortgin thrust his belt dagger deep into the earth of the field as if he were planting it in one of the blue coated riders. "I'll need more than my two legs."

"Just so. And there is what we all seek." Koris jerked a thumb at the ducal party.

"Beyond the bridge the road takes a cut through a small woods," Simon thought aloud.

Koris' pseudo-face expressed malicious appreciation of that hint. "They'll soon be through with the chatter. We'd best move."

They crawled away from their vantage point, crossed the river ford, and found the woods track. The roads leading north were not well kept. Yvian's rule in this district had been covertly opposed by noble and commoner alike. Away from the main highways all passages tended to be only rough tracks.

On either side banks rose, brush and grass covered. It was not a safe place for any wayfarer, doubly suspect for anyone in the Duke's livery.

Simon settled into concealment on one side of that cut, Koris chose a stand closer to the river, prepared to head off any retreat. And Vortgin was across from Simon. They had only to wait.

The leader of the messengers was no fool. One of his men rode ahead, studying every bush the wind stirred, every clump of suspiciously tall grass. He passed between the hidden men and trotted on. After him came the one who bore the horn, and a companion, while the fourth man brought up the rear.

Simon shot as the rearguard drew level with his position. But the man who fell from the expertly aimed dart was the lead scout.

The leader swung his mount around with the skill of an expert horseman, only to see the rearguard collapse from his saddle coughing blood.

"Sul . . . Sul . . . Sul!" The battle cry Simon had last heard in the doomed seaport rose shrilly. A dart creased Simon's shoulder, ripping leather and burning skin—the leader must have cat's eyes.

The remaining shieldman tried to back his leader in that attack, until Vortgin arose out of hiding and threw the dagger he had played with. The weapon whirled end over end until its heady knob struck the back of the other's head at the base of his skull and he went down without a protesting sound.

Hooves pawed the air over Simon's head. Then the horse overbalanced and crashed back, pinning his rider under him. Koris sprang out of hiding and the hooked pole battered down upon the feebly struggling man.

They set to work to strip the riders, secure their mounts. Luckily the horse which had fallen, struggled to its feet, frightened and blowing but without any great injury. The bodies were dragged out of sight into the brush and the mail shirts, the helmets and the extra weapons were bound on the saddles before the horses were led to the deserted sheep fold where the fugitives had sheltered.

There the men walked into a hot quarrel. The withered crone, the dark beauty in rent gold and scarlet fronted each other hot-eyed. But their raised voices fell silent as Simon came through a gap in the rotting fence. Neither spoke until they brought up the horses and their burdens. Then the girl in red gave a little cry and pounced upon one of those bundles of leather and mail.

"I want my own shape—and now!" She spat at the witch.

Simon could understand that. At Briant's age a role as he had been forced to assume would be more galling than slavery. And none of them could wish to keep on wearing the decidedly unattractive envelopes the woman from Estcarp had spun for them, even though they had been so delivered out of Kars.

"Fair enough," he endorsed that. "Can we change by our—or rather *your* will, lady? Or is there a time period on this shape business?"

Through her tangle of rough locks the witch frowned. "Why waste the time? And we are not yet out of the reach of Yvian's messengers—though apparently you have dealt with some of them." She picked up one of the surcoats as if to measure it against her own bent person.

Briant glowered, gathering an armload of male clothing to him. The pouting lips of his girl's face set stubbornly. "I go away from here as myself, or I don't go at all!" he announced and Simon believed him.

The woman from Estcarp gave in. From beneath her ragged bodice she pulled a bag and shook it at Briant. "Off with you to the stream then. Wash with a handful of this for your soaping. But be careful of it, for this supply must serve us all."

Briant snatched the bag, and, with the clothing, he gathered up his full skirts to scuttle away as if he feared his new possessions might be torn from him.

"What about the rest of us?" Simon demanded indignantly, ready to take off after the runaway.

Koris secured the horses to the moldering fence. His villainous face could not look anything but hideous, but somehow he managed to suggest honest amusement in his laughter. "Let the cub get rid of his trappings in peace, Simon. After all, he hasn't protested before. And those skirts must have irked him."

"Skirts?" echoed Vortgin in some surprise. "But . . ."

"Simon is not of the old race." The witch combed her hair with her long nails. "He is new to our ways and shape changing. You are right, Koris," she glanced oddly at the Captain, "Briant can be left to make his transformation in peace."

The garments looted from the Duke's unfortunate

messengers hung loosely on the young warrior who
returned at a far bolder gait from the stream. He tossed a
ball of red stuff to the back of the shelter and stamped
earth over it with an energy which approached attack as
Simon and the rest went to the water.

Koris rubbed and laved his rusty hooked pole before
he dipped his body, and continued to hold the Ax of
Volt as he scrubbed himself. They made a choice from
the tumbled clothing, Koris again assuming the mail
shirt he had worn out of Kars since no other would fit
him. But he shrugged one of the surcoats over it, a
precaution followed by both his companions.

Simon handed the bag to the witch when they re--
turned and she nursed it for a moment in one hand, then
restored it to its former hiding place. "You are a brave
company of warriors. Me, I am your prisoner. With
your hoods and your helms Estcarp does not show so
strong in you. Vortgin, you alone have the print of the
old race. But were I to be seen in my true face I would
damn you utterly. I shall wait before I break this
shape."

So it was that they rode out of that hiding place, four
men in the Duke's colors and the crone perched behind
Briant. The horses were fresh, but they held the pace to
a comfortable trot as they worked a path across the
country, avoiding the open roads until they reached a
point where Vortgin must turn east.

"North along the trade roads," the witch leaned
from her seat behind Briant to urge. "If we can alert the
Falconers they should see fugitives safely through the
mountains. Tell your people to leave their gear and
bring with them only their weapons and food, what may
be carried on pack animals. And may the Power ride
with you, Vortgin, for those you can urge into Estcarp
will be blood for our veins!"

Koris pulled the horn strap from his shoulder and passed it over. "This may be your passport if you flush any of Yvian's forces before you get into the back country. Luck be yours, brother, and seek out the Guards in the North. There is a shield in their armory to fit your shoulder!"

Vortgin saluted and kicked his horse into a flurry of speed eastward.

"And now?" the witch asked Koris.

"The Falconers."

She cackled. "You forget, Captain, old and shriveled as I seem, with all the juices age-sucked from me, still am I female and the hold of the hawk men is barred to me. Set Briant and me across the border and then seek out your women-hating bird men. Rouse them up as best you may. For a border abristle with sword points will give Yvian something else to think about. And if they can afford our cousins safe passage, they will put us deep in their debt. Only," she plucked at the surcoat on Briant's shoulders, "I would say to you throw these name signs of a lord you do not serve away, or you may find yourself pinned to some mountain tree before you have time to make your true nature known."

Simon was not surprised this time to find they were being observed by a hawk, nor did he think it odd to hear Koris address the bird clearly, giving their true identies and explaining their business in the foothills. He covered the back trail while the Captain took the lead, the witch and Briant riding between them. They had parted with Vortgin in midafternoon and it was now close to sunset, their only food during the day the rations found in the saddlebags of the captured horses.

Now Koris pulled up until the others joined him. While the Captain spoke he still faced into the rising mountains and it seemed to Simon as if he had lost a little of his robust confidence.

"This I do not like. That message must have been relayed by the bird's communicator, and the frontier guards could not have been too far away. They should have met us before now. When we were in the Eyrie they were eager enough to promote a common cause with Estcarp."

Simon eyed the slopes ahead uneasily. "I do not take a trail such as this in the dark without a guide. If you say, Captain, that they are not following custom, then that is all the more reason for staying clear of their territory. I would say camp at the first likely spot."

It was Briant who broke in then, his head up, his attention for the bird wheeling overhead.

"That one does not fly right!" The youngster, dropping the reins of his horse, held his hands together to mimic the wings of a bird. "A true bird goes so—and a falcon so—many times have I watched them. But this one, see—flap, flap, flap—it is not right!"

They were all watching the circling bird now. To Simon's eyes it was the same sort of black and white feathered sentry as had found them outside the Hole of Volt, as he has seen on the saddle perches of the Falconers. However he would be the first to admit that he knew nothing of birds.

"Can you whistle it down?" he asked Koris.

The Captain's lips pursed and clear notes rang on the air.

At that same moment Simon's dart gun went up. Koris turned with a cry and struck at Simon's arm, but the shot had already been fired. They saw the dart strike, piercing just the point of the white Vee upon the bird's breast. But there was no faltering in its flight, no sign that it had taken any hurt from the bolt.

"I told you it is no bird!" cried Briant. "Magic!"

They all looked to the witch for an explanation, but her attention was riveted on that bird, the dart still protruding from its body, as it made low lazy circles overhead.

"No magic of the Powers." That answer seemed forced out of her against her will. "What this is, I cannot tell you. But it does not live as we know life."

"Kolder!" Koris spat.

She shook her head slowly. "If it is Kolder, it is not nature-tampering as it was with the men of Gorm. What it is I cannot tell."

"We'll have to get it down. It is lower since that dart struck it; perhaps the weight pulls it." Simon said, "Let me have your cloak," he added to the witch, dismounting.

She handed him that ragged garment and looping it over his arm Simon began to climb the wall beside the narrow track they had followed to this place. He hoped that the bird would remain where it was, content to fly above them. And he was sure it drew nearer earth with every circle.

Simon waited, flipping the cloak out a little. He flung it, and the bird flew unwarily into the improvised net. When Simon tried to draw it back the captive fell free, to fly blindly on and smash head first against the rock wall.

Tregarth leaped down to scoop up what lay on the ground. Real feathers right enough—but under them! He gave a whistle almost as clear and carrying as Koris' bird summons, for entangled in the folds of torn skin and broken feathers was a mass of delicate metal fittings, tiny wheels and wires, and what could only be a motor of strange design. Holding it in his two hands he went back to the horses.

"Are you sure the Falconers use only real hawks?" he asked of the Captain.

"Those hawks are sacred to them." Koris poked a finger into the mess Simon held, his face blank with amazement. "I do not think that this thing is any of their fashioning, for to them the birds are their power and they would not counterfeit that lest it either turn upon them or depart utterly."

"Yet someone or something has tossed into the air of these mountains hawks which are made, not hatched," Simon pointed out.

The witch leaned closer, reaching out a finger to touch as Koris had done. Then her eyes raised to Simon's and there was a question in them, a shadow of concern.

"Outworld—" she spoke hardly above a whisper. "This is not bred of our magic, or of the magic of our time and space. Alien, Simon, alien . . ."

Briant interrupted her with a cry and pointing a finger. A second black and white shape was over their heads, swooping lower. Simon's free hand went to the gun, but the boy reached down from his saddle to strike at Tregarth's wrist and spoil his aim.

"That is a real bird!"

Koris whistled and the hawk obeyed that summons in the clean strike of its breed, settling on a rock crown, the tip of the same pinnacle against which the counterfeit had dashed itself to wreckage.

"Koris of Estcarp," the Captain spoke to it, "but let him who flies you come swiftly, winged brother, for there is ill here and perhaps worse to come!" He waved his hand and the falcon took once more to the air, to head straight for the peaks.

Simon put the other thing into one of his saddle bags.

In the Eyrie he had been intrigued by the communication devices which the true falcons bore. A machine so
delicate and so advanced in technical ability was out of
place in the feudal fortress of its users. And what of the
artificial lighting and heating systems of Estcarp, or the
buildings of the Sulcarkeep, of that energy source Osberic had blown up to finish the port? Were all these
vestiges of an earlier civilization which had vanished
leaving only traces of its inventions behind? Or—were
they grafts upon this world from some other source?
Simon's eyes may have been on the trail they rode but
his wits were tumbling the problem elsewhere.

Koris had spoken of Volt's non-human race preced-
ing mankind here. Were these remnants of theirs? Or
had the Falconers, the mariners of Sulcarkeep, learned
what they wished, what served their purposes best from
someone, or something else, perhaps overseas? He
wanted a chance to examine the wreckage of the false
hawk, to try and assess from it if he could the type of
mind, or training, which could create such an object.

The Falconers emerged from the mountain slopes as
if they had stepped from the folds of the ground. And
they waited for the party from Kars to approach, neither
denying them passage, nor welcoming them.

"Faltjar of the southern gate," Koris identified their
leader. He swept his own helm from his head to display
his face plainly in the fading light. "I am Koris of
Estcarp, and I ride with Simon of the Guards."

"Also with a female!" The return was cold and the
Falcon on Faltjar's saddle perch shook its wings and
screamed.

"A lady of Estcarp whom I must put safely beyond
the mountains," corrected the Captain in a tone as cold
and with the sharpness of a rebuke. "We make no claim

upon you for shelter, but there is news which your Lord of Wings should hear.''

"A way through the mountains you may have, Guard of Estcarp. And the news you may give to me; it shall be retold to the Lord of Wings before moonrise. But in your hail you spoke of ill here and worse to follow. That I must know, for it is my duty to man the southern slopes. Does Karsten send forth her men?''

"Karsten has thrice horned all of the old race and they flee for their lives. But also there is something else. Simon, show him the false hawk.''

Simon was reluctant. He did not want to yield up that machine until he had more time to examine it. The mountaineer looked upon the broken bird he took from the saddlebag, smoothing a wing with one finger, touching an open eye of crystal, pulling aside a shred of feathered skin to see the metal beneath.

"This flew?'' he demanded at last, as if he could not believe in what he saw and felt.

"It flew as one of your birds, and kept watch upon us after the fashion of your scouts and messengers.''

Faltjar drew his forefinger caressingly down the head of his own bird as if to assure himself that it was a living creature and not such a copy.

"Truly this is a great ill. You must speak yourself with the Lord of Wings!'' Clearly he was torn between the age-old customs of his people and the necessity for immediate action. "If you did not have the female—the lady,'' he corrected with an effort, "but she may not enter the Eyrie.''

The witch spoke. "Let me camp with Briant, and you ride to the Eyrie, Captain. Though I say to you, bird man, the day comes soon when we must throw aside many old customs, both we of Estcarp and you of the mountains, for it is better to be alive and able to fight, than to be bound by the chains of prejudice and dead! There is a riving of the border before us such as this land has never seen. And all men of good will must stand together."

He did not look at her, nor answer, though he half sketched a salute, giving the impression that that was a vast concession. And then his hawk took to the air with a cry, and Faltjar spoke directly to Koris.

"The camp shall be made in a safe place. Then, let us ride!"

PART IV: VENTURE OF GORM

I

THE RIVING OF THE BORDER

A column of smoke penciled into the air, broken by puffs as more combustible materials caught. Simon reined up on the rise to gaze back at the site of another disaster for the Karsten forces, another victory for his own small, hard-riding, tough-punching troop. How long their luck would hold, none of them could guess. But as long as it did, they would continue to blast into the plains, covering up the escape lines of those set-faced, dark-haired people from the outlands who came in family groups, in well armed and equipped bodies, or singly at a weaving pace dictated by wounds and exhaustion. Vortgin had done his work well. The old race, or what was left of it, was withdrawing over a border the Falconers kept open, into Estcarp.

Men without responsibilities for families or clans, men who had excellent cause to want to meet Karsten levies with naked blades, stayed in the mountains, providing a growing force to be led by Koris and Simon. Then by Simon alone as the Captain of the Guard was summoned north to Estcarp to recommand there.

This was guerilla warfare as Simon had learned it in another time and land, doubly effective this time because the men under him knew the country as those sent against them did not. For Tregarth discovered that these silent, somber men who rode at his back had a queer affinity with the land itself and with the beasts and the birds. Perhaps they were not served as the Falconers were by their trained hawks, but he had seen odd things happen, such as a herd of deer move to muddle horse tracks, crows betray a Karsten ambush. Now he listened, believed, and consulted with his sergeants before any strike.

The old race were not bred to war, though they handled sword and gun expertly. But with them it was a disagreeable task to be quickly done and forgotten. They killed cleanly with dispatch and they were incapable of such beastliness as the parties from the mountains had come upon where fugitives had been cut off and captured.

It was once when Simon left such a site, white, controlling his sickness by will power alone, that he was startled by a comment from the set-faced young man who had been his lieutenant on that foray.

"They do not do this of their own planning."

"I have seen such things before," Simon returned, "and that was also done by human beings to human beings."

The other who had held his own lands in the back country and had escaped with his bare life from that holding some thirty days earlier, shook his head.

"Yvian is a soldier, a mercenary. War is his trade. But to kill in such ways is to sow black hate against a future reaping. And Yvian is lord in this land; he would not willingly rip apart his own holding and bring it to ruin—he is too keen-witted a man. He would not give orders for the doing of such deeds."

"Yet we have seen more than one such sight. They could not all be the work of only one band commanded by a sadist, or even two such."

"True. That is why I think we now fight men who are possessed."

Possessed! The old meaning of that term in his own world came to Simon—possession by demons. Well, that a man could believe having seen what they had been forced to look upon. Possessed by demons—or—the memory of the Sulcarkeep road flooded into his mind; possessed by a demon—or emptied of a soul! Kolder again?

From then on, much as it revolted him, Simon kept records of such finds, though never was he able to catch the perpetrators at their grisly work. He longed to consult with the witch, only she had gone north with Briant and the first wave of fugitives.

He launched through the network of guerrilla bands a request for information. And at nights, in one temporary headquarters after another, he pieced together bits and patches. There was very little concrete evidence, but Simon became convinced that certain commanders among the Karsten forces did not operate according to their former ways, and that the Duke's army had been infiltrated by an alien group.

Aliens! As always that puzzle of inequality of skills continued to plague him. Questioning of his refugees told him that the energy machines which they had always known had come from "overseas" ages past: "overseas", energy machines brought by the Sulcar traders, adapted by the old race for heat and light, the Falconers also from "Overseas" with their amazing communicators borne by their hawks. And the source of the Kolder was also "overseas"—a vague term—a common source for all?

What he could learn he dispatched by messenger to Estcarp, asking for anything the witches might have to tell in return. The only thing he was sure of was that as long as his own force was recruited from those of the old race, he had no need to fear infiltration himself. For that quality which gave them kinship with the land and the wild things granted them in addition the ability to smell out the alien.

Three more false hawks had been detected in the mountains. But all had been destroyed in their capture and Simon had only broken bits to examine. Where they came from and for what purpose they had been loosed was a part of all the other mystery.

Ingvald, the Karstenian lieutenant, pushed up beside him now to look down upon the scene of destruction they had left.

"The main party with the booty is well along the hill track, Captain. We have plundered to some purpose this time, and with that fire laid to cross our trail, they will not even know how much has come into our hands! There are four cases of darts as well as the food."

"Too much to supply a flying column." Simon frowned, his mind snapping back to the business at hand. "It would seem that Yvian hopes to make a central post somewhere hereabouts and base his foray parties there. He may be planning to move a large force borderwards."

"I do not understand it," Ingvald said slowly. "Why did this all blow up so suddenly out of nothing? We are not—were not—blood brothers of the coastwise people. They drove us inland when they came from the sea. But for ten generations we have been at peace with them, each going our way and not troubling the other. We of the old race are not inclined to war and there was no reason for this sudden attack upon us. Yet when it came it moved in such a way as we may only believe that it had long been planned."

"But, not, perhaps, by Yvian." Simon set his horse to a trot matched by Ingvald's mount so they rode knee to knee. "I want a prisoner, Ingvald, a prisoner of such a one as has been amusing himself in those ways we saw in the farm meadow of the fork roads!"

A spark gleamed deep in the dark eyes meeting his. "If such a one is ever taken, Captain, he shall be brought to you."

"Alive and able to talk!" Simon cautioned.

"Alive and able to speak," agreed the other. "For it is in our minds too, that things can be learned from one of that sort. Only never do we find them, only their handiwork. And I think that that is left deliberately as a threat and a warning."

"There is a puzzle in this," Simon was thinking aloud, playing once more with his ever-present problem. "It would seem that someone believes we can be beaten into submission by brutality. And that someone or something does not understand that a man can be fired to just the opposite by those methods. Or," he added after a moment's pause, "could this be done deliberately to goad us into turning our full fury against Yvian and Karsten, to get the border aflame and all Estcarp engaged there, then to strike elsewhere?"

"Perhaps a little of both," Ingvald suggested. "I know, Captain, that you have been seeking for another presence in the Karsten forces, and I have heard of what was found at Sulcarkeep and the rumors of man-selling to Gorm. We are safe in this much: no one who is not truly human can come among us without our knowledge—just as we have always known that you are not of our world."

Simon started, but turned to see the other smiling quietly.

"Yes, Outlander, your tale spread—but after we knew you were not of us—though in some strange way your own akin to our blood. No, the Kolder cannot sneak into our councils so easily. Nor can the enemy venture among the Falconers, for the hawks would betray them."

Simon was caught by that. "How so?"

"A bird or an animal can sense that kind of alien quicker than even one who has the Power. And those like now to the men of Gorm would find both bird and beast against them. So the Hawks of the Eyrie serve their trainers doubly and make safe the mountains."

But before the day was behind them Simon was to learn that that vaunted safety of the mountains was only as strong as those frail bird bodies. They were examining the supplies looted from the train and Simon set aside a portion intended for the Eyrie, when he heard the hail of a camp sentry and the answer of a Falconer. Welcoming the chance to let the latter transport the hawkmen's share and so save his men a trip, Simon came forward eagerly.

The rider had not followed custom. His bird-head helm was closed as if he rode among strangers. It was not that alone which stopped Simon before he gave greeting. The men of his band were alert, drawing in in a circle. Simon felt it, too, that prickle of awaking surmise, just as he had known it before.

Without stopping to reason, he hurled himself at the silent rider and his hands caught at the other's weapon belt. Simon knew fleeting wonder that the hawk perched on the saddle horn did not rouse as he attacked its master. His lunge caught the Falconer by surprise, and the fellow had no time to draw his arms. But he made a quick recovery, slumping his whole weight on

Simon, bearing him under him to the ground, where mailed gloved hands tore for Tregarth's throat.

It was like tangling with a steel-muscled, iron-fleshed thing, and within seconds Simon knew that he had attempted the impossible—what was encased in the Falconer's covering could not be subdued with bare hands. Only he was not alone; other hands plucked that fighter off him, held the man pinned to the ground, though the stranger struggled wildly.

Simon, rubbing his scratched throat, got to his knees.

"Unhelm!" He gasped the order, and Ingvald worked at the helm straps, jerking them free at last.

They gathered around the men who held the captive down, for his struggles did not stop. The Falconers were an inbred race with a dominate physical type—reddish hair and brown-yellow eyes like their feathered servants. By his looks this was a true man of the breed. Yet Simon and every man in that clearing knew that what they held was no normal member of the mountain country.

"Rope him tight!" Simon ordered. "I think, Ingvald, we have found what we have been wishing for." He went over to the horse which had carried the pseudo-hawkman into their camp. The animal's hide glistened with sweat, threads of foam spun at the bit hooks; it might have been ridden in a grueling race. And its eyes were wild, showing rims of white. But when Simon reached for the reins it did not try to escape, standing with a drooping head as great shudders moved its sweat-soaked skin.

The hawk had remained quiet, no flap of wings or hissing beak to warn Simon off. He reached up and plucked the bird from its perch, and the minute his fingers closed upon that body he knew he did not hold a living creature.

With it in his hand he turned to his lieutenant. "Ingvald, send Lathor, Karn," he named the two most accomplished scouts in his command. "Let them ride to the Eyrie. We must know how far the rot has spread. If they find no damage done there, let them give warning. For proof of their tale," he stooped to pick up the bird helm of their prisoner, "let them take this. I believe it is of Falconer making, yet," he walked over to the bound man, still silent, still watching them with eyes of mad hate, "I cannot quite believe that this is one of them."

"We do not take him also?" asked Karn, "or the bird?"

"No, we open no doors which are not already breached. We need safe disposal for this one for a space."

"The cave by the waterfall, Captain." Waldis, a boy of Ingvald's homestead who had tracked his master to the mountains, spoke up. "One sentry at the entrance can keep it safe and none know of it save us."

"Good enough. You will see to it, Ingvald."

"And you, Captain?"

"I am going to backtrail this one. It may be that he did ride from the Eyrie. If that is true, the sooner we know the worst the better."

"I do not think so, Captain. At least if he did, it was not by any straight trail. We are well to the westward of the hold. And he entered from the path leading to the sea. Santu," he spoke to one who had helped to rope the prisoner, "do you go and take outpost on this trail and send in Caluf who first challenged him."

Simon threw the saddle on his own horse, and added

a bag with rations. On top he thrust in the dummy falcon. Whether this was one of the counterfeit flying things, he could not tell as yet, but it was the first intact one they had. He finished just as Caluf ran in.

"You are sure he came from the west?" Simon pressed the question.

"I will swear it on the Stone of Engis if you wish, Captain. The hawkmen do not care greatly for the sea, though they serve the traders at times as marines. And I did not know they patrolled the shore cliffs. But he rode straight between those notched rocks which give upon the way to the cove we mapped five days ago, and he moved as one who knew the trail well."

Simon was more than a little disturbed. The cove of their recent discovery had been a ray of hope for the establishment of better communication with the north. It was not endangered by reefs and shoals such as fanged too much of the coastline and Simon had planned for the use of small vessels to harbor there, transporting north refugees, and returning with supplies and arms for the border fighters. If that cove was in enemy hands he wanted to know it, and at once.

As he left the clearing, with Caluf and another riding behind him, Simon's mind was again working on two levels. He noted the country about him with an alert survey for landmarks and natural features which might be used in future defensive or offensive action. But beneath that surface activity he was pushing under the constant preoccupation with safety, food, shelter—the job at hand—his own private concerns.

Once, in prison, he had had time to explore the depths within himself. And the paths he had hewn had been bleak, freezing him into a remoteness of spirit which had never thawed since that day. The give and take of barracks life, of companionship in field service he could assume as a cover, but nothing ate below that cover—or he had not allowed it to.

Fear he understood. But that was a transitory emotion which usually spurred him into action of one sort or another. In Kars he had been attracted in another way, and had fought free. Once he had believed that when he took Petronius' gate he would be a complete man again. But so far that was not true. Ingvald had spoken of demon possession, but what if a man did not possess himself?

He was always a man standing apart watching another occupied with the business of living. Alien— these men he led knew it in him. Was he another of the odd mistaken pieces strewn about this world, pieces which did not fit, one with the machines out of their time and the riddle of the Kolder? He sensed that he was on the brink of some discovery, one which would mean much to not only himself but to the cause he had chosen.

Then that second, prying, stand-aside self was banished by the Captain of raiders as Simon caught sight of a branch of a tree, warped by mountain storms, as yet lacking leaves. It was stark against the afternoon sky and the burden it bore, dangling in small, neatly fashioned loops, was starker yet.

He spurred ahead and sat gazing up at the three small bodies swaying in the breeze, the gaping beaks, the glazed eyes, the dangling, crooked claws still bearing their bracelets of scarlet jesses and small, silvery discs. Three of the true falcons, their necks wrung, left to be found by the next traveler along the way.

"Why?" Caluf asked.

"A warning, maybe, or something more." Simon

dismounted and tossed his reins to the other. "Wait here. If I am not back within a reasonable time, return to Ingvald and report. Do not follow, we cannot afford to waste men uselessly."

Both men protested, but Simon silenced them with a decisive order before he entered the brush. There was evidence in plenty of those who had been there, broken twigs, scraps of boots on moss, a piece of torn jess strap. He was moving closer to the shore; the sound of the surf could be heard, and what he sought had certainly come from the cove.

Simon had been over that path twice, and he set himself to recall a mental picture of the country. Unfortunately the small valley which gave on the shore was lacking in cover. And the crags on either side were as bald. He would have to try one of those, which meant a roundabout route and some tough climbing. Doggedly he got to it.

As he had crept up to Volt's Hole so did he travel now, crevice, ledge, hand and foothold. Then he crawled on his belly to the edge and looked down into the cove.

Simon had expected many things—a bare strip of sand with no sign of any invasion, a party from Karsten, an anchored ship. But what he saw was very different. At first he thought of the illusions of Estcarp—could what lay below be projected from his own mind, some old memory brought to life for his bafflement? Then a closer inspection of that sharp, clean curve of metal told him that, while it bore some faint resemblance to craft he had known, this was as different from any thing in his previous experience as the counterfeit hawk was from the real.

The thing was clearly a sea-going craft, though it had

no sign of any superstructure, mast, or method of propulsion. Sharply pointed both fore and aft, it was shaped as might be a cross section, taken length-wise, of a torpedo. There was an opening on its flat upper surface and men stood by that, three of them. The outline of their heads against the silver sheen of the ship were those of the Falconer bird helms. But Simon was equally sure no true Falconers wore them.

Once again the eternal mystery of this land, for the traders' ships at Sulcarkeep had been masted vessels of a nonmechanical civilization; this ship could be taken out of the future of his own world! How could two so widely differing levels of civilization exist side by side? Were the Kolder responsible here also? Alien, alien— once more he was on the very verge of un- derstanding—of guessing—

And for that instant he relaxed his vigilance. Only a stout helm plundered from Karsten stores saved his life. The blow which struck at him out of nowhere dazed Simon. He smelled wet feathers, something else—half blinded and dizzy he tried to rise—to be struck again. This time he saw the enemy wing out to sea. A falcon, but true or false? That question he carried with him into the black cloud which swallowed him up.

II

TRIBUTE TO GORM

The throbbing beat of a pain drum filled his skull, shaking on through his body. At first, Simon, returning reluctantly to consciousness, could only summon strength enough to endure that punishment. Then he knew that the beat was not only inside him, but without also. That on which he lay shook with a steady rhythmic pound. He was trapped in the black heart of a tom-tom.

When he opened his eyes, there was no light, and when he tried to move Simon speedily discovered that his wrists and ankles were lashed.

The sensation of being enclosed in a coffin became so overpowering that he had to clamp teeth on lips to prevent crying out. And he was so busy fighting his own private war against the unknown, that it was minutes before he realized that wherever he might be, he was not alone in captive misery.

To his right someone moaned faintly now and again. On his left another retched in abject sickness, adding a new stench to the thick atmosphere of their confinement. Simon, oddly reassured by those sounds, unpromising as they were, called out:

"Who lies there? And where are we; does anyone know?"

The moaning ended in a quick catch of breath. But

the man who was sick either could not control his pangs, or did not understand.

"Who are you?" That came in a weak trail of whisper from his right.

"One from the mountains. And you? Is this some Karsten prison?"

"Better that it were, mountain man! I have lain in the dungeons of Karsten. Yes, I have been in the question room of such a one. But better there than here."

Simon was busy sorting out recent memories. He had climbed to a cliff top to spy upon a cove. There had been that strange vessel in harbor there, then attack from a bird which might not have been a bird at all! Now it added up to only one answer—he lay in the very ship he had seen!

"Are we in the hands of the man-buyers out of Gorm?" he asked.

"Just so, mountain man. You were not with us when those devils of Yvian's following gave us to the Kolder. Are you one of the Falconers they snared later?"

"Falconers! Ho, men of the Winged Ones!" Simon raised his voice, heard it echo hollowly back from unseen walls. "How many of you lie here? I, whom am of the raiders, ask it!"

"Three of us, raider. Though Faltjar was borne hither limp as a death-stricken man, and we do not know if yet he lives."

"Faltjar! The guard of the southern passes! How was he taken—and you?"

"We heard of a cove where ships dared land and there was a messenger from Estcarp saying that perhaps supplies might be sent to us by sea if such could be found. So the Lord of Wings ordered us to explore. And we were struck down by hawks as we rode. Though they were not our hawks who battled for us. Then we awoke on shore, stripped of our mail and weapons, and they brought us aboard this craft which has no like in the world. I say that, who am Tandis and served five years as a marine to Sulcarmen. Many ports have I seen and more ships than a man can count in a week of steady marking, yet none kin to this one.''

"It is born of the witchery of Kolder," whispered the weak voice on Simon's right. "They came, but how can a man reckon time when he is enclosed in the dark without end? Is it night or day, this day or that? I lay in Kars prison because I offered refuge to a woman and child of the old race when the Horning went forth. They took all of us who were young from that prison and brought us to a delta island. There we were examined.''

"By whom?" Simon asked eagerly. Here was some one who might have seen the mysterious Kolder, from whom he might be able to get some positive information concerning them.

"That I cannot remember." The voice was the merest thread of sound now and Simon edged himself as far as he could in his bonds to catch it at all. "They work some magic, these men from Gorm, so that one's head spins around, spilling all thoughts out of it. It is said that they are demons of the great cold from the end of the world, and that I can believe!

"And you, Falconer, did you look upon those who took you?"

"Yes, but you will have little aid from what I saw, raider. For those who brought us here were Karsten men, mere husks without proper wits—hands and strong backs for their owners. And those owners already wore the trappings they had taken from our backs, the better to befool our friends.''

"One of them was taken in his turn," Simon told him. "For that be thankful, hawkman, for perhaps a part of the unraveling of this coil may lie with him." Only then did he wonder if there were ears in those walls to listen to the helpless captives. But if there were, perhaps that one scrap of knowledge would serve to spread uneasiness among their captors.

There were ten Karsten men within that prison hold, all taken from jails, all caught up for some offense or other against the Duke. And to them had been added the three Falconers captured in the cove. The majority of the prisoners appeared to be semi-conscious or in a dazed condition. If able to recall any of the events leading up to their present captivity, such recollections ended with their arrival at the island beyond Kars, or on the beach of the cove.

As Simon persisted in his questioning however, a certain uniformity, if not of background, then of offenses against the Duke and temperament among these prisoners began to emerge. They were all men of some initiative, who had had a certain amount of military training, ranging from the Falconers who lived in a monastic military barracks for life and whose occupation was frankly fighting, to his first informant from Kars, a small landowner in the outlands who commanded a body of militia. In age they were from their late teens to their early thirties, and, in spite of some rough handling in the Duke's dungeons, they were all able-bodied. Two were of the minor nobility with some schooling. They were the youngest of the lot, brothers picked up by Yvian's forces on the same charge of aiding one of the old race who had been so summarily outlawed.

None of those here were of that race, and everyone

declared that in all parts of the duchy men, women and children of that blood had been put to death upon capture.

It was one of the young nobles, drawn by Simon's patient questioning from his absorption with his still unconscious brother, who provided the first bit of fact for the outworld man to chew upon.

"That guard who beat down Garnit, for which may the Rats of Nore forever gnaw him night and day, told them not to bring Renston also. We were blood brothers by the bread from the days we first strapped on swords, and we went to take him food and weapons that he might try for the border. They tracked us down and took us, though we left three of them with holes in their hides and no breath in their bodies! When one of the scum the Duke's men had with him would have bound Renston too, he told it was no use, for there was no price for those of the old blood and the men buyers would not take them.

"The fellow whined that Renston was as young and strong as we and that he ought to sell as well. But the Duke's man said the old race broke but they would not bend; then he ran Renston through with his own sword."

"Broke but would not bend," Simon repeated slowly.

"The old race were once one with the witchfolk of Estcarp," the noble added. "Perchance these devils of Gorm cannot eat them up as easily as they can those of another blood."

"There is this," the man beside Simon added in his half-whisper, "why did Yvian turn so quickly on the old race? They have left us alone, unless we sought them out. And those of us who companied with them

found them far from evil, for all their old knowledge
and strange ways. Is Yvian under orders to do as he did?
And who gives such orders and why? Could it be, my
brothers in misfortune, that the presence of those others
among us was in some manner a barrier against Gorm
and all its evil, so that they had to be routed out that
Gorm may spread?''

Shrewd enough, and close to Simon's own path of
thought. He would have questioned still further but,
through the soft moans and wordless complaints of
those still only half conscious, he heard a steady hissing, a sound he strove hard to identify. The thick odors
of the place would make a man gag, and they provided a
good cover for a danger he recognized too late—the
entrance of vapor into the chamber with a limited air
supply.

Men choken and coughed, fought for air with
strangling agony and then went inert. Only one thought
kept Simon steady: the enemy would not have gone to
the trouble of loading fourteen men in their ship merely
to gas them to death. So Simon alone of that miserable
company did not fight the gas, but breathed slowly,
with dim memories of the dentist's chair in his own
world.

"... gabble ... gabble ... gabble ..."
Words which were no words, only a confused sound
made by a highpitched voice—carrying with them the
snap of an imperative order. Simon did not stir. As
awareness of his surroundings returned, an inborn instinct for self-preservation kept him quiet.

"... gabble ... gabble ... gabble ..."
The pain in his head was only a very dull ache. He
was sure he was no longer on the ship; what he lay upon
did not throb, nor move. But he had been stripped of his
clothing and the place in which he lay was chill.

He who spoke was moving away now; the gabble retreated without an answer. But so clearly had the tone been one of an order that Simon dared not move lest he betray himself to some silent subordinate.

Twice, deliberately, he counted to a hundred, hearing no sound during that exercise. Simon lifted his eyelids and then lowered them again quickly against a stab of blazing light. Little by little his field of vision, limited as it was, cleared. What he saw in that narrow range was almost as confounding as had been his first glimpse of the strange ship.

His acquaintance with laboratories had been small, but certainly the rack of tubes, the bottles and beakers on shelves directly before him could be found only in a place of that nature.

Was he alone? And for what purpose had he been brought here? He studied, inch by inch, all he could see. Clearly he was not lying at floor level. The surface under him was hard—was he on a table?

Slowly he began to turn his head, convinced that caution was very necessary. Now he was able to see an expanse of wall, bare, gray, with a line at the very end of his field of vision which might make a door.

So much for that side of the room. Now the other. Once more he turned his head and discovered new wonders. Five more bodies, bare as his own, were laid out, each on a table. All five were either dead or unconscious, and he was inclined to believe the latter was true.

But there was someone else there. The tall thin figure stood with his back to Simon, working over the first man in line. Since a gray robe, belted in at the waist covered all of his, her, or its body, and a cap of the same stuff hid the head, Simon had no idea of race or type of creature who busied himself with quiet efficiency there.

A rack bearing various bottles with dangling tubes was rolled over the first man. Needles in those tubes were inserted into veins, a circular cap of metal was fitted over the unresisting head. Simon, with a swift jolt of pure fear, guessed that he was watching the death of a man. Not the death of a body, but that death which would reduce the body to such a thing as he had seen slain on the road to Sulcarkeep and had helped to slay himself in defense of that keep!

And he also determined that it was not going to be done to him! He tested hand and arm, foot and leg, moving slowly, his only luck being that he was the last in that line and not the first. He was stiff enough, but he was in full control of his muscles.

That gray attendant had processed his first man. He was moving a second rack forward over the next. Simon sat up. For a second or two his head whirled, and he gripped the table on which he had lain, prayerfully glad it had neither creaked nor squeaked under his change of position.

The business at the other end of the room was a complicated one, and occupied the full attention of the worker. Feeling that the table might tip under him, Simon swung his feet to the floor, breathing strongly again only when they were firmly planted on the smooth cold pavement.

He surveyed his nearest neighbor, hoping for some sign that he too, was rousing. But the boy, for he was only a youngster, lay limp with closed eyes, his chest rising and falling at unusually slow intervals.

Simon stepped away from the table toward that set of shelves. There alone could he find a weapon. Escape from here, if he could win the door unhindered, was too chancy a risk until he knew more of his surroundings. And neither could he face the fact that in running he would abandon five other men to death—or worse than death alone.

He chose his weapon, a flask half filled with yellow liquid. It seemed glass but was heavy for that substance. The slender neck above the bulbous body gave a good handhold, and Simon moved lightly around the line of tables to the one where the attendant worked.

His bare feet made no sound on the material on the flooring as he came up behind the unsuspecting worker. The bottle arose with the force of Simon's outrage in the swing, crashing upon the back of that gray-capped head.

There was no cry from the figure who crumpled forward, dragging with it the wired metal cap it had been about to fit on the head of the waiting victim. Simon had reached for the fallen man's throat before he saw the flatness on the back of the head through which dark blood welled. He heaved the body over and pulled it free of the aisle between tables to look down upon the face of one he was sure was a Kolder.

What he had been building up in his imagination was far more startling than the truth. This was a man, at least in face, very like a great many other men Simon had known. He had rather flat features with a wide expanse of cheekbone on either side of a nose too close to bridgeless, and his chin was too small and narrow to match the width of the upper half of his face. But he was no alien demon to the eye, whatever he might house within his doomed skull.

Simon located the fastenings of the gray robe and pulled it off. Though he shrank from touching the mess in the cap, he made himself take that also. There was a runnel of water in a sink at the other end of the room and there he dropped the head gear for cleansing. Under the robe the man wore a tightfitting garment with no fastenings nor openings Simon could discover, so in the end he had to content himself with the robe for his sole clothing.

There was nothing he could do for the two men the attendant had already made fast to the racks, for the complicated nature of the machines was beyond his solving. But he went from one man to the next of the other three and tried to arouse them, finding that, too, impossible. They had the appearance of men deeply drugged, and he understood even less how he had come to escape their common fate, if these *were* his fellow prisoners from the ship.

Disappointed, Simon went to the door. The closed slab had no latch or knob he could see, but experimentation proved that it slid back into the right-hand wall and he looked out upon a corridor walled, ceilinged, and paved in the same monotone of gray which was in use in the laboratory. As far as Simon could see it was deserted, though there were other doors opening off its length. He made for the nearest of these.

Inching it open with the same caution with which he had made his first moves upon regaining his senses, he looked in upon a cache of men the Kolder had brought to Gorm, if this was Gorm. Lying in rows were at least twenty bodies, these still clothed. There were no signs of consciousness in any, though Simon examined them all hurriedly. Perhaps he could still gain a respite for those in the laboratory. Hoping so, he dragged the three back and laid them out with their fellows.

Visiting the laboratory for the last time Simon rummaged for arms, coming up with a kit of surgical knives, the longest of which he took. He cut away the rest of the clothing from the body of the man he had killed and laid him out on one of the tables in such a way that the battered head was concealed from the doorway. Had he known any method of locking that door he would have used it.

With the knife in the belt of his stolen robe, Simon washed out the cap and gingerly pulled it on, wet as it was. Doubtless there were a hundred deadly weapons in the various jars, bottles, and tubes about him, only he could not tell one from the others. For the time being he would have to depend upon his fists and his knife to remain free.

Simon went back to the corridor, closing the door behind him. How long would the worker he had killed be left undisturbed? Was he supervised by someone due to return shortly, or did Simon have a better allowance of time?

Two of the doors in the corridor would not yield to his push. But where the hall came to a dead end he found a third a little way open and slipped into what could only be living quarters.

The furniture was severe, functional, but the two chairs and the box bed were more comfortable than they looked. And another piece which might be either a desk or a table drew him. His puzzlement was a driving force for his mind refused to connect the place in which he stood with the same world which had produced Estcarp, the Eyrie and crooked-laned Kars. One was of the past; this was of the future.

He could not open the compartments of the desk, though there was a sunken pit at the top of each in which a finger tip could be handily inserted. Baffled, he sat back on his heels after trying the last.

There were compartments in the walls also, at least

the same type of finger hole could be seen there. But they, too, were locked. His jaw set stubbornly as he thought of trying his knife as a prying lever.

Then he spun around, back against the wall, staring into a room still empty of all but that severely lined furniture. Because out of the very empty air before him came a voice, speaking a language he could not understand, but by the inflection asking a question to which it demanded an immediate answer.

III

GRAY FANE

Was he under observation? Or merely listening to something akin to a public address system? Once Simon had assured himself that he was alone in the room, he listened closely to words he could not understand and must interpret by inflection alone. The speaker repeated himself—at least Simon was convinced he recognized several sounds. And did that repetition mean that he was seen?

How soon before an investigation would be launched by the unseen speaker? Immediately, when no reply was made? It was clearly a warning to be on his way, but which way? Simon went back into the corridor.

Since this end of the passage was a blank wall he must try the other, repassing the other doors. But there again he met with unbroken gray surface. With memories of the hallucinations of Estcarp, Simon ran his hands across that blank expanse. But if there was any opening there it was concealed by more than eye-confusing skill. His conviction—that the Kolder, who or whatever they might be, were of a different breed altogether from the witches, achieving their magic according to another pattern—became fixed. They based their action on skills without, rather than a Power within.

To the men of Estcarp much of the technical knowledge of his own world would have ranked as magic. And perhaps alone among the Guards of Estcarp at this moment was Simon fitted to rationalize and partly understand what lay here in Gorm, better prepared to face those who used machines and the science of machines than any witch who could call a fleet up out of wooden ships.

He crept along the hallway, running his hands along first one wall and then the other, seeking any irregularity which might be a clue to an exit. Or did that door lie within one of the rooms? His luck certainly could not hold much longer.

Again from the air overhead came a ringing command in the strange tongue, the vehemence of which could not be denied. Simon, sensing danger, froze where he was, half expecting to be engulfed by a trapdoor or trapped in some suddenly materializing net. In that moment he discovered his exit, but not in the way he had hoped, as on the other side of the corridor a portion of the wall slipped back to show lighted space beyond. Simon pulled the knife from his belt and faced that space, ready for an attack.

The silence was broken again by that bark of disembodied voice; he thought that perhaps his real status had not yet been suspected by the masters of this place. Perhaps, if they did see him, the robe and cap he wore tagged him as one of their own who was acting oddly and had been ordered to report elsewhere.

Deeming it best to act in his chosen role as long as he could, Simon approached that new door with more outward assurance and less commando caution. He nearly panicked, however, when the door closed behind him and he discovered that he was neatly imprisoned in a box. It was not until he brushed against one of the walls and felt through it that faint vibration, that he guessed he was in an elevator, a discovery which for some reason steadied him. More and more he accepted the belief that the Kolder represented a form of civilization close to that he had known in his own world. It was far more steadying to the nerves to be ascending or descending to a showdown with the enemy in an elevator than to stand, for example, in a mist-filled room and watch a friend turn to a hideous stranger in a matter of moments.

Yet, in spite of that feeling of faint familiarity with all this, Simon had no ease, no relaxation of a certain inward chill. He could accept the products of Kolder hands as normal, but he could not accept the atmosphere of this place as anything but alien. And not only alien, for that which is strange need not necessarily be a menace, but in some manner this place was utterly opposed to him and his kind. No, not alien, one part of him decided during that swift journey to wherever the Kolder waited, but unhuman, whereas the witches of Estcarp were human, no matter whatever else they might also be.

The thrumming in the wall ceased. Simon stood away from it, unsure as to where the door would open. His certainty that it would open did not waver and was justified a moment later.

This time there were sounds outside, a muted humming, the snap of distant voices. He emerged warily to stand in a small alcove apart from a room. Partial recognition outweighed strangeness for him once again. A wide expanse of one wall was laid out as a vast map. The trailing, deeply indented shorelines, the molded mountain areas he had seen before. Set here and there upon the chart were tiny pinpoints of light in various colors. Those along the shore about the vanished hold of Sulcar and the bay in which Gorm lay were a dusky violet, while those which pricked on the plains of Estcarp were yellow, the ones in Karsten green, and those of Alizon red.

A table, running the full length of that map, stood below it, bearing at spaced intervals machines which clattered now and then, or flashed small signal lights. And seated between each two of such machines, with their backs toward him, their attention all for the devices they tended, were others wearing the gray robes and caps.

A little apart was a second table, or outsized desk, with three more of the Kolder. The center one of this trio wore a metal cap on his head from which wires and spider-thread cables ran to a board behind him. His face was without expression, his eyes were closed. However, he was not asleep for, from time to time, his fingers moved with swift flicks of the tips across a panel of buttons and levers set in the surface before him. Simon's impression of being in a central control of some concentrated effort grew with the seconds he was left to view the scene undisturbed.

The words which were barked at him this time did not come from the air, but from the man on the left of that capped figure. He gazed at Simon, his flat face with its overspread of upper features, displaying first impatience and then the growing realization that Simon was not one of his own kind.

Simon sprang. He could not hope to reach that end table, but one of those who tended the machines before the map was in his range. And he brought his hand edge down in a blow which might have cracked backbone, but instead rendered the victim unconscious. Holding the limp body as a shield, Simon backed to the wall of the other doorway, hoping to win to that exit.

To his amazement the man who had first marked his arrival there made no move to obstruct him, physically. He merely repeated slowly and deliberately in the language of the continental natives:

"You will return to your unit. You will report to your unit control."

As Simon continued his crabwise advance upon the door, one of the men who had been a neighbor of his captive returned an astounded face from Tregarth to the men at the end table, then back to Simon. The rest of his fellows looked up from their machines with the same surprise as their officer got to his feet. It was clear they had expected only instant and complete obedience from Simon.

"You will return to your unit! At once!"

Simon laughed. And the result of his response was startling indeed. The Kolder, with the exception of the capped man who took no notice of anything, were all on their feet. Those of the center table still looked to their two superiors at the end of the room as if awaiting orders. And Simon thought that if he had shrieked in agony they would not have been so amazed—his reaction to their orders had completely baffled them.

The man who had given that command, dropped his hand on the shoulder of his capped companion, giving him a gentle shake, a gesture which even in its restraint expressed utmost alarm. So summoned to attention, the capped man opened his eyes and looked about impatiently, then in obvious amazement. He stared at Simon as if sighting at a mark.

What came was no physical attack, but a blow of force, unseen, not to be defined by the untutored outworlder. But a blow which held Simon pinned breathless to the wall unable to move.

The body he had been using as a shield slid out of his heavy-weighted arms to sprawl on the floor, and even the rise and fall of Simon's chest as he breathed became a labor to which he had to give thought and effort. Let him stay where he was, under the pressure of that invisible crushing hand, and he would not continue to live. His encounters with the Power of Estcarp had sharpened his wits. He thought that what trapped him now was not born of the body, but of the mind, and so it could only be countered by the mind in turn.

His only taste of such power had been through the methods of Estcarp and he had not been trained to use it. But setting up within him what strength of will he could muster, Simon concentrated on raising an arm which moved so sluggishly he was afraid he was doomed to failure.

Now that one palm was resting flat against the wall where the energy held him, he brought up the other. With complaining muscles as well as will of mind, he strove to push himself out and away. Did he detect a shade of surprise on the broad face below the cap?

What Simon did next had the backing of no conscious reasoning. It was certainly not by his will that his right hand moved up level with his heart and his fingers traced a design in the air between him and that capped master of force.

It was the third time he had seen that design. Before the hand which had drawn it was one of Estcarp, and the lines had burned fire bright for only an instant.

Now it flashed again, but in a sputtering white. And at that moment he could move! The pressure had lessened. Simon ran for the door, making good a momentary escape into the unknown territory beyond.

But it was only momentary. For here he faced armed men. There was no mistaking that rapt concentration in the eyes turned to him as he erupted into the corridor where they were on duty. These were the slaves of the Kolder, and only by killing could he win through.

They drew in with the silent, deadly promise of their kind, their very silence heavy with menace. Simon chose quickly and darted to meet them. He skidded to the right and tackled the man next to the wall about the shins, bringing him down in such a way as to guard his own back.

The smooth flooring of the passage was an unexpected aid. The impact of Simon's tackle carried both past the man's two companions. Simon stabbed up with his knife and felt the sear of a blade across his own ribs under his arms. Coughing, the guard rolled away, and Simon snatched the dart gun from his belt.

He shot the first of the others just in time and the stroke of the sword aimed for his neck sank instead into the wounded man. That brought him a precious second to sight on the third and last of the enemy.

Adding two more dart guns to his weapons he went on. Luckily this hall ended in no concealed doors but a stair, cut of stone and winding up against a wall also of stone, both of them in contrast to the smooth gray surfacing of the passages and rooms through which he had already come.

His bare feet gritted on that stone as they took the steps. At a higher level he came out in a passage akin to those he had seen in the hold of Estcarp. However functional-futuristic the inner core of this place might be, its husk was native to the buildings he knew.

Simon took cover twice, his gun ready, as detachments of the Kolder-changed natives passed him. He could not judge whether a general alarm had been given, or whether they were merely engaged in some routine patrol, for they kept to a steady trot and did not search any side ways.

Time in these corridors where there was no change of light had no meaning. Simon did not know whether it was day or night, or how long he had been within the fortress of the Kolder. But he was keenly conscious of hunger and thirst, of the cold which pierced the single garment he wore, of the discomfort of bare feet when one had always gone shod.

If he only had some idea of the inner plan of the maze through which he was trying to escape. Was he on Gorm? Or in that mysterious city of Yle which the Kolder had founded on the mainland coast? In some more hidden headquarters of the invaders? That it was an important headquarters he was certain.

Both a desire for a temporary hiding place and the need for supplies brought him to explore the rooms on this upper level. Here were none of the furnishings he had seen below. The carved wooden chests, the chairs, the tables were all of native work. And in some of the chambers there were signs of hurried departure or search, now overlaid with dust as if the rooms had been deserted for a long time.

It was in such a one that Simon found clothing which fitted after a fashion. But he still lacked mail or any other weapons than those he had taken from the fighters in the hall. He craved food more than anything else and began to wonder if he must return to the dangerous lower levels to find it.

Though he was considering descent Simon continued to follow up any ramp or set of steps he chanced upon. And he saw that in this sprawling pile all the windows had been battened tight so that only artificial light made visible his surroundings, the light being dimmer in ratio to the distance he put between him and the quarters of the Kolder.

A last and very narrow flight of stairs showed more use and Simon kept one of the guns ready as he climbed to a door above. That swung easily under his hand, and he looked out upon a flat rooftop. Over a portion of this a second sheltering awning had been erected and lined up under which were objects which did not astonish Simon after what he had seen below. Their stubby wings were thrust back sharply from their blunt noses and none could carry more than a pilot and perhaps two passengers, but they were surely aircraft. The mystery of how Sulcarkeep had been taken was solved, providing the enemy had a fleet of those to hand.

Now they presented Simon with a way of escape if he had no other chance. But escape from where? Watching that improvised hangar for any sign of a guard, Simon stole to the nearest edge of the roof, hoping to see something in the way of a landmark to give him a clue to his whereabouts.

For a moment he wondered if he could be back in a restored Sulcarkeep. For what was spread below was a harbor, with anchored ships and rows of buildings set along streets which marched to the wharves and the water. But the plan of this city was different from the town of the traders. It was larger and where the Sulcarmen had had their warehouses with fewer living quarters, these streets reversed that process. Though it was midday by the sun there was no life in those streets, no sign that any of the houses were inhabited. Yet neither did they show those signs of decay and nature's encroachment which would mark complete desertion.

Since the architecture resembled that of Karsten and

Estcarp with only minor differences, this could not be that Yle erected by the Kolder. Which meant that he *must* be now on Gorm—maybe in Sippar—that center of the canker which the Estcarp forces had never been able to pierce!

If that city below was as lifeless as it appeared, it should be easy enough for him to get to the harbor and locate some means of boat transportation to the eastern continent. However with the building below him so well sealed to the outer world, perhaps this roof was the only exit, and he had better explore its outlets.

The pile on which he stood was the highest building in the whole small city; perhaps it was the ancient castle where those of Koris' clan had ruled. If the Captain were only with him now the problem might be simplified by half. Simon toured three sides and discovered that there were no other roofs abutting on this one, that a street or streets, fronted each side.

Reluctantly he came to the shelter which housed the planes. To trust to a machine he did not know how to pilot was foolhardy. But that was no reason not to inspect one. Simon had grown bolder since he had gone unchallenged this long. However he took precautions against surprise. Wedged into the latch of the roof door, the knife locked it to all but a battering down.

He returned to the plane nearest him. It moved into the open under his pushing, proving to be a light craft, easily handled. He pulled up a panel in its stub nose and inspected the motor within. It was unlike any he had seen before, and he was neither engineer nor mechanic. But he had confidence enough in the efficiency of those below to believe that it could fly—if he were able to control it.

Before he explored farther Simon examined the four

other machines, using the butt of one of the dart guns to smash at their motors. If he did have to trust to the air he did not want to be the target for an attack-chase.

It was when he raised his improvised hammer for the last time that the enemy struck. There had been no battering at the wedged door, no thunder of guard feet on the stairs. Again it was the silent push of that invisible force. It did not strive to hold him helpless this time, but to draw him to its source. Simon caught at the disabled plane for an anchor. Instead he drew it after him out into the open—he could not halt his march down the roof.

And it was not taking him back to the door! With a stab of panic Simon realized now that his destination was not the dubious future of the levels below, but the quick death which awaited a plunge from the roof!

With all his will he fought, his reluctant steps taken one at a time, with periods of agonizing struggle between. He tried again the trick of the symbol in the air which had served him before. Perhaps because he was not now fronting the person of his enemy it gave him no relief.

He could slow that advance, put off for seconds, minutes, the inevitable end. A try for the doorway failed; it had been a desperate hope that the other might take his action for a gesture of surrender. But now Simon knew they wanted him safely dead. The decision he would have made had he commanded here.

There was the plane he had meant to use in a last bid. Well, now there was no other escape! And it was between him and the roof edge towards which he was urged.

It was such a little chance, but he had no other. Simon yielded two steps to the pressure, he gave another quickly as if his strength were waning. A third—his hand was on the opening to the pilot's compartment. Making the supreme effort in this weird battle he threw himself within.

The pull brought him against the far wall and the light craft rocked under his scrambling. He stared at what must be the instrument board. There was a lever up at the end of a narrow slot, and it was the only object which seemed to be movable. With a petition to other Powers than those of Estcarp, Simon managed to raise a heavy hand and pull that down its waiting slot.

IV

CITY OF DEAD MEN

He had perhaps childishly expected to be whisked aloft, but the machine ran straight forward, gathering speed. Its nose plowed across the low parapet with force enough to somersault the whole plane over. Simon knew he was falling, not free as his tormenter had intended, but encased in the cabin.

There was another swift moment of awareness that that fall was not straight down, that he was descending at an angle. Hopelessly, he jerked once more at that lever, pulling it halfway up the slot.

Then there was a crash, followed by nothing but blackness without sight, sound, or feeling.

A spark of red-amber watched him speculatively out of the black. It was matched by a faint repetitive sound—the tick of a watch, the drip of water? And thirdly there was the smell. It was that latter which prodded Simon into action. For it was a sweetish stench, thick and sickening in his nostrils and throat, a stench of old corruption and death.

He was sitting up, he discovered, and there was a faint light to show the wreckage which held him in that position. But the hounding pressure which had battered him on the upper roof was gone; he was free to move if he could, to think.

Save for some painfully bruised areas, he had apparently survived the crash without injury. The machine must have cushioned the shock of landing. And that red eye out of the dark was a light on the board of the lever. The drip was close by.

So was the smell. Simon shifted in his seat and pushed. There was a rasp of metal scraping metal and a large section of cabin broke away. Simon crawled painfully out of his cage. Overhead was a hole framed with jagged ends of timbers. As he watched, another piece of roofing gave way and struck on the already battered machine. The plane must have fallen on the roof of one of the neighboring buildings and broken through that surface. How he had escaped with life and reasonably sound limbs was one of the strange quirks of fate.

He must have been unconscious for some time as the sky was the palid shade of evening. And his hunger and thirst were steady pains. He must have food and water.

But why had not the enemy located him before this? Certainly anyone on the other roof could have spotted the end of his abortive flight. Unless—suppose they did not know of his try with the plane—suppose they only traced him by some form of mental contact. Then they would only know that he had gone over the parapet, that his fall had ended in a blackout which to them might have registered as his death. If that were true then he was indeed free, if still within the city of Sippar!

First, to find food and drink, and then discover where he was in relation to the rest of the port.

Simon found a doorway, one which gave again on stairs leading downward toward the street level, as he had hoped. The air here was stale, heavily tainted with that odor. He could identify it now and it made him hesitate—disliking what must lie below to raise such a stench.

But down was the only way out, so down he must go.

The windows here were unsealed and light made fading patches on each landing. There were doors, too, but Simon opened none of them, because it seemed to him that around them that fearsome, stomach-churning smell was stronger.

Down one more flight, and into a hall which ended in a wide portal he thought must give on the street. Here Simon dared to explore and in a back room he found that leathery journey bread which was the main military ration of Estcarp, together with a pot of preserved fruit still good under its cap. The moldering remains of other provisions were evidence that no one had foraged here for a long time. Water trickled from a pipe to a drain and Simon drank before he wolfed down the food.

It was difficult to eat in spite of his hunger for that smell clung to everything. Although he had been only in this one building outside the citadel Simon suspected that his monstrous suspicion was the truth; save for the central building and its handful of inhabitants, Sippar was a city of the dead. The Kolder must have ruthlessly disposed of those of the conquered of no use to them. Not only slain them, but left them unburied in their own homes. As a warning against rebellion of the few remaining alive? Or merely because they did not care? It would appear that the last was the most likely, and that odd feeling of kinship he had for the flat-faced invaders died then and there.

Simon took with him all the bread he could find and a bottle filled with water. Curiously enough the door leading to the street was barred on the inside. Had those who had once lived here locked themselves in and committed mass suicide? Or had the same pressure methods driven them to their deaths as had been used to send him over the upper roof?

The street was as deserted as he had seen it from that

same roof. But Simon kept close to one side, watching every shadowed doorway, the mouth of every cross lane. All doors were shut; nothing moved as he worked his way to the harbor.

He guessed that if he tried any of those doors he would find them barred against him, while within would lie only the dead. Had they perished soon after Gorm had welcomed Kolder to further the ambitions of Orna and her son? Or had that death come sometime later, during the years since Koris had fled to Estcarp and the island had been cut off from humankind? It would not matter to anyone save perhaps a historian. This remained a city of the dead—the dead in body, and in the keep, the dead in spirit—with only the Kolder, who might well be dead in another fashion, keeping a pretense of life.

As he went Simon memorized route of street and house. Gorm could only be freed when the central keep was destroyed, he was certain of that. But it seemed to him that leaving this waste of empty buildings about their lair had been a bad mistake on the part of the Kolder. Unless they had some hidden defenses and alarms rigged in these blank walled houses, it might be no trick at all to bring a landing party ashore and have them under cover.

There were those tales of Koris' concerning the spies Estcarp had sent to this island over the years. And the fact that the Captain himself had been unable to return because of some mysterious barrier. After his own experience with Kolder weapons Simon had an open mind. Only he *had* been able to break free, first in that headquarters room and secondly by the use of one of the planes. The mere fact that the Kolder had not tried to hunt him down was proof of a kind they must believe him finished for good.

But it was hard to think that someone or something did not keep watch in the silent city. So he kept to cover until he reached the wharves. There were ships there, ships battered by storms, some driven half ashore, their rigging a rotting tangle, their sides scored and smashed in, some half waterlogged, with only their upper decks above the surface of the harbor. None of these had sailed for months, or years!

And the width of the bay lay between Simon and the mainland. If this dead port was Sippar, and he had no reason to believe that it was not, then he was now facing that long arm of land on which the invaders had built Yle, ending in the finger of which Sulcarkeep had been the nail. Since the fall of the traders' stronghold it was very probable that the Kolder forces now controlled that whole cape.

If he could find a manageable small craft and take to the sea, Simon would have to take the longer route eastward down the bottle-shaped bay to the mouth of the River Es and so to Estcarp. And he was plagued by the idea that time no longer fought upon his side.

He found his boat, a small shell stored in a warehouse. Though Simon was no sailor he took what precautions and made what tests he could to ensure its seaworthiness. And waited until full dark before he took oars, gritting his teeth against the pain of his bruises, as he pulled steadily, setting a crooked course among the rotting hulks of the Gormian fleet.

It was when he was well beyond those and had dared to step his small mast, that he met the Kolder defense head on. He saw or heard nothing as he fell to the bottom of the boat, his hands over his ears, his eyes closed against that raging tumult of silent sound and invisible light which beat outward from some point within his brain. He had thought his ordeal with the will pressure had made him aware of the Kolder power, but this scrambling of a man's brain was worse.

Was he only minutes within that cloud, or a day, or a year? Dazed and dumb, Simon could not have told. He lay in a boat which swung with the waves but obeyed sluggishly the wind touch on its sail. And behind him was Gorm, dead and dark in the moonlight.

Before dawn Simon was picked up by a coastal patrol boat from the Es, and by that time he had recovered his wits, though his mind felt as bruised as his boat. Riding relays of swift mounts he went on to Estcarp city.

Within the keep, in that same room where he had first met the Guardian, he joined a council of war, retelling his adventures within Gorm, his contacts with the Kolder to the officers of Estcarp, and those still-faced women who listened impassively. As he spoke he hunted for one among the witches, without finding her in that assembly.

When he had done, they asked few questions, allowing him to tell it in his own way, Koris tight-lipped and stone-featured as he described the city of the dead, the Guardian beckoned forward one of the other women.

"Now, Simon Tregarth, do you take her hands, and then think upon this capped man, recall in your mind every detail of his dress and face," she ordered.

Though he could see no purpose in this, Simon obeyed. For one generally did obey, he thought wryly, the witches of Estcarp.

So he held those hands which were cool and dry in his, and he mentally pictured the gray robe, the odd face where the lower half did not match the upper, the metal cap, and the expression of power and then of bafflement which had been mirrored on those features when Simon had fought back. The hands slipped out of his and the Guardian spoke again:

"You have seen, sister? You can fashion?"

"I have seen," the woman answered. "And what I have seen I can fashion. Since he used the power between them in the duel of wills the impression should be strong. Though," she looked down at her hands, moving each finger as if to exercise it in preparation for some task, "whether we can use such a device is another matter. It would have been better had blood flowed."

No one explained and Simon was not given time to ask questions for Koris claimed him as the council broke up, and marched him off to the barracks. Once within that same chamber he had had before they left for Sulcarkeep, Simon demanded of the Captain:

"Where is the lady?" It was irritating not to be able to name her whom he knew; that peculiarity of the witches irked him more now than ever. But Koris caught his meaning.

"She is checking the border posts."

"But she is safe?"

Koris shrugged. "Are any of us safe, Simon? But be sure that the women of Power take no unnecessary risks. What they guard within them is not lightly spent." He had gone to the western window, his face turned into the light there, his eyes searching as if he willed to see more than the plain beyond the city. "So Gorm is dead." The words came heavily.

Simon pulled off his boots and stretched out on the bed. He was weary to every aching bone in his body.

"I told you what I saw and only what I saw. There is life walled into the center keep of Sippar. I found it nowhere else, but then I did not search far."

"Life? What sort of life?"

"Ask that of the Kolder, or perhaps the witches," returned Simon drowsily. "Neither are as you and I, and maybe they reckon life differently."

He was only half aware that the Captain had come away from the window, was standing over Simon so that his wide shoulders shut away the daylight.

"I am thinking, Simon Tregarth, that you are different too." Again the words were heavy, without any ring. "And seeing Gorm, how do you reckon its life—or death?"

"As vile," Simon mumbled. "But that shall also be judged in its own time," and wondered at his choice of words even as he fell asleep.

He slept, awoke to eat hugely, and slept again. No one demanded his attention nor did he rouse to what was going on in the keep of Estcarp. He might have been an animal laying up rest beneath his hide as the bear lays up fat against hibernation. When he awoke thoroughly once again it was alertly, eagerly, with a freshness he had not felt for so long, since before Berlin. Berlin—what—where was Berlin? His memories were curiously overlaid nowadays with new scenes.

And the one which returned to haunt him the most was that of the room of that secluded house in Kars where threadbare tapestries patterned the walls and a woman looked at him with wonder in her eyes as her hand shaped a glowing symbol in the air between them. Then there was that other moment when she stood sick at heart and curiously alone after she had made her sordid magic for Aldis, tarnishing her gift for the good of her cause.

Now as Simon lay tingling with life in every nerve

and cell of him, the ache of his bruises, the strain of his hunger and his striving gone out of him, he moved his right hand up until it lay over his heart. But beneath it now he did not feel the warmth of his own flesh; rather did he cradle in memory something else, as a singing which was no song drew from him, into the other hand he had grasped, a substance he did not know he possessed.

Over all else, the life in the border raiding parties, the experience of Kolder captivity, did those quiet and passive scenes hold him now. Because, empty of physical action though they had been, they possessed for him a hidden excitement he shrank from defining or explaining too closely.

But he was summoned soon enough to attention. During his sleep Estcarp had marshalled all its forces. Beacons on the heights had brought messengers from the mountains, from the Eyrie, from all those willing to stand against Gorm, and the doom Gorm promised. A half dozen Sulcar vessels, homeless, had made port in coves the Falconers charted, the families of their crews landed in safety, the ships armed and ready for the thrust. For all were agreed that the war must be taken to Gorm before Gorm brought it to them.

There was a camp at the mouth of the Es, a tent set up in it on the very verge of the ocean. From its flap of door they could see the shadow of the island appearing as a bank of cloud upon the sea. And, waiting signal beyond that point where the broken ruins of their keep were sea-washed and desolate, hovered the ships, packed with the Sulcar crew, Falconers, and border raiders.

But the barrier about Gorm must be broken first and that was in the hands of those who welded Estcarp's Power. So, not knowing why he was to be one of that company, Simon found himself seated at a table which might have been meant for a gaming board. Yet there was no surface of alternate colored blocks. Instead, before each seat there was a painted symbol. And the company who gathered was mixed, seemingly oddly chosen for the high command.

Simon found that his seat had been placed beside the Guardian's and the symbol there overlapped both places. It was a brown hawk with a gilded oval framing it, a small, three pointed cornet above the oval. On his left was a diamond of blue-green enclosing a fist holding an ax. And beyond that was a square of red encasing a horned fish.

To the right, beyond the Guardian, were two more symbols which he could not read without leaning forward. Two of the witches slipped into the seats before those and sat quietly, their hands palm down upon the painted marks. There was a stir to his left and he glanced up to know an odd lift of spirit as he met a level gaze which was more than mere recognition of his identity. But she did not speak and he copied her silence. The sixth and last of their company was the lad Briant, pale-faced, staring down at the fish creature before him as if it lived and by the very intensity of his gaze he must hold it prisoner in that sea of scarlet.

The woman who had held Simon's hands as he thought of the man on Gorm came into the tent, two others with her, each of whom carried a small clay brazier from which came sweet smoke. These they placed on the edge of the board and the other woman set down her own burden, a wide basket. She threw aside its covering cloth to display a row of small images.

Taking up the first she went to stand before Briant. Twice she passed the figure she held through the smoke and then held it at eye level before the seated lad. It was a finely wrought manikin with red-gold hair and such a life-look that Simon believed it was meant to be the portrait of some living man.

"Fulk." The woman pronounced the name and set the image down in the center of the scarlet square, full upon the painted fish. Briant could not pale, his transparent skin had always lacked color, but Simon saw him swallow convulsively before he answered.

"Fulk of Verlaine."

The woman took a second figure from her basket, and, as she came now to Simon's neighbor, he could better judge the artistic triumph of her work. For she held between her hands, passing it through the smoke, a perfect image of she who had asked for a charm to keep Yvian true.

"Aldis."

"Aldis of Kars," acknowledged the woman beside him as the tiny feet of the figure were planted on the fist with the ax.

"Sandar of Alizon." A third figure for the position farthest to his right.

"Siric." A potbellied image in flowing robes for that other right-hand symbol.

Then she brought out the last of the manikins, studying it for a moment before she gave it to the smoke. When she came to stand before Simon and the Guardian she named no names but held it out for his inspection, for his recognition. And he stared down at the small copy of the capped leader in Gorm. To his recollection the resemblance was perfect.

"Gorm!" He acknowledged it, though he could not give the Kolder a better name. And she placed it carefully on the brown and gold hawk.

V

GAME OF POWER

Five images set out upon the symbols of their lands, five perfect representations of living men and woman. But why and for what purpose? Simon looked right again. The tiny feet of the Aldis manikin were now encircled by the hands of the witch, those of the Fulk figure by Briant's. Both were regarding their charges with absorption, on Briant's part uneasy.

Simon's attention swung back to the figure before him. Dim memories of old tales flickered through his mind. Did they now stick pins in these replicas and expect their originals to suffer and die?

The Guardian reached for his hand, caught it in the same grip he had known in Kars during the shape changing. At the same time she fitted her other hand in a half circle about the base of the capped figure. He put his to match so that now they touched finger tips and wrists enclosing the Kolder.

"Think now upon this one between whom and you has been the trial of power, or the tie of blood. Put from your mind all else but this one whom you must reach and bend, bend to our use. For we win the Game of Power upon this board in this hour—or it—and we—fail for this time and place!"

Simon's eyes were on that capped figure. He did not know if he could turn them away if he wished. He supposed that he had been brought into this curious procedure because he alone of those of Estcarp had seen this officer of Gorm.

The tiny face, half shadowed by the metal cap, grew larger, life size. He was fronting it across space as he had fronted it across that room in the heart of Sippar.

Again the eyes were closed, the man was about his mysterious business. Simon continued to study him, and then he knew that all the antagonism he had known for the Kolder, all the hate born in him by what he had found in that city, by their treatment of their captives, was drawing together in his mind, as a man might shape a weapon of small pieces fitted together into one formidable arm.

Simon was no longer in that tent where sea winds stirred and sand gritted on a brown painted hawk. Instead he stood before that man of the Kolder in the heart of Sippar, willing him to open his closed eyes, to look upon him, Simon Tregarth, to stand to battle in a way not of bodies, but of wills and minds.

Those eyes did open and he stared into their dark pupils, saw lids raise higher as if in recognition, of knowledge of the menace which was using him as a gathering point, a caldron in which every terror and threat could be brought to a culminating boil.

Eyes held eyes. Simon's impressions of the flat features, of the face, of the metal cap above it, of everything *but* those eyes, went, bit by bit. As he had sensed the flow of power out of his hand into the witch's in Kars, so did he know that which boiled within him was being steadily fed by more heat than his own emotions could engender, that he was a gun to propel a fatal dart.

At first the Kolder had stood against him with confidence; now he was seeking his freedom from that

eye-to-eye tie, mind-to-mind bond, knowing too late
that he was caught in a trap. But the jaws had closed and
struggle as he might the man in Gorm could not loosen
what he had accepted in an arrogant belief in his own
form of magic.

Within Simon there was a sharp release of all the
tension. And it shot from him to that other. Eyes were
fear-submerged by panic, panic gave way to abject
terror, which burned in and in until there was nothing
left for it to feed upon. Simon did not have to be told
that what he faced now was a husk which would do his
bidding as those husks of Gorm did the bidding of their
owners.

He gave his orders. The Guardian's power fed his;
she watched and waited, ready to aid, but making no
suggestions. Simon was certain of his enemy's obedience as he was of the life burning in him. That which
controlled Gorm would be crippled, the barrier would
go down, as long as this tool worked unhindered by his
fellows. Estcarp now had a robot ally within the fortress.

Simon lifted his head, opened his eyes, and saw the
painted board where his fingers still clasped the Guardian's about the feet of the small figure. But that manikin was no longer perfect. Within the hollow of the
metal cap the head was a shapeless blob of melted wax.

The Guardian loosened her clasp, drew back her
hand to lie limp. Simon turned his head, saw on his left
a strained and blanched face, eyes dark smudged, as
she who had centered the power upon Aldis fell back in
her seat. And the lady before her was also head ravaged.

That image named for Fulk of Verlaine lay flat and
Briant was huddled in upon himself, his face hidden in

his hands, his lank, colorless hair sweat-plastered to his skull.

"It is done." The silence was first broken by the Guardian. "What the Power can do, it has done. And this day we have wrought as mightily as ever did the blood of Estcarp! Now it is given to fire and sword, wind and wave, to serve us if they will, and if men will use them!" Her voice was a thin thread of exhaustion.

She was answered by one who moved to the board to stand before her, accompanied by the faint clink of metal against metal which marked a man in full war gear. Koris carried on his hip the hawk crested helm; now he raised the Ax of Volt.

"Be sure, lady, that there are men to use each and every weapon Fortune grants us. The beacons are lighted, our armies and the ships move."

Simon, though the earth under his feet had a tendency to sway when he planted his feet upon it and levered himself up, arose. She who had sat on his left moved quickly. Her hand went out, but it did not touch his before it fell back upon the board once more. Nor did she put into words that denial he could read in every tense line of her body.

"The war, now completed according to your Power," he spoke to her as if they were alone, "is of the fashion of Estcarp. But I am not of Estcarp, and there remains this other war which is of my own kind of power. I have played your game to your willing, lady; now I seek to play to mine!"

As he rounded the table to join the Captain, another arose and stood hesitating, one hand on the table to steady him. Briant regarded the image before him and his face was bleak, for the figure, though fallen, was intact.

"I never claimed the Power," he said dully in his soft voice. "And in this warfare it would seem I have been a failure. Perhaps it will not be so with sword and shield!"

Koris stirred as if he would protest. But the witch who had been in Kars spoke swiftly:

"There is a free choice here for all who ride or sail under Estcarp's banner. Let none gainsay that choice."

The Guardian nodded agreement. So the three of them went out from the tent on the sea shore: Koris, vibrant, alive, his handsome head erect on his grotesque shoulders, his nostrils swelling as if he scented more than sea salt in the air; Simon, moving more slowly, feeling a fatigue new to his overdriven body, but also buoyed by a determination to see this venture to its end; and Briant, settling his helm over his fair head, coiling the metal ring scarf about his throat, his eyes straight ahead as if he were driven, or pulled, by something far greater than his own will.

The Captain turned to the other two as they reached the boats waiting to pull out to the ships. "You come with me on the flagship, for you, Simon, must serve as a guide, and you—" he looked to Briant and hesitated. But the youngster, with a lift of chin and stare of eye which was a challenge, met that appraisal defiantly. Simon sensed something crosswise between the two which was of their own concern as he waited for Koris to meet that unvoiced defiance.

"You, Briant, will put yourself among my shield men and you will stay with them!"

"And I, Briant," the other answered with something approaching impudence, "shall stay at your back, Captain of Estcarp, when there is good cause to do so. But I fight with my own sword and wield my own shield in this or any other battle!"

For a moment it seemed that Koris might dispute that, but they were hailed from the boats. And when they splashed through the surf to board, Simon noted that the younger man took good care to keep as far from his commander as the small craft allowed.

The ship which was to spearhead the Estcarp attack was a fishing vessel and the Guards were jammed aboard her almost shoulder to shoulder. The other mismatched transports fell in behind her as they took to the bay waters.

They were close enough to see the fleet rotting in Gorm harbor when the hail from the Sulcar vessels crossed the water and the trading ships with their mixed cargo of Falconers, Karsten refugees, and Sulcar survivors rounded a headland to draw in from the sea side.

Simon had no idea of where he had crossed the barrier on his flight from Gorm, and he might be leading this massed invasion straight into disaster. They could only hope that the Game of Power had softened up the defense in their favor.

Tregarth stood at the prow of the fishing smack, watching the harbor of the dead city, waiting for the first hint of the barrier. Or would one of those metal ships, protected past any hope of attack from Estcarp, strike at them now?

Wind filled their sails, and, overladen as the ships were, they cut the waves, keeping station as if drilled. A hulk from the harbor, still carrying enough rags aloft to catch the wind, its anchor ropes broken, drifted across their course, a wide collar of green weed lying under the water line to slow it.

On its deck there was no sign of life as it bore on its wallowing way. From a Sulcar ship arched a ball, rising lazily into the air, dropping down to smash upon the deck of the derelict. Out of that ragged hole in the planking came red tongues of clean flame, feasting avidly on the tinder dry fittings, so the ship, burning, drifted on to sea.

Simon grinned at Koris, a brittle excitement eating at him. He could be sure now that they were past the first danger point.

"We have overrun your barrier?"

"Unless they have moved it closer to land, yes!"

Koris rested his chin on the head of Volt's Ax as he surveyed the dark fingers of wharves before what had once been a flourishing city. He was grinning too, as a wolf shows its fangs before the first slash of the fight.

"It would appear that this time the Power worked," he commented. "Now let us be about our part of the business."

Simon knew a twinge of caution. "Do not underestimate them. We have but passed the first of their defenses, perhaps their weakest." His first elation was gone as quickly as it had come. There were swords, axes, dart guns about him. But in the heart of the Kolder keep was a science centuries ahead of such weapons—which might at any moment produce some nasty surprise.

As they came farther into the harbor, faced now by the need for finding passage to the wharves in and among the vessels moldering at anchor, there continued to be no sign of any life in Sippar. Only some of the brooding and forbidding silence of the dead city fell upon the invaders, dampening their ardor, taking a slight edge off their enthusiasm and their feeling of triumph at having passed the barrier.

Koris sensed that. Working his way back through the mass of men waiting to be landed, he found the captain of the ship and urged a quick thrust at the shore. Only to be reminded tartly that while the Captain of Estcarp's

Guard might be all powerful on land, he should leave the sea to those who knew it, and that the master of this particular ship had no intention of fouling his vessel with any of the hulks before them.

Simon continued to eye the shoreline, studying the mouth of each empty street, glancing now and then aloft to that blind hulk which was the heart of Sippar in more ways than one. He could not have said just what he feared—a flight of planes, an army emerging from the streets to the quays. To be met by nothing at all was more disconcerting than to face the high odds of Kolder weapons carried by hordes of their slaves. This was too easy, and he could not find full faith in the Game of Power; some core of him refused to believe that because a small image had ended with a melted head, they had defeated all that lay in Gorm.

They made the shore without incident, those of Sulcar landing farther down the coast to cut off any reinforcements which might be drawn from other points on the island. They scouted up the streets and lanes down which Simon had come days earlier, trying locked doors, investigating dark corners. But as far as they could discover nothing lived nor moved within the husk of Gorm's capital.

And they were well up to the center hold when the first resistance came, not from the air, nor from any invisible wave, but on foot with weapons in hand as the men of this world had fought for generations.

Suddenly the streets were peopled with fighters who moved swiftly, but without sound, who voiced no battle cries, but came forward steadily with deadly purposes. Some wore the battle dress of Sulcarmen, some of Karsten, and Simon saw among them a few of the bird helms of Falconers.

That silent rush was made by men who were not only

expendable, but who had no thought of self-protection, just as those in the road ambush had fought. And their first fury carried them into the invasion force with the impact of a tank into a company of infantrymen. Simon went to his old game of sniping, but Koris charged with the Ax of Volt, a whirling, darting engine of death, to clear a path through the enemy lines, and another back again.

The slaves of the Kolder were no mean opponents, but they lacked the spark of intelligence which would have brought them together to re-form, to use to better advantage their numbers. They knew only that they must attack while any strength was left in them, while they still kept on their feet. And so they did, with the insane persistence of the mindless. It was sheer butchery which turned even the veteran Guardsmen sick while they strove to defend themselves and to gain ground.

Volt's Ax no longer shone bright, but, stained as it was, Koris tossed it in the air as a signal for the advance. His men closed ranks leaving behind them a street which was no longer empty, though it was without life.

"That was to delay us." Simon joined the Captain.

"So do I think. What do we expect now? Death from the air such as they used at Sulcarkeep?" Koris looked into the sky, the roofs above them gaining his wary attention.

It was those same roofs which suggested another plan to his companion.

"I do not think you will be able to break into the hold at ground level," he began and heard the soft rumble of laughter from within the Captain's helm.

"Not so. I know ways herein which perhaps even the Kolder have not nosed out. This was *my* burrow once."

"But I have also a plan," Simon cut in. "There are ropes in plenty on the ships, and grappling hooks. Let one party take to the roofs, while you search out your burrows, and perhaps we can close jaws upon them from two sides."

"Fair enough!" Koris conceded. "Do you try the sky ways since you have traveled them before. Choose your men, but do not take above twenty."

Twice more they were attacked by those silent parties of living-dead, and each time more of their own men were left as toll when the last of the Kolder-owned were cut down. In the end the Estcarp forces parted ways. Simon and some twenty of the Guard broke in a door and climbed through the miasma of old death to a roof. Tregarth's sense of direction had not betrayed him; the neighboring roof showed a ragged hole, the mark of his landing in the plane.

He stood aside for the sailors who cast their grapples to the parapet of that other roof above their heads and across an expanse of street. Men tied their swords to them, made sure of the safety of their weapon belts, eyed that double line across nothingness with determination. Simon had recruited none who could not claim a good head for heights. But now when he faced the test he had more doubts than hopes.

He made that first ascent, the tough rope scraping his palms as he climbed, putting a strain on his shoulders he believed from moment to moment he could not endure.

The nightmare ended sometime. He uncoiled a third rope from about his waist, and tossed its weighted end back to the next man in line, taking a turn with the other end around one of the pillars supporting the hangar and so helping to draw him up.

Those planes he had disabled stood where he had left

them, but open motor panels and scattered tools testified to work upon them. Why the job had not been
finished was another mystery. Simon told off four men
to guard the roof and the rope way, and with the rest
began the invasion of the regions below.

The same silence which had held elsewhere in the
town was thick here. They passed along corridors,
down stairs, by shut doors, with only the faint sound of
their own quiet tread to be heard. Was the hold deserted?

On they went into the heart of the blind, sealed
building, expecting at any moment to encounter one of
the bands of the possessed. The degree of light grew
stronger; there was an undefinable change in the air
which suggested that if these levels were deserted now
it had not long been so.

Simon's party came to the last flight of stone steps
which he remembered so well. At the bottom that stone
would be coated with the gray walling of the Kolders.
He leaned out over the well, listening. Far, far below
thcrc was a sound at last, as regular in its thump, thump
as the beat of his own heart.

VI

THE CLEANSING OF GORM

"Captain," Tunston had moved up to join him, "what do we meet below?"

"Your foreseeing in that is as good as mine," Simon answered half absently, for it was in that moment that he realized he did *not* sense any danger to come at all, even in this strange place of death and half life. Yet there was something below, or they would not hear that.

He led the way, his gun ready, taking those steps cautiously, but at a fast pace. There were closed doors which were locked against their efforts to open them, until they came into the chamber of the wall map.

Here that beat arose from the floor under their feet, was drummed out by the walls, to fill their ears and their bodies with its slow rhythm.

The lights on the map were dead. There remained no line of machines on the table, tended by gray-robed men, though metal fastenings, a trailing wire or two marked where they had rested. But at that upper table there still sat a capped figure, his eyes closed, immobile, just as Simon had seen him on his first visit to this place.

At first Simon believed the man dead. He walked to the table watching the seated Kolder alertly. To his best knowledge this was the same man whom he had tried to

265

visualize for the artist of Estcarp. And he was fleetingly pleased at the accuracy of his memory.

Only—Simon halted. This man was not dead, though those eyes were closed, the body motionless. One hand lay upon the control plate set in the table top and Simon had just seen a fingertip press a button there.

Tregarth leaped. He had an instant in which to see those eyes open, the face beneath the metal twist in anger—and perhaps fear. Then his own hands closed upon the wire which led from the cap the other wore to the board in the wall behind. He ripped, bringing loose several of those slender cables. Someone cried out a warning and he saw a barreled weapon swing into line with his body as the Kolder went into action.

Only because that cap and its trailing veil of wire interfered with the free action of he who wore it was Simon to continue to live. He slapped out with his dart gun across the flat face with its snarling mouth which uttered no sound, its stark and hating eyes. The blow broke skin, brought blood welling from cheek and nose. Simon caught the other's wrist, twisting it so that a thin film of vapor spurted up into the vault of the ceiling, and not into his own face.

They crashed back into the chair from which the Kolder had risen. There was a sharp snap, fire flashed across Simon's neck and shoulder. A scream, muted and suppressed rang in his ears. The face beneath its sweep of blood was contorted with agony, yet still the Kolder fought on with steel-muscled strength.

Those eyes, larger, and larger, filling the hall— Simon was falling forward into those eyes. Then there were no more eyes, just a weird fog-streaked window into another place—perhaps another time. Between pillars burst a company of men, gray robed, riding in machines strange to him. They were firing behind them as they came, unmistakably some remnant of a broken force on the run and hardly pressed.

In a narrow column they struggled on, and with them he endured desperation and such a cold fury as he had not known existed as an emotion to wrack mind and heart. The Gate—once through the gate—*then* they would have the time: time to rebuild, to take, to be what they had the will and force to be. A broken empire and a ravaged world lay behind them—before them a fresh world for the taking.

The beset fugitives were swept away. He saw only one pallid face flushed red about a wound where his first blow had landed. Clinging about them both was the smell of scorching cloth and flesh. How long had that vision of the valley lasted—it could not have been a full second! He was still fighting, exerting pressure so that he might crack the other's wrist against the chair. Twice he struck it so, and then the fingers relaxed and the vapor gun fell out of their grip.

For the first time since that one scream the Kolder made a sound, a broken whimpering which sickened Simon. A second fading vision of those fleeing men—a moment of passionate regret which was like a blow to the man who involuntarily shared it. They thrashed across the floor to bring the Kolder up against a spitting wire. Simon slammed the other's metal cap hard against the floor. For the last time a fragment of recognition reached from the man to him and in that scrap of time he knew—perhaps not what the Kolder were—but from whence they had come. Then there was nothing at all, and Simon pulled away from the flaccid body to sit up.

Tunston stooped and tried to pull the cap from the

head which rolled limply on the gray-robed shoulders. They were all a little daunted when it became apparent that that cap was no cap at all, but seemingly a permanent part of the body it crowned.

Simon got to his feet. "Leave it!" he bade the Guard. "But make sure none touch those wires."

It was then that he was aware that that throb in wall and floor, that feeling of life was gone, leaving behind it a curious void. The Kolder of the cap might himself have been the heart, which, ceasing to beat, had killed the citadel as surely as his race had killed Sippar.

Simon made for the alcove where the elevator had been. Had all power ceased so that there was no way to reach the lower levels? But the door of the small cell was open. He gave command here to Tunston, and taking two of the Guardsmen with him, pushed the door shut.

Again luck appeared to be with those out of Estcarp, for the closing of the panel put into action the mechanism of the lift. Simon expected to front the level of the laboratory when that door opened once again. Only, when the cage came to a stop, he faced something so far removed from his expectations that for a moment he stood staring, while both of the men with him exclaimed in surprise.

They were on the shore of an underground harbor, strongly smelling of the sea and of something else. The lighting which had prevailed elsewhere in the pile was centered upon a runway washed by the water on both sides, pointing straight out into a bowl of gloom and dark. And on that quay were the tumbled bodies of men, men such as themselves with no gray robes among them.

Where the living dead who had met them in the street

battles had gone armed and fully clad, these were either naked or wore only the tattered rags of old garments about their bodies, as if a need for clothing had no longer concerned them for a long time.

Some had crumpled beside small trucks on which boxes and containers were still heaped. Others lay in line as if they had been marching in ranks when struck down. Simon walked forward and stooped to peer at the nearest. It was clear that the man was truly dead, had been so for a day at least.

Gingerly, avoiding the heaped bodies, the three from Estcarp made their way to the end of the quay, finding nowhere among the dead any armed as fighting men. And none were of Estcarp blood. If these had been the slaves of the Kolder, they were all of other races.

"Here, Captain." One of the Guards lagging behind Simon had halted beside a body and was looking at it in wonder. "Here is such a man as I have never seen before. Look at the color of his skin, his hair; he is not from these lands!"

The unfortunate Kolder slave lay on his back as if in sleep. But his skin, totally exposed save for a draggle of rag about his hips, was a red-brown, and his hair was tightly curled to his scalp. It was plain that the Kolder had cast their man nets in far regions.

Without knowing why, Simon walked clear to the end of that wharf. Either Gorm had originally been erected over a huge underground cavern, or the invaders had blasted this out to serve their own purposes, purposes Simon could only believe were connected with the ship on which he had been a prisoner. Was this the secluded dock of the Kolder fleet?

"Captain!" The other Guard had tramped a little ahead, uninterested in the bodies among which he

threaded a fastidious path. Now he stood on the end of
that tongue of stone beckoning Simon forward.

There was a stirring of the waters; waves lapped
higher on the wharf, forcing all three men to retreat.
Even in that limited light they could see something
large rising to the surface.

"Down!" Simon snapped the command. They did
not have time to return to the lift; their best hope was to
play one with the bodies about them.

They lay together, Simon pillowing his head on his
arm, his gun ready, watching the turmoil. Water spilled
from the bulk of the thing. Now he could make out the
sharp bow with its matching needle stern. His guess had
been right: this was one of the Kolder ships come to
harbor.

He wondered if his own breathing sounded as loud as
that of his men beside him did to him. They were more
fully clothed than the dead about them; could sharp
eyes pick out the gleam of their mail and nail them with
some Kolder weapon before they could move in defense?

Only that silver ship, having once surfaced, made no
other move at all, rolling in the waves within the cavern
as if it were as dead as the bodies. Simon watched it
narrowly and then started, as the man beside him whispered and touched his officer's arm.

But Simon did not need that admonition to watch.
He, too, had sighted that second boiling upheaval of
waves. In those the first ship was pushed toward the
quay. It was plain now that she answered no helm.
Hardly daring to believe that the vessel was unmanned,
they still kept in hiding. It was only when the third ship
bobbed into sight and sent the other two whirling with
the force of its emergence, that Simon accepted the

evidence and got to his feet. Those ships were either unmanned or totally disabled. They drifted without guidance, two coming together with a crash.

No openings showed on their decks, no indications that they carried crews and passengers. The story that the quay told was different, however. It suggested a hasty loading of vessels, intended to attack, or to make a withdrawal from Gorm. And had only an attack been the purpose would the slaves have been killed?

To board one of those floating silver splinters without preparation would be folly. But it would be best to keep an eye upon them. The three went back to the cage which had brought them there. One of the ships struck against the wharf, sheered it off, and wallowed away.

"Will you remain here?" He asked a question of his men rather than gave an order. The Guard of Estcarp should be inured to strange sights, but this was no place to station an unwilling man.

"Those ships—we should learn their secrets," one of the men returned. "But I do not think they will sail out from here again, Captain."

Simon accepted that oblique dissent. Together they left the underground harbor to the derelicts and the dead. Before they took off in the cage, Simon inspected its interior for controls. He wanted to reach some level where he might contact Koris' party, not return to the hall of the map once again.

Unfortunately the walls of that box were bare of any aid to direction. Disappointed they closed the door behind them waiting to be returned aloft. As the vibration in the wall testified to their movement, Simon recalled vividly the corridor of the laboratory and wished he could reach it.

The cage came to a stop, the door slid back, and the

three within found themselves looking into the startled faces of other men, armed and alert. Only those few seconds of amazement saved both parties from a fatal mistake, for one of the group without called Simon's name and he saw Briant.

Then a figure not to be mistaken for any but Koris shouldered by the others.

"Where do you spring from?" he demanded. "The wall itself?"

Simon knew this corridor where the Estcarp force was gathered: the place he had been thinking of. But why had the cage brought him here as if in answer to his wish alone? His wish!

"You have found the laboratory?"

"We have found many things, few of which make any sense. But not yet have we found any Kolder! And you?"

"One of the Kolder and he is now dead—or perhaps all of them!" Simon thought of the ships below and what they might hold in their interiors. "I do not believe that we have to fear meeting them here now."

Through the hours which followed Simon was proved a true prophet. Save for the one man in the metal cap, there was no other of the unknown race to be discovered within Gorm. And of those who had served the Kolder there were only dead men left. Found, those were in squads, in companies, or by twos and threes in the corridors and rooms of the keep. All lay as they had dropped, as if what had kept them operating as men had suddenly been withdrawn and they had fallen into the nothingness which should have been theirs earlier, the peace which their masters had denied them.

The Guards found other prisoners in the room beyond the laboratory, among them some who had shared captivity with Simon. These awoke sluggishly from their drugged sleep, unable to remember anything after they had been gassed, but thanking such gods as each owned that they had been brought to Gorm too late to follow the sorry path of the others the Kolder had engulfed.

Koris and Simon guided Sulcar seamen to the underground harbor, and in a small boat, explored the cavern. They found only rock wall. The entrance to the pool must lie under surface, and they believed it had been closed to the escape of the derelict ships.

"If he who wore the cap controlled it all," surmised Koris, "then his death must have sealed them in. Also, since he is the one you battled from afar through the Power, he might have already been giving muddled orders to lead to confusion here."

"Perhaps," Simon agreed absently. He was thinking of what he had learned from that other in his last few seconds of life. If the rest of the Kolder force were sealed into those ships, then indeed Estcarp had good reason to rejoice.

They got a line to one of the vessels and brought it alongside the wharf. But the fastenings of the hatch baffled them and Koris and Simon left the Sulcarmen to puzzle it out, returning to the keep.

"This is another of their magics." Koris slid the door of the lift closed behind them. "But seemingly one the capped man did not control, seeing as how we can use it now."

"You can control this as well as he ever did," Simon leaned back against wall, weariness washing over him. Their victory was inconclusive; he had an inkling of the chase yet before him, but would those of Estcarp believe what he had to tell them now? "Think upon the corridor where you met me, picture it in your mind."

"So?" Koris pulled off his helm; now he set his shoulders against the opposite wall and closed his eyes in concentration.

The door opened. They looked out upon the laboratory corridor and Koris laughed with a boy's amusement at an exciting toy.

"This magic I can work also, I, Koris, the Ugly. It would seem that among the Kolder the Power was not limited only to women."

Simon closed the door once again, pictured in his mind the upper chamber of the wall map. Only when they reached that did he answer his companion's observation.

"Perhaps that is what we now have to fear from the Kolder, Captain. They had their own form of power, and you have seen how they used it. This Gorm may now be a treasure house of their knowledge."

Koris threw his helm on the table below the map, and leaning on his ax regarded Simon levelly.

"It is a treasure house you warn against looting?" He picked that out quickly.

"I don't know," Simon dropped heavily into one of the chairs, and resting his head on his fists, stared down at the surface on which his elbows were planted. "I am no scientist, no master of this kind of magic. The Sulcarmen will be tempted by those ships, Estcarp by what else lies here."

"Tempted?" Someone had echoed that word and both men looked around. Simon got to his feet as he saw who seated herself quietly a little from them, Briant beside her as if playing her shieldman.

She was helmed and in mail, but Simon knew that she could disguise herself with shape-changing and still he would know her always.

"Tempted," again she repeated. "Well do you choose that word, Simon. Yes, we of Estcarp shall be tempted; that is why I am here. There are two edges to this blade and we may cut outselves on either if we do not take care. Should we turn aside from this strange knowledge, destroy all we have found, we may be making ourselves safe, or we may be foolishly opening a way for a second Kolder attack, for one cannot build a defense unless he has a clear understanding of the weapons to be used against him."

"Of the Kolder," Simon spoke slowly, heavily, "you will not have to fear too much. There was but a small company of them in the beginning. If any escaped here, then they can be hunted back to their source and that source closed."

"Closed?" Koris made a question of that.

"In the last struggle with their leader he revealed their secret."

"That they are not native to this world?"

Simon's head swung around. Had she picked that out of his mind, or was that some information she had not seen fit to supply before?

"You knew?"

"I am not a reader of minds, Simon. But we have not known it long. Yes, they came to us—as you came—but, I think, from other motives."

"They were fugitives, fleeing disaster, a disaster of their own making, having set their own place aflame behind them. I do not think that they dared to leave their door open behind them, but that we must make sure of. The more pressing problem is what lies here."

"And you think that if we take their knowledge to us the evil which lies in it may corrupt. I wonder. Estcarp has lived long secure in its own Power."

"Lady, no matter what decision is made, I do not

think that Estcarp shall remain the same. She must either come fully into the main stream of active life, or she must be content to withdraw wholly from it into stagnation, which is a form of death.''

It was as if they two talked alone and neither Briant nor Koris had a part in the future they discussed. She met him mind to mind with an equality he had not sensed in any other woman before.

"You speak the truth, Simon. Perhaps the ancient solidity of my people must break. There shall be those who will wish for life and a new world, and those who shall shrink from any change from the ways which mean security. But that struggle still lies in the future. And it is only a growth of this war. What would you say should be done with Gorm?''

He smiled wearily. ''I am a man of action. Out of here I shall go to hunt down that gate which the Kolder used and see that it is rendered harmless. Give me orders, lady, and they shall be carried out. But for the time being I would seal this place until a decision can be made. There may be an attempt on the part of others to take away what lies here.''

"Yes. Karsten, Alizon, both would relish the looting of Sippar.'' She nodded briskly. Her hand was at the breast of her mail shirt and she drew it away with the jewel of power in it.

"This is my authority, Captain,'' she spoke to Koris. "Let it be as Simon has said. Let this storehouse of strange knowledge be sealed, and let the rest of Gorm be cleansed for a garrison, until such time as we can decide the future of what lies here.'' She smiled at the young officer. ''I leave it in your command, Lord Defender of Gorm.''

VII

A VENTURE OF NEW BEGINNINGS

A dusky red spread slowly up from the collar of Koris'
mail shirt, reaching the line of his fair hair. Then he
answered and the bitter lines about his well-cut mouth
were deep, adding years to his young face.

"Are you forgetting, lady," he brought the blade of
Volt's Ax down flatwise on the table with a clang,
"that long ago Koris the Misshapen was driven from
these shores?"

"And what happened to Gorm thereafter, and to
those who did that driving?" she asked quietly. "Have
any said 'misshapen Captain of Estcarp'?"

His hand tightened on the haft of his weapon until the
knuckles were white and sharp. "Find another Lord
Defender for Gorm, lady. I swore by Nornan that I
would not return here. To me this is a doubly haunted
place. I think that Estcarp has had no reason to com-
plain of her Captain; also I do not believe this war
already won."

"He is right, you know," Simon cut in. "The Kolder may be few, most of them may be trapped in those
ships below. But we must trace them back to their gate
and make sure that they do not consolidate shattered
forces to launch a second bid for rulership. What about
Yle? And do they have a garrison in Sulcarkeep? How
deeply are they involved in Karsten and Alizon? We

may be at the beginning of a long war instead of grasping victory."

"Very well," she stroked the jewel she held. "Since you have such definite ideas, become governor here, Simon."

Koris spoke swiftly before Tregarth could answer. "To me that is a plan to which I agree. Hold Gorm with my blessing, Simon, and do not think that I shall ever rise in the name of my heritage to take it from you."

But Simon was shaking his head. "I am a soldier. And I am from another world. Let dog eat dog as the saying goes—the Kolder trail is mine." He touched his head; if he closed his eyes now he knew he would see not darkness but a narrow valley through which angry men fought a rearguard action.

"Do you venture into Yle and Sulcarkeep and no farther?" Briant broke silence for the first time.

"Where would you have us go?" Koris asked.

"Karsten!" If Simon had ever thought the youth colorless and lacking in personality he was to doubt his appraisal at that moment.

"And what lies in Karsten which is of such moment to us?" Koris' voice held an almost bantering note. Yet there was something else beneath the surface of that tone which Simon heard but could not identify. There was a game here afoot, but he did not know its purpose or rules.

"Yvian!" The name was flung at the Captain like a battle challenge and Briant eyed Koris as if waiting to see him pick it up. Simon glanced from one young man to the other. As it had been earlier when he and the witch had talked across the board, so was it now: these two fenced without thought of their audience.

For the second time red tinged Koris' cheeks, then ebbed, leaving his face white and set, that of a man committed to some struggle he hated but dared not shirk. For the first time he left the Ax of Volt lying forgotten on the table as he came swiftly about the end of the board, moving with that lithe grace which always contrasted with his ill-formed body.

Briant, a queer expression of mingled defiance and hope giving life to his features, waited for his coming, stood still as the Captain's hands fell on his shoulders in a grip which could not have been anything but bruising.

"This is what you want?" the words came from Koris as if jerked one by one by torture.

At the last moment perhaps Briant tried to evade. "I want my freedom," he replied in a low voice.

Those punishing hands fell away. Koris laughed with such raking bitterness that Simon protested inwardly against the hurt that sound betrayed.

"Be sure, in time, it shall be yours!" The Captain would have stepped away if Briant had not seized in turn upon Koris' upper arms with the same urgency of hold the other had shown earlier.

"I want my freedom only that I may make a choice elsewhere. And I have decided upon that choice—do you doubt that? Or is it again that there is an Aldis who has the power I cannot reach for?"

Aldis? A glimmering of what might be the truth struck Simon.

Koris' fingers were under Briant's chin, turning the thin young face up to his. This once was the Captain able to look down and not up at a companion.

"You believe in sword thrust for sword thrust, do you not?" he commented. "So Yvian has his Aldis; let them have the good of each other while they may. But I think that Yvian has made a very ill choice of it. And since one ax made a marriage, another may undo it!''

"Marriage in the gabble gabble of Siric only," flashed Briant, still a little defiant, but not struggling in the Captain's new hold.

"Need you have told *me* that," Koris was smiling. "Lady of Verlaine?"

"Loyse of Verlaine is dead!" Briant repeated. "You get no such heritage with me, Captain."

A tiny frown line appeared between Koris' brows. "That you need not have said either. Rather is it that such as I am must buy a wife with gauds and lands. And never afterwards be sure of the bargain."

Her hand whipped from his arm to his mouth, silencing him. And there was red anger in both her eyes and her voice when she replied:

"Koris, Captain of Estcarp need never speak so of himself, least of all to a woman such as I, without inheritance of lands or beauty!"

Simon moved, knowing that neither were aware of the other two in that room. He touched the witch of Estcarp gently on the shoulder and smiled down at her.

"Let us leave them to fight their own battle," he whispered.

She was laughing silently after her fashion. "This talk of mutual unworthiness will speedily be a step to no talking at all and so to a firm settlement of two futures."

"I take it that she *is* the missing heiress of Verlaine, wedded by proxy to Duke Yvian?"

"She is. By her aid alone I came scatheless out of Verlaine, I being captive there for a space. Fulk is not a pleasant enemy."

Afire to every shade of her voice, Simon's smile became grim.

"I think that Fulk and his wreckers shall be taught a lesson in the near future; it will curb their high spirits," he commented, knowing well her way of understatement. It was enough for him that she admitted she owed her escape from Verlaine to the girl across the room. For a woman of the Power such an admission hinted of danger indeed. He had a sudden overwhelming desire to take one of the Sulcar ships, man it with his mountain fighters, and sail southward.

"Doubtless he shall," she agreed to his statement concerning Fulk with her usual tranquillity. "As you have said, we are still in the midst of a war, and not victors at the end of one. Verlaine and Karsten, too, shall be attended to in their proper seasons. Simon, my name is Jaelithe."

It came so abruptly, that for a full moment he did not understand her meaning. And then, knowing the Estcarpian custom, of the rules which had bound her so long, he drew a deep breath of wonder at that complete surrender: her name, that most personal possession in the realm of the Power, which must never be yielded lest one yield with it one's own identity to another!

As Koris' ax lay on the table, so she had left her jewel behind her when she had moved apart with Simon. For the first time he realized that fact also. She had deliberately disarmed herself, put aside all her weapons and defenses, given into his hands what she believed was the ordering of her life. What such a surrender had meant to her he could guess, but only dimly—and that he knew also, awed. He felt as stripped of all talents and ability, as misshapen, as Koris deemed himself.

Yet he moved forward and his arms went out to draw

her to him. As he bent his head to hers, searching for waiting lips, Simon sensed that for the first time the pattern had changed indeed. Now he was a part of a growing design, his life to be woven fast with hers, into the way of this world's. And there would be no breaking it for the remainder of his days. Nor would he ever wish to.

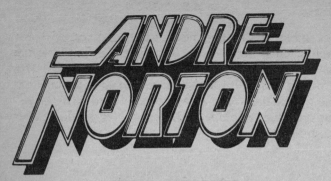

ANDRE NORTON

FORERUNNER SERIES

| ☐ 24624-9 | **FORERUNNER FORAY** | $2.50 |

THE WITCH WORLD SERIES

☐ 87879-2	**WEB OF THE WITCH WORLD #2**	$2.75
☐ 77558-6	**SORCERESS OF THE WITCH WORLD #6**	$2.75
☐ 82346-7	**TREY OF SWORDS #7**	$2.75

☐ 22368-0	**EXILES OF THE STARS**	$2.50
☐ 33711-2	**HIGH SORCERY**	$2.50
☐ 35844-6	**ICE CROWN**	$2.50
☐ 47443-8	**LAVENDER-GREEN MAGIC**	$2.75
☐ 69685-6	**QUEST CROSSTIME**	$2.50
☐ 76804-0	**THE SIOUX SPACEMAN**	$2.50
☐ 78435-6	**THE STARS ARE OURS!**	$2.50
☐ 84466-9	**UNCHARTED STARS**	$2.50
☐ 95966-0	**THE ZERO STONE**	$2.75
☐ 37294-5	**IRON CAGE**	$2.75
☐ 43676-5	**KEY OUT OF TIME**	$2.95

Please send the titles I've checked above. Mail orders to:

BERKLEY PUBLISHING GROUP
390 Murray Hill Pkwy., Dept. B
East Rutherford, NJ 07073

NAME_____

ADDRESS_____

CITY_____

STATE_____ZIP_____

Please allow 6 weeks for delivery.
Prices are subject to change without notice.

POSTAGE & HANDLING:
$1.00 for one book, $.25 for each
additional. Do not exceed $3.50.

BOOK TOTAL	$_____
SHIPPING & HANDLING	$_____
APPLICABLE SALES TAX (CA, NJ, NY, PA)	$_____
TOTAL AMOUNT DUE PAYABLE IN US FUNDS. (No cash orders accepted.)	$_____

COLLECTIONS OF SCIENCE FICTION AND FANTASY

☐ 85444-3	**UNICORNS!** Jack Dann & Gardner Dozois, eds.	$2.95
☐ 51532-0	**MAGICATS!** Jack Dann and Gardner Dozois, eds.	$2.95
☐ 06977-0	**BODY ARMOR: 2000** Joe Haldeman, Charles G. Waugh, Martin Harry Greenberg, eds.	$3.50
☐ 14264-8	**DEMONS!** Jack Dann & Gardner Dozois, eds.	$3.50
☐ 77532-2	**SORCERERS!** Jack Dann & Gardner Dozois, eds.	$2.95
☐ 77786-4	**SPACEFIGHTERS** Joe Haldeman, Charles G. Waugh, Martin Harry Greenberg, eds.	$3.50

Available at your local bookstore or return this form to:

ACE
THE BERKLEY PUBLISHING GROUP, Dept. B
390 Murray Hill Parkway, East Rutherford, NJ 07073

Please send me the titles checked above. I enclose _____ Include $1.00 for postage
and handling if one book is ordered; add 25¢ per book for two or more not to exceed
$3.50. CA, NJ, NY and PA residents please add sales tax. Prices subject to change
without notice and may be higher in Canada. Do not send cash.

NAME_____

ADDRESS_____

CITY_____STATE/ZIP_____

(Allow six weeks for delivery.)